THE
GRAMMARIAN

THE
GRAMMARIAN

a novel by

ANNAPURNA POTLURI

COUNTERPOINT
BERKELEY

Excerpts from *The History of Doing* by Radha Kumar. Copyright © 1993 by Radha Kumar.

Excerpts from *India* by Pierre Loti. Copyright © 1913 by P. Loti, Translated from the French by George A. F. Inman. Copyright © 1993 by George A. F. Inman.

Excerpts from *The Lusiad: Or, the Discovery of India, an Epic Poem* by Luis de Camões, translated by William Julius Mickle. Copyright © 1798 by William Julius Mickle.

Excerpts from *Urdu Letters Of Mirza Asadu'llah Khan Ghalib* by Mirza Asadu'llah Khan Ghalib, translated and annotated by Daud Rahbar. Copyright © 1987 by Daud Rahbar.

Excerpts from Bharati—*Patriot Poet Prophet* by S. Ramakrishnan. Copyright © 1982 by S. Ramakrishnan.

Library of Congress Cataloging-in-Publication Data:

Potluri, Annapurna, 1979-
    The Grammarian / Annapurna Potluri.
        pages cm
    ISBN 978-1-61902-102-0 (hardcover)
1. Philologists--Fiction. 2. French--India--Fiction. 3. Families--India--Fiction. 4. Self-realization--Fiction. 5. India--Social life and customs--20th century--Fiction. I. Title.

PS3616.O8446G73 2013
813'.6--dc23

Paperback ISBN: 978-1-61902-279-9

Cover design by Ann Weinstock
Interior design by meganjonesdesign.com

Printed in the United States of America

COUNTERPOINT
2560 Ninth Street Suite 318
Berkeley, CA 94710
www.counterpointpress.com

This book is dedicated to my beloved grandmother Satyavati Challagulla, and in loving memory of my grandparents Nagamalleswara Rao Challagulla and Annapurnamma and Ramachandra Rao Potluri.

2012

NEW YORK

"Seulement ces paroles: Je me trouve justement condamné."
"Mere words. I consider myself justly convicted."

THE RED AND THE BLACK

STENDHAL

PROLOGUE

1896

TWO SUMMERS BEFORE, Paris was abuzz with rumors of the American inventor Thomas Edison's "Peephole Kinetoscope," through which reporters in New York City and London had already been seduced by the image of Carmencita. It would be five years until Parisians would have a firsthand look, at the Exposition Universelle, but for the time being, the news reports in France served to stir excitement. After the reporters, men who had the twenty-five cents to see her through the small hole in the box holding a rather large and unwieldy machine watched Carmencita roll her hips without remorse or shame into their subconscious. Zaftig, clad in white, Carmencita, who had thrilled the crowds at Koster and Bial's on 34th Street, lifted her skirts joyously to music unheard by her viewers, her small feet in white heels skipping along effortlessly as the potato-starch grain of the film moved over her like a sparkling, sheer veil covering the voyeur's eyes. Edison's machine could take 46 photographs per second. These photographs were shown in rapid succession, and thus Carmencita was able to pirouette into the viewer's mind, as did the visions of Sandow the strong man flexing, or James Corbett knocking out Peter Courtney in the sixth round in an Orange, New Jersey, boxing ring.

Antoine Lumière, a painter and owner of a photography shop, had been invited by Edison that Paris summer to see an exhibition of the Kinetoscope, and upon returning to Lyons, he recounted what he had seen to his sons Auguste and Louis. Auguste was the older brother by two years, and the two bore a striking resemblance to each other. They would inherit their father's interest in photography and the burgeoning science of filmmaking.

In less than two years, the Lumière brothers had improved Edison's process and had prepared a sampling of six short films: *Entry of Cinematographe*, *The Sea*, *Arrival of a Train*, *A Demolition*, *Ladies & Soldiers on Wheels*, and *Leaving the Factory*; viewers found *The Sea* particularly moving: four men running along a jetty, jumping into a tumult of waves. On the waves, rolling white crests, silent and powerful, carried the men back to land. To pay for the equipment, its maintenance and a hall in which to show the films, the brothers charged Parisians one frank for ten minutes of film. But for that amount, a Parisian could as easily treat himself to an evening at a music hall. Disheartened by the public's complaint of overcharging, Louis said, "The cinema is an invention without any future," and attempting to at least pay for the fees they had to cover when they failed to sell out the hall, the Lumières took their invention on the road to London and Bombay, where their *cinématographe* device and the films it recorded were to be exhibited to the foreign public.

Reading about the *cinématographe* in the London newspapers his butler brought from town, in the long leap-year February of 1896, Shiva Adivi sent word to his friend Jamsetji Tata, a Parsi Gujurati.

Tata lived in Bombay and had been working there as a businessman amidst the 1857 rebellion and had heavy Persian eyelids, as per his ancestry. Adivi wanted to see the *cinématographe*, and he hadn't been to Tata's home, the Esplanade House, in some time; he enjoyed his old friend's great collection of Chinese and Japanese art. Tata also had an

X-ray photograph that he had obtained by writing William Röntgen a letter of admiration—flattered, Röntgen sent Tata an image of his wife Anna's hand, showing in shades of blue her long bones visible beneath the flesh with the interruption of her wedding ring. Esplanade House itself was classically Moorish. Tata's sons were British educated and had been working in their father's business, expanding the millworks that had begun in Nagpur on the first day of 1877 after their father had studied the industry of the Lancashire mills. The first Tata mill was named the Empress Mill, in honor of Victoria, empress of India.

Tata received the idea with exuberance: "My dear Adivi," he replied, via the post, "I would be thrilled if you would be my guest during your stay in Bombay. I too have heard of the *frères Lumière*, as my son would say—he's always off to Pondichéry these days—overseeing the fabric mills.

"Regarding the *cinématographe*: I am also very curious about this contraption. The word is that it shall be here in July. If I can be of any aid in your travel plans, you will let me know. Otherwise, myself and Hirabai look forward to your visit. Our best to your dear wife and children."

THE MONSOON SEASON began in June, and Adivi watched much of it from the raised verandah of his home; he stood on the cool stone watching the rain hit the soil and the rocks heavily and constantly for days and days. His wife and mother stayed indoors most of the time: his wife Lalita, the young mother still taking care to put coal-colored *kajal* on her eyes; his mother, the widow, in a simple white sari. Both of them herding his daughters, Anjali and Mohini, through the day in a routine of feedings, games, naps and gentle scoldings. They took care of his small daughters and, wary of water-borne germs, felt it was best to keep them from the rain. The female world of child-rearing had left him feeling alienated from his family in the last few years, and he was eager to get away and see Tata, a friend he had made in the mill industry before he was married.

Having children did not alter his views on the universe, or change his ideas of what was and was not possible in this life. The only way in which he changed was in his own understanding of what his capacity for love was. With his first daughter, Anjali, his love became depthless, an ocean that swept over his senses, his emotions, his better judgment; he became fiercely protective, and constantly worried. This much was true: he could not love anyone more than his daughters. For Adivi, having daughters was like holding sand in his palms while wading in the ocean; too soon, they would wash away from him, out of his grasp, shed his name, defy his word; his girls were his for precious little time. Glad though he was to go away on holiday, he would miss them—their squealing, excitable laughter, the weight of their fat, silky little bodies in his arms, the way they were alternately lovingly protective of each other and then fought mercilessly, their funny little ways. He had big, wild dreams for his girls: he would send them to England for university as he had once wanted to do. His girls would be beautiful and kind like their mother. He would teach them poetry.

This would be his first trip for pleasure since his honeymoon in Jaipur, the pink city, seven years before. Then, he had been a young man without a mustache and with a new bride whose hair was thick and black and reflected the light like a lake. They had only just met. When they stood on the roof of Nahargarh Fort in the evening overlooking

Rajasthan, she turned to look at him, her face framed by inky black braids, and he wanted to tell her she looked beautiful but he was too shy. At night when they lay next to each other, he wrapped her hair around his hand. Now it was too late to tell her, not because she had lost her beauty but because it wasn't the same anymore. It had lost its youthful translucency and reformed itself into an earthy maternity that was more powerful than its earlier incarnation but no longer exclusively his.

In late June, he said good-bye to his family and felt a bit light on his feet. He mounted a horse-drawn carriage to set off for the long journey to the Madras train station. The railways were established primarily to ease British business, and though plans were in effect to build a station at Waltair, the stone had not yet been laid. His longtime butler, Subba Rao, kept him company along the route, but they exchanged few words; their stations in life prevented them from speaking freely.

When they arrived at Madras Central Station, Subba Rao hired coolies to lift the trunks into the first-class car. They were filled with Adivi's Saville Row suits and homemade sweets made by servants under his mother's strict guidance—more than once the servants threw up their hands in frustration, allowing his mother, Kanakadurga, to take over the cooking. Subba Rao shook hands with Adivi and dropped into a shallow bow, "Have a pleasant stay in Bombay, Sir."

"Thank you Subba Rao. I will send word of when I will return once I get to Bombay."

"Yes, Sir. The household staff would like to extend our fond greetings to Mr. Tata."

"Yes Subba Rao." He gave Subba Rao dinner money for himself and the coach driver and then reached back into his wallet and gave him a few more bills. "Buy chocolates for the girls in town—Anjali likes the milk chocolates from the import store near Asilmetta, and be sure to give the horses some bananas tonight."

He slept much of the way up north, enjoying the scenery. When he felt especially restless, he would walk to the water closet and run cold water in the basin, remove his suit jacket, roll up his sleeves and splash his face.

ADIVI WOKE AS the train closed in on Venice. The slowing rocking of the train made his body jerk to and fro more pronouncedly, and as his head was thrown forward, his hair fell over his forehead. Drowsy and disoriented, he looked out the window and saw a Venetian horizon moving in on him, and only moments later realized he was now in Bombay, its magnificent Gothic Victoria Station looming in the distance. Soon he would set foot on the Bombay soil. The station had been completed some fifteen years before, in the style of what was called, in fashionable circles, Indian Gothic. Adivi stood to retrieve his hand trunk; he would have station coolies bring down the rest.

When the train finally came to a stop, he was surprised to see his friend's face out the window grates and felt flattered that Tata had come to receive him personally. Tata would not tell Adivi as much, but it was not for the sake of friendship or hospitality alone that he came to receive him; Tata enjoyed any excuse to take a trip to the station with its statue of the queen on its dome, its red roof and turrets. When it was being built, he would frequent the construction site, enjoying it at each stage, watching his city grow. Adivi descended the train and Tata greeted him with open arms and directed his servants to unload his friend's luggage.

The room at the Esplanade House Adivi was given was Spanish themed, and as he retired for the evening, the oil lanterns illuminated two dark, Mediterranean beauties. A framed print of Goya's *Naked Maja* adorned one wall: a virginal woman with soft eyes, her face framed with obsidian ringlets, her body the color of the inside of a shell, a pane of light over her heart. On the opposite wall was Velázquez's *The Toilet of Venus*, Venus's body supple and lovely, turned away from the painter's gaze, an unapproachable glamour about her with her red hair, a winged, cherubic Cupid holding up a mirror into which she gazed contentedly.

In the mornings, he took his coffee with Tata in his sitting room. Tata subscribed to the British and European papers and the Hindi ones as well as the local, Marathi-language ones.

Reading an update of the Indian National Congress in one of the Hindi papers, Adivi snorted. "More than ten bloody years since they formed and they've still done nothing."

"Oh, I don't know, Adivi, these things take time."

"My friend, I agree that some of the current practices and regulations need to be reformed, but these people want to rule the country? They can't even get themselves in order. Tilak is on about Hindu nationalism even if it means that all these . . . these uneducated peasants can marry their eight—nine-year-old daughters off! Half of Congress I'm sure aren't positive they want the English out, they've elected an Irish president, and all the while Gokhale is sitting in the back with his ledger board counting the number of radishes planted per square foot of soil in some bloody backwater or counting the number of spots on spinach leaves . . . will that man never grasp the big picture? Is he simply trying to bore the English out of India? . . . sometimes it seems these so-called freedom fighters are just riding the back of Irish nationalism . . . "

"It isn't child marriage that Tilak is opposed to; he opposes the idea of the legitimacy of British rule, Adivi. You must admit it is a terribly principled stance! He has a point." Tata sipped the last of his coffee. "Even reasonable laws perhaps should not be put forth if the government advocating them is unreasonable . . . " He rose, stretching. "At any rate, we can't worry about INC politics today, Adivi." He set down his coffee cup and smiled. "Tonight is the Lumière exhibition—it is at the Watson in the Kala Ghoda—I've hired a coach for tonight," Tata beamed, "it is a nice excuse to wear something extra smart."

THE COACH WOVE through the streets of Bombay, and Adivi noticed that the signage on the sky-blue Keneseth Eliyahoo Synagogue was in English, Marathi and Hebrew. It had been built a few years prior by Jacob Elias David Sassoon, the son of Baghdadi Jewish immigrants, who named the synagogue after his father. Like the train station, it had a Gothic influence.

"The inside is incredible," Tata offered, noticing his friend admiring the building. "Gold gilt work, an arched mezzanine, beautiful Middle Eastern tile floors, colored stain-glass windows . . . truly spectacular."

"Ah . . . how beautiful," Adivi answered, not looking away.

The synagogue was in the Kala Ghoda—Black Horse—district, so named because of the obsidian stone used in the imposing statue of Edward VII, prince of Wales, mounted on a dark stallion in the district's main intersection, his shoulders thrown back in triumph.

"Amazing that Victoria is still alive, isn't it?" Tata said, nodding in the direction of the statue. "Wonder if you'll ever get your chance, old boy." The prince was fifty-nine years old but still under the rule of his mother. "Well, I suppose his time is busied with hunting." The prince had recently had all the clocks at Sandringham House set a half hour faster than Greenwich Mean Time to allow himself more time in the day to hunt with his dogs, including his beloved Sandringham black Labradors.

"She is one tough old lady . . . " Adivi replied, distracted. He only thought of the evening ahead. Tonight he was going to see the Lumière brothers' films. Adivi was looking forward to *The Train* the most: the vision of the filmed train was so intense that the audiences of Paris and London jumped for fear of being run over by it. They passed too the newly built library, the Bibliotheque Dinshaw Petit, built by another prominent Parsi, whose slight and long-deceased forefather had kept the affectionate nickname French traders had given him. Tata pointed to it, "A new French-language library."

Tata and Adivi arrived at the hotel an hour before the screening was to begin to start the evening with tea and refreshments—the hotel was known for its English–style tea service with scones and cucumber sandwiches. The Watson was a new hotel, a grand cast-iron building designed by Rowland Mason Ordish, who had just finished the Albert Bridge on the Thames. Every room in the place had its own balcony, and there was a ballroom in the atrium. The Watson's dark-skinned door-man approached the Tata coach, and as per his instructions opened the door, but when he saw Tata and Adivi, he knitted his eyebrows.

"Well, move aside, boy," Tata muttered, putting one leg out.

"Sir, I am sorry, the Watson caters to European clientele only."

Tata rose to his height outside the coach, and Adivi followed suit. "Have you any idea who I am?" Tata was a modest man and rarely resorted to such shows of arrogance, but his pride was injured and he resented being embarrassed in front of his friend.

"Mr. Tata Sir, I do realize who you are, and I apologize, but I cannot let you in Sir. I am on strict orders from Mr. Watson himself."

"Tata," Adivi said, standing next to his friend, "do not waste your time with this coolie." He pushed forward, only to have the doorman lay a hand firmly on his arm.

"Sir, you cannot enter." The doorman looked up, seeing other coaches with white clientele arriving. "Sir, please. I do not want to embarrass you. Please be on your way. I have to cater to these arriving guests."

Adivi felt the blood rise into his face; he grabbed the doorman's wrist. "Get your bloody nigger hand off me!"

Tata stepped between them. "I demand to speak with Watson now. We have tickets to see the Lumière exhibition, and we will bloody well see it."

The doorman spoke to a coolie in rushed, irritable Marathi and then bowed slightly to an English couple arriving. "Madam, Sir," he acknowledged, holding the door for them. The coolie had scrambled inside, and the doorman asked Tata and Adivi to wait.

Some white guests arrived, the ladies in evening dresses, the gentlemen in suits. Outside, posters boasted the Lumière screening: "Only engagement in India! Living Photographic Pictures in Life-Size Reproductions by Mssrs. Lumière Brothers on the night of July the 7th! See the moving picture show that has caused a sensation in Europe! Audiences jumping in their seats! Only at the Watson Hotel, Kala Ghoda, Bombay. Screenings at 6 PM, 7 PM, 9 PM, and 10 PM."

Some long minutes afterward, a tall British man with dark hair opened the hotel doors and spoke with the doorman, who pointed at

Tata and Adivi. Raising an eyebrow and inhaling, he turned to Tata. "Mr. Tata. My name is David Brown; I manage the staff here at the Watson. I have been informed of your situation and I regret to inform you gentlemen that under no conditions are Indians allowed as guests of the hotel."

"We have tickets," Adivi snarled. "I have come all the way from Waltair to see this exhibition. "

"Sir," Brown touched the tip of his mustache. "I am quite busy this evening as you can imagine. The Watson will be happy to refund you the price of your ticket. If that is all . . . ." Brown turned back to the hotel.

"That is not all, Sir!" Tata had never felt so angry. "Now, I demand to speak to your superior!"

Brown clicked his heels, turning back. "Sir, I am not going to ask you again. You must leave the premises immediately, or I shall be forced to summon the police. If either of you have any intentions of getting inside the Watson, I would be happy to take your name down for the next time we have an opening for a dishwasher."

BOTH MEN REMAINED silent on the trip back to the Esplanade House. Tata's regal profile looked forward in defiance; Adivi gazed out the window, allowing them both the privacy of their shame. Tata reached into the breast pocket of his suit, pulled out the tickets and slowly began to tear them, the pieces falling like snow to the floor.

The only Indians that night who would behold the Lumière films would be the servants working the night shift, who slept in the hallways of the hotel and saw bits of the 10 PM show when the English waitresses called them to go to the storeroom to bring up more ice or gin.

"THEY ARE REAL bastards," Tata muttered finally, his head shaking in disgust. "Real bastards."

"Do not take it to heart, Tata. One idiot who owns one hotel. He can go to hell."

Tata shook his head; his hands trembled with anger. "No. No, my friend. Their time is up."

Adivi spoke softly. "He is just one idiot, Jamsetji."

TATA AND ADIVI returned to Esplanade House and ate their dinner quietly, talking about the stormy monsoon rains outside, which had caused the coach to sway on the return trip. Lighting and thunder illuminated the walls of the dining room and punctuated their conversation with loud claps.

"Shivani!" Tata called the cook to bring in coffee after the meal, and this too they took quietly until Tata said softly, "I shall build a hotel near Watson's. Grander, more beautiful, open to all except him." The line of his mouth was straight but the corners inched slightly upward. He finished his coffee and sighed. Tata stood up. "My friend, you will excuse me. I am quite tired tonight. You will ask Shivani should you need anything else. Good night."

"Good night," Adivi offered, his sad eyes gazing out the windows of the Esplanade House, nature offering a show that was grand but not the one he had hoped for that evening. He walked to his room and lay down, still dressed, listening to the thunder. He turned his head toward the window, looking at silvery lines of lightning before closing his eyes. He conjured the image of a steely and intrepid locomotive emerging from the cloud of its own smoky exhaust.

Adivi put his hand on his chest. His heart was still broken.

❋ 1 ❋

EN ROUTE TO THE PRESIDENCY OF FORT ST. GEORGE,
SOUTH INDIA, OCTOBER 1911

I T ALL SUITED his sensibilities so, the silver tea sets that made a
merry tinkling with the to and fro of the train, the quiet efficiency of
the stewards, the reading car with its collection of newspapers. He had
been, upon arrival in Bombay, determined to keep faithful to European
dress; he thought it a burden worth bearing—as a European and especially as a Parisian—to be, at all times, a picture of style and elegance,
whatever the inconveniences posed by travel or heat. After some days in
the cars of this country's great black steam trains, however, and finding
his finest suits falling victim to perspiration marks and oil stains from
the station foods, he succumbed. The train stopped in Pune for several
hours, and he left the station and purchased an ill-fitting but comfortable, lightweight kurta: a long, summer-weight white jacket, with a pair
of slacks cut from the same fabric.

Seeing him in Indian dress, one of his fellow passengers, a British
engineer, raised his eyebrows and said, "Ah, Dr. Lautens, you've gone
native, I see," and Lautens peered over his worn copy of de Saussure's
Cours de Linguistique Générale and grinned.

"What are you reading, Dr. Lautens?" the engineer asked.

"The Bible," Lautens replied, smiling.

In his bag were other books too. English and Hindi dictionaries,
a book of Sanskrit roots, the Griffith translation of the *Ramayana*

13

and the Fauche one, for purposes of comparison, and Loti's *L'Inde (Sans les Anglais)*—his wife bought the latter and gave it to him, saying that he would at least have one other Frenchman traveling with him. It seemed so improbable to him this feeling—that here, this place not remotely stark or stoic, here, with a hundred people seemingly always around him, this place, a soaring urban space all bucolic at its blurred boundaries and where untethered animals mingled through the aisles of the city, the half-naked sadhus with the long grey beards and the Hindu rosaries, and that nearly ever-present splash of sunshine, exposing everything, and the constant sounds of the train: the roar of the engine, the boys walking through with coffee and tea, the old women fruit vendors, the endlessly inquisitive natives, here where the humidity, heat and dust all clouded the periphery of Alexandre's vision with the sheer crowdedness of the place—but there it was: he felt lonely. It was so foreign a sentiment to him that when he long lastly defined it, he found it surprising. And yet being neither a native nor an Englishman (his countrymen were few—and concentrated in French possessions like Pondichéry), he preferred to maintain a distance from everyone and remained wary, as he long had, of quickly forged friendships.

It was his fourth day on the train journey to the South—that great expanse of salty-aired land that still posed a mystery to most Europeans with its tribes and closed societies, its culture like a picture stopped in time. He breathed it in—India always smelled like it was burning, that hot dust and kerosene and petrol smell, as if under the earth was a smoldering fire, just there, beneath the surface. From Victoria Station in Bombay, and then away from the Arabian Sea, to Pune, Secundrabad. In Hyderabad he would transfer to Madras on the

Southern Mahratta Line, and from his next stop in Warangal he would ride along the Bay of Bengal to Waltair.

THE BRITISH ENGINEER always left his food half-finished. "The food and the bloody heat conspire to kill a man here. It is impossible; if you want my advice, stay away from the food and out of the sun, though of course I suppose one really can't avoid either completely. I try to eat only to the point of not being hungry; the rest I leave." He rested his fingertips on the rim of his hat; he always wore his hat and a three-piece suit, no matter the heat.

Though Alexandre had never considered himself a glutton, or even a gourmet, he had found that the thing he missed with particular intensity was the food of his country. Longing for the foods of home— completely unattainable in this part of the world—made him feel at times as if his mind was going. And hours went by before he could force away this useless reverie and bring himself back to the reality of the train: the brown faces that watched him in his window seat, his attaché case with his journals, books, and the first several pages of a manuscript in progress. Inevitably, the train's food steward would come around with the dinner *thali*—a main dish, usually of vegetables, surrounded with rice and small dishes of lentils, greens and pickles. This food offered its own particular satisfaction, and though it had begun to bore him now, he knew someday he would miss it too. At first he found it overly spicy, but he had grown accustomed to it, somewhat, and washed the heat down with heavy, white dollops of yogurt and fresh mango slices or jackfruit. The fruit here was unearthly in its sweetness and its richness, and it offered him a unique delight that was unmatched in Europe.

Tired as he was, and as thoughtful and pensive an adult as he had recently become, there was, just beneath the surface of his conscious thinking, in Alexandre, a kinetic, adolescent shudder, the boyish thrill of adventure to unknown lands. Since Bombay, he could not control his restless right foot and an ever so slight upward turn of the corners of his lips; all in all, he rather loved the view of that continual show of village after village outside his window, which Alexandre, new as he was to the subcontinent, found endlessly fascinating but which his train companions blocked from their sight by drawing the window shades down and concerning themselves instead with the imported newspapers from the places they called home: a white stone home off St. James Park, or those English villages with gardens of tea roses, those places that smelled in the summer of the salty North Atlantic.

Just now, as they passed through the fertile villages around Bijapure, a steward came around, in his steady hands a silver service carrying cream, sugar, tea and biscuits.

"No, I said one biscuit not two," the British engineer shouted. He waved his hand dismissively over the tea and biscuits set down before him and looked at Alexandre, sighing as if exhausted and shaking his head disapprovingly.

The steward looked bored, not shaken in the least by the engineer's sharp upbraiding. "I'm sorry, Sir," he said, removing one of the biscuits amidst the engineer's fussy, fluttering fingers.

"These people need instruction to perform even the most menial task, it seems sometimes!" the engineer said, looking at Alexandre, his long tapered fingers delicately holding the teacup.

Alexandre was supremely put off by such a sort of feminine fastidiousness regarding food, and for his part found no fault in the steward's service. Alexandre averted his eyes from the engineer's, taking deep pleasure in denying the Saville-Rowe dandy his companionship. Alexandre threw a meaningful, sympathetic glance at the tea steward.

Alexandre was not an Englishman; he shared with these people only his skin color. And there being no other Frenchman on the train, Alexandre at that moment declared himself a man without a nation, simply himself, Alexandre Lautens, and felt suddenly a wild and intoxicating freedom. He was a scholar, not a soldier, and he felt bound only to the kingdom of scholarship, of ideas, not those lines on maps that only men obeyed. All of those men, some small and some great: presidents, popes, despots, dictators. Even so stupid an animal as a pigeon had more freedom, not bound by the laws imposed by border guards where France met Spain. But a man must find his papers, those credentials given by other men, as if identity were not a birthright but a government issuance, merely a collection of yellowing papers.

Sitting in that train in a country utterly foreign to him, at that moment, Alexandre had successfully shaken off the shackles of society no more imagined than a prisoner's steel handcuffs. His body did not betray that newfound lightness, nor the soaring freedom he felt, but his eyes under his thick, dark eyebrows glittered with the color and sparkle of cut sapphires. Smiling at the engineer, Alexandre snapped a biscuit in half and pushed a piece in his mouth, eating happily, ravenously, the way his children ate oranges on Christmas morning.

THIS FOREIGN LAND went by, and drowsiness set on Alexandre as the world outside turned dark. It was odd, he thought, how quickly one could retire from the life he knew and held dear. Even the essentials of existence had quickly fallen away like the peel of a fruit, and soon he was left only with the meat, left only with himself. Two months ago, before he embarked on this voyage, he could not have imagined a life without Madeline, without her pale, long form and messy brown hair across his pillow. He remembered how her hips felt in his hands. Rose water and baby powder on her skin, and on the bedsheets, on Matthieu and Catherine when they would nestle in bed together, all of them fighting for her loving. He did miss her. But not as much as he claimed in the letters he had sent her from the port in Bombay and from the village post offices along the train route. Perhaps it was because life here seemed a thing apart, as if it were not a continuum of that Parisian existence. He missed the children in the same way, and yet moments would go by when he could scarcely remember that he was a father. And then shuddering, he would recall, from some deep well of that former life, how dearly he once held those moments: carrying Matthieu on his shoulders, buying Catherine ribbons or a piece of chocolate, kissing them good night, setting adrift paper sailboats in ponds, flying red kites in an endless blue, summer sky.

He thought perhaps Madeline did not miss him as she claimed, perhaps she too had moved away from their life together, and taken a lover, and perhaps this same man kissed his children good night, bounced them on his knee. After all, he had been away for some time: after he collected the necessary travel papers, he had first to take the train to Calais from Paris, and then a cargo-laden ferry from Calais to Dover. From Dover he traveled to London, where he stayed for four days before boarding a ship, which took three weeks to arrive in Bombay and then, at long last, he found himself on this train, headed south and then east. How impossibly large life seemed when he considered all the possibilities, how small when a choice was made.

CATALOGING A LANGUAGE is a never-ending task—words are added, or fall into ill repute or disuse. Innocuous terms become vulgar. The profane is edified. Grammar varies, has within it different registers—literary, formal, the easy speak of peasants. It is difficult anywhere. But the linguistic climate of India made this exercise infinitely more difficult, and—when Alexandre doubted the reason for his travel, when he felt frustrated with his work—quite nearly impossible. There were as many languages as there were gods in India, and that was very, very many. When a linguist was fortunate, a direct translation for a complicated word existed, and linguists were rarely fortunate. Most complicated were verbs—the translation for a single verb tense in one language could take three or four words to only approximate the meaning in another. Speakers would impose the correct structures of their native languages on learned ones.

He thought back to college, when he embarked—much to the amusement of his friends and family—on learning Sanskrit.

"*Sanskrit* means 'refined,'" his college classics lecturer, Dr. Bonventre, had said. Bonventre's office windows were draped with curtains made of saris and he had a large stone statue of a dancing Ganesha on his bookshelf.

"Pāṇini, five hundred years before Christ, had identified 3,959 rules of Sanskrit morphology. *Three thousand, nine hundred fifty nine!*" Bonventre lifted himself up on his toes, looking skyward in amazement. " . . . he codified a hodgepodge of vernaculars, rarefied the language until it was, when spoken properly, an elegant, mathematical poem." In India, Alexandre could sometimes hear the language coming from inside temples that lined the train route, spoken as it was over the ringing prayer bells. Pāṇini must not have had much time left for anything other than the study of the language, Alexandre thought.

Dr. Bonventre wrote *Sanskrit* on the chalkboard and then drew a slash after the *n*. "The name comes from *sa*, 'self-fulfilled,' plus *skar*, 'educated' or 'cultured.' The name *Sanskrit* is the result of the sound change laws, called *sandhi*, with which you will be well acquainted by the end of this term."

And so Alexandre logged these words, these sentences, their strange structures, so unlike those found in the languages of the West and charming in their own way, and often musical, with a melody that fell into the cadence of those native varieties of French and English too, making familiar languages somehow strange and exotic.

ONLY A FEW months before, the Germans had sent their warship the *Panther* to Morocco; the world was smaller, tenser; wars were waged over bits of land, scrambling for tokens of empire, seeing now in the light of modernity how little there was to own on earth. Some few months later, an American politician named Bingham, while wandering South America's hills, had stumbled upon the ancient city of Machu Picchu. The photographs had been published in the European press: a city so high up it could be mistaken for heaven itself, buildings of stone, the mythical city of Vilcabamba, of which Bingham had heard rumors. The Agence Havas spoke to Bingham and he said, "In the variety of its charms and the power of its spell, I know of no place in the world which can compare with it." No place. Lautens remembered. The glory of the Louvre was dimmed now, after *La Joconde* had gone missing; from the safety of a corner neighboring a Correggio, it had been stolen. Warships named after wildcats, dormant cities in the sky, the abduction of a mysterious woman. The world grew smaller and larger at the same time.

INSIDE THE TRAIN car, hushed conversations carried on in the glow of reading lights; Alexandre could hear, from a neighboring car, the wail of an infant.

It was autumn in Paris now, and Madeline took an umbrella with her, an overcoat to protect her from the grey skies, the ever-looming threat of rain, the early fall of night. She wore boots to arm herself against the slush of fallen foliage; she walked the children to school. She would wear a hat, hiding a tightly pinned bun. The cold air made her cheeks pink. Men looked at her—there was no one to escort her, to mark her as his own, to protect her from their leering. She was beautiful half because of true prettiness and half because she believed so deeply in her beauty.

She made dinner in the evening. There was, in their home, in the evenings, the warm, quiet hum of happiness. Madeline drank wine while she cooked. She would turn her head back and kiss Alexandre while stirring stew. The children played, they grabbed her legs, required kisses when they fell, someone to cut their meat. Alexandre had been jealous when Matthieu was born, though he never said as much. Madeline put them to bed with stories and songs and lavish kisses. She undressed and slipped into the sheets next to him and Alexandre would breath in a garden of roses, clean linens drying in the sun, put his hand on her hip, touch the silk of her nightgown, close his eyes in the darkness, watch Paris sleep under the light weight of a blue and black night, daylight slipping away, the city growing quiet. Then Madeline would turn into his chest; he knew his children were asleep in their

beds. His family was safe. The house was quiet. Tomorrow was promised. Alexandre could not, so long ago, imagine life any other way or
have wished it differently.

Now, Alexandre was lulled to sleep by the heat and the train's
incessant rocking, its rhythmic sounds and motion.

LATE AFTERNOON, ON the fifth day of his train journey, the train
was held in a village station outside of Dharwar. The remnants of a
railway collision two days before had yet to be moved off the tracks.
From the station platform, as Alexandre stretched his legs, he could
see in the distance mangled black railcars on their sides. Loud, coffee-
colored workmen pulled the steel remains of the train off the tracks and
into a nearby field.

Alexandre returned to his seat. Too distracted to read or write,
he began to daydream. The previous summer, the Lautens family had
spent a week at Madeline's family home in Provençe. During the great
flood that year, in January and February, many of Alexandre's classes
had to be canceled and he stayed home with Madeline and the children,
and since then he had planned a summer holiday so the children could
shake off any lingering feelings of their prolonged confinement and
escape a city that was still in disrepair.

The days in Provençe were active with endless cycling, and on the
last day the heat was wonderful on their tired skin, and he lay in his
bathing suit on the sand. The beach was nearly empty. His muscles
ached. The water was clear and blue, and while the children giggled,
building their sand castle, he leapt up suddenly, and grabbing Madeline,
carried her to the water and threw her in. She gasped and laughed as the
coldness swept over her boyish form, which was graceful in a skirted

white swimsuit with pink flowers. He dove in after her. She climbed his body like a vine and he saw that feminine expression so long familiar to him: a woman ready to be seduced. His hair, which had only just begun to sprout silver at the temples, clung wet and black to his head. He kissed her mouth in the sea. The children ran in after them, and he caught Matthieu when he ran into the water; she, Catherine's chubby, warm little body. They swam with the children and later walked along the water's edge, looking for seashells. Alexandre's was the throbbing heart of his home.

Matthieu found a starfish, and when he did, Catherine cried. Alexandre held her and she pounded her head angrily into his chest as he and Madeline laughed. They ate freshly caught fish for dinner with white wine, local vegetables, and warm, crusty bread; the soil in that region, the closeness of the ocean, made everything taste better, more delicate. In the air: thyme and lavender. He put the children to bed, still in their swimsuits, Matthieu still holding his prized find, Catherine exhausted from her own rage. He fell asleep deliciously tired, with his fingers interlaced with Madeline's. They left sand on the sheets. Her skin smelled like salt. He hadn't remembered ever feeling so content.

As the black steam engine continued southward, great and roaring, the smell of salt grew greater, and he was often overcome by the memory of his son sleeping, his taut pink fingers clutching a starfish.

The light grew low in India now, as evening came, yet again. The debris of the accident up ahead and been removed from the tracks, and Alexandre's train lurched cautiously forward. He opened the cumbersome window of his car, unhinging the metal fasteners, and happily breathed in the warm, floral air, opening the top of his shirt to feel the breeze against his chest. Alexandre lit a cigarette. He could hear the black-suited dining steward making his rounds, the clinking of the dishes as they knocked into each other with the movement of the train. He could smell the hot food. It was pleasant but predictable. Tonight he would not join his fellow passengers; around him he saw them moving down to the dining car. A few upper-class Indians with children at Cambridge and Oxford, Anglo-Indians who would never be at home in that land of Shakespeare and Chaucer, the English military men and administrators, their families, all changed into their best suits and dresses to dine. He wished rather to eat alone with his daydreaming. At times like this, he found it hard to maintain a polite amount of curiosity about strangers; they were merely partners in this journey, and he saw no need to make more of what amounted to a coincidence of no particular importance.

He wasn't typically a recluse—Alexandre liked the company of others. But this train ride had been ruined for him on the second day when, as he was unconsciously muttering to himself while writing, a man in a bowler hat in the neighboring seat raised an eyebrow and, looking at him with icy coldness, said, "Please keep your thoughts to yourself. Your ramblings are disturbing my reading. No one else is interested in what you are writing there." The man then disappeared behind his newspaper.

Alexandre had been too surprised to respond beyond a lamely raised eyebrow and "Excuse me?" before returning once again to his notebook. Alexandre's mind went reeling—that that man, that wretched man probably went to church, and sat there every Sunday, superior and loathsome. An hour of piety each week but so lacking in compassion for his fellow man, this fellow rider along this journey, how ridiculous it seemed to Alexandre. That small, nasty exchange had colored his whole trip, and the night that it happened he fantasized about slitting the man's throat.

After dinner, it was routine for the men to gather in the gentlemen's lounge car for drinks and cigars. There they could wear their shirtsleeves and loosen their ties. Alexandre had joined them the night before, but their talk bored him endlessly—it was all the same—a cousin to the Parisian parlor room conversation that he had always tried so hard to avoid: gossip about the upper-class English families they all knew or at least knew of—the Hawleys, the Bakers, the Austins. Their estates and summer homes in Simla and Dharamsāla and other hill stations and their relations back home, and the various details and luck of their financial interests at home and abroad, complaining without self-regard of the ridiculousness of the native Indians. The English talked with the glee of gossiping schoolgirls about their fallen countrymen who had taken up with native women. They were able to maintain an exterior of manners around natives of high standing—doctors, lawyers and academics—but when no native was in sight, even those Indians were often referred to as coolies and darkies. Full from dinner, Alexandre made his excuses to the crowd heading toward the lounge car, and pulled from his attaché case his Pierre Loti.

Alone in the train car now, Alexandre opened the window, lacing his fingers through the protective iron bars. Alongside the train, a band of pretty, painted *hijras* in bright, colorful saris winked at him, blowing kisses and holding out their large, masculine hands for change. Their eyes were lined in black coal and fluttered seductively. Alexandre smiled drowsily; flashes of gold and pink and red and blue went by. He felt the wind blowing through his thick hair, and closed his eyes.

THE TRAIN AT long last entered the southern provinces.

This was a part of India that, while ruled by the British, was more meagerly populated by them than was the north of the country, and a degree of the native chaos in politics and culture remained. The men were darker, the women thicker, and very few of the North Indians with their Mediterranean coloring were to be found here. When they were in the South, they too, and perhaps more markedly, held their southern brothers in contempt. To the European, these shades of brown and black were less distinct. Alexandre was hundreds of miles west of Bombay, a thousand miles southwest of Calcutta, a light-year, a bout of daydreaming, the better part of a hemisphere from Paris.

❉ 2 ❉

THE DAYS BEGAN a clear grey—the light almost white—before sliding gently into blue and yellow, the morning sun pushing at first gently and then forcefully into the windows of his train car. The station hands in the villages shouted in Kannada. In the afternoons, the air and land became gold, and everything was colored by this strong sun, at once beautiful and dangerous to the European constitution. English women, at risk of heatstroke and fainting, retired at this time of day to the safety of the ladies' cars, away from the sweltering heat.

India was a green place: jackfruit trees, coconuts and bananas, jasmines, roses, moonflowers, grasses the colors of the sea, or like blades of silver; tomato, aubergine, okra, fruits and vegetables for which no English or French names existed, hyacinth, mangoes the lyrical shape of a woman's breast, rice and wheat, bougainvillea. This part of India sprawled out great and wide, in shades of brown and green, before melting into a peerless line of seawater that crashed in waves like diamonds, emeralds and sapphires. The view moved somehow seamlessly from buildings in the grand style of London, Amsterdam and Paris, to magnificent Hindu temples and Mughal mansions, to shantytowns and water-filled rice paddies and barren fields of brown made sterile by enforced indigo, opium and tobacco production. As the train rolled along the eastern coastline of the continent, Alexandre watched the ocean melt into the sand, which pulled at the water and surrendered it like a woman's fickle hand, opening and closing and at long last submitting to the water's departure as the evening came in, and the tide fell low under the silvery light of the moon.

And then the Indian night. Quiet, blue and black and clear, the dark eyes of the Indians sparkling in the omnipresent light of candles and oil lamps outside the train's windows. The strong smells of fried street foods, of evening blossoming flowers, the stringent rules of English society letting loose under the slow departure of the fatiguing heat whilst retaining something sultry and sensual in the dark alleys and secret doorways lending protection from a receding sun. Most of Indian life, it seemed, was lived after hours; as a Parisian, Alexandre found this very familiar.

Alexandre found himself wildly sentimental. India had made him sensitive to life in a way he hadn't been for so long. His life back in Paris had grown so routine, and the comfort in that routine had made way for a dreary, sleepy monotony. Going day to day as if sleepwalking—sometimes happily and rarely sadly.

In 1889, Alexandre had felt that peculiar dream of flight, there, on the Ferris wheel at the Exposition Universelle in Paris. It was his first memory of that particular feeling of being alive so different from simply being awake. He was very young then, still wearing short pants and made to watch over his sisters as they ate chocolates while walking up the stairs of the Eiffel Tower. As he got older, he realized that that state of vitality was not only impossible day to day, but inadvisable. How could anyone go about like that all the time? So sensitive, always striving and learning and listening, always seeing beauty and horror, how terrifying it all seemed. Adulthood, it seemed to Alexandre a somber and sober expanse—that long stretch between a winged youth and the eccentricities and frailty of old age.

MADELINE WAS SEVENTEEN months older than Alexandre. He had met her when she was twenty-one; he was nineteen, and an arrogant young man of the sort that in his adulthood he was weary of. There was little to be said for his younger self beyond that he possessed a keen intellect and a quiet ambition. His physical beauty was more girlish then; all else was unremarkable, and not different from other young men of his generation. He was sometimes brutish and coarse. He thought too much of himself and too little of the minds of his parents and teachers.

He was a student at the Sorbonne back then; he met her ankles first. He met those perfectly sculpted ankles, which led to perfectly sculpted calves as Madeline balanced herself on a rolling ladder in the philology department's library. He had for some days made a habit of asking for hard-to-reach books so that he might admire her without her knowing. Though (as she later told him) she had grown suspicious of his eclectic book requests, she obligingly smiled and went to retrieve the ladder. More often than not, they were not books he needed, and they rested for hours on his desk at the library while he studied morphology and Madeline. She had then, and still had now, wonderful taste in shoes and stockings. One day, he followed the single black seam up the back of her legs and up her skirt, and he cocked his neck to sneak a look at the slip he would sometimes catch a glimpse of. She kicked him in the face.

Her pale green satin shoe landed squarely on his nose. She did not say anything, just stared at him with her large green eyes, demanding an apology, which he gave her, stumbling over his quickly sought words. He asked her her name.

"Madeline."

And he knew her name and felt now he knew her. Madeline, like a sylph, and again and again Madeline. In the library and later, waiting for him in cafés, always Madeline. And now, knowing her name, he felt he knew all he needed to know about her, her name like a ribbon enveloping that body—softer than a boy's but not quite womanly. It was that same peculiar feeling of possession he felt when his children were born and he would look into their blue eyes and say their names and feel them become what they were called. Now Matthieu, now Catherine, gazing back at their father's too-handsome face and becoming his children under that quotidian but astonishing feat: that baptism of being named.

The next day he returned to the library with gauze on his face, and a bunch of fresh yellow tulips with a note of apology, and a request that she meet him later in a nearby café on the street Monsieur le Prince. He remembered feeling a wonderful sensation of being some beautiful woman's lover as he ran up the library's stairs with flowers, his overcoat flapping against his back, a light rain making the air wet. Another librarian, matronly and disapproving, snorted and crossed her arms over her chest when he handed Madeline the tulips.

She laughed at him when he tried to kiss her outside the café. Then, those dismissive reactions made her more alluring; Alexandre, with his archangel face, was rarely rejected by women. Later in life he would find her smugness withering.

"You cannot kiss a girl with a bandage on your nose, and plus, I don't want to be kissed—not by you, not now."

He was indignant. "When?!" He was a beautiful boy, and the reluctance on the part of any woman he was making advances on only amounted in his mind to a show of propriety. Real disdain he was not prepared for.

"You'll have to wait . . . anyhow . . . I feel I would be taking advantage of a mere boy . . . and one stupid enough to get caught looking up a woman's skirt."

Some months later, when her guard had dropped and the bandages on his nose had long come off, she showed him the library after hours. Years later, he could still see her pale hand agitating the formidable library lock on its heavy door. They went in to the dark, and with only small panes of moonlight and streetlight making their squares on the floor, she climbed the ladder and let him make his way up her legs guided by the seam on the back of her stockings. She giggled and clutched the ladder. He knew he wanted to marry her when she stopped giggling and at long last sighed.

A dark native steward in an English butler's costume walked the aisles of the train. His hands, in immaculate white gloves, were striking against the black of his uniform, the bluish hue of his impossibly dark skin.

"Coffee or tea, Sir?" he asked, his timbre affected, his bored eyes heavily lashed. The tips of his full mustache had been waxed, and his thick hair had been combed in the manner of a matinee idol's waves. He carried two silver pitchers with an ease that did not suggest their weight.

"Coffee, please," Lautens said, offering him his emptied cup. The steward filled the cup gracefully, his other arm bent behind his back.

THE TRAIN HAD stopped many times since leaving Bombay. Usually, Alexandre would wander the platform, trying Indian street food and buying fruit. He would stretch his legs, his back, his neck, before long lastly reboarding the train as the conductor, with all the flourish of his English and American counterparts, cried, waving his handkerchief, "Alll aboarrrd!"

But this stop was his. At last Waltair was declared in red lettering on signboards. He slowly and carefully read the Telugu signage. His body felt exhausted; the final few minutes of waiting as the train slowed into the station were the longest moments of the entire journey. Finally it happened and the train stopped, pulling the passengers' bodies forward before throwing them back against their seats. Men found their briefcases, women their parasols, children were ushered out by tired governesses. They nodded politely at those fellow passengers who would remain on for destinations farther south. And then suddenly his heart began to pound wildly in his chest. He pulled his attaché case from beneath his chair, and with legs that moved at first uneasily beneath him he disembarked.

Bulky stewards, also in English costume, unloaded his cases. When he finally descended to the platform, the task of collecting his belongings and meeting up with Adivi's servants seemed to have been miraculously worked out for him in rapid-fire shouting in native tongue between a man in a red European jacket on the platform and the train's head steward, a man with a white cummerbund and black bowtie.

Within seconds of descending the train, Alexandre felt that Indian heat no longer mediated by the enclosure of a train car, and he felt sweat trickling down his face and on his forearms and thighs; his clothes stuck to his skin and the ever-present dust clung to his face and in his lungs, a dry, spicy non-air that stuck in his throat. Feeling the dirt on his face and in his fingernails and nose, and sweat dripping off his chin, so many brown bodies, human and animal closed in on him, Alexandre felt nauseous and dizzy and, for the first time since his departure, a sudden and painful desire to return home.

THREE INCHES, HELD between the tip of a girl's index finger and that of her thumb, almost holding in her hand the roaring Atlantic sea, and the Pacific too, which moaned and thrashed like a temperamental god, and between: burgeoning concrete cities, fields of golden wheat, canyons, soaring mountain ranges, those ancient forests: the United States. A mere three inches between her fingertips. Anjali Adivi touched the tips of the map in the newspaper, a tiny dot in the state of California, indicating the town of Oroville, where white Americans had for decades moved toward the battering western ocean and the gold promised on its shores.

All around her, her mother and the household servants were readying themselves for their guest.

Oroville was where Ishi was found. He was the last of the Yana, who lived in the Sierra Nevadas, where once they ate fish and fruit. When the gold prospectors came, the Yana retreated to the cover of sylvan concealment. Ishi's mother and all the rest of his people had died. Starving, his hair shorn in mourning, he stumbled down the foothills and into the white towns below the forests.

It was morning in Waltair, and she was alone now. She could hear the servants in the kitchen preparing for the arrival of the academic.

Anjali held the newspaper in her hands and felt a fast swelling of some powerful emotion: tears filled her eyes and she began, there, alone in the garden, to cry for Ishi, the last of his tribe. She imagined herself without family or friends or kindness, only an object of scientific curiosity. The last speaker of his language, the histories he would take with him, all soon to be gone with this single man; he would take with him the story of his people, and sing for the last time certain songs. He was the only one on earth to know his given name, this brown-skinned Calàf. Anjali's lip quivered at the thought of that lonely man wandering from the forest to the foothills below, and to the scientists and museum curators who received him, and Anjali hoped Ishi would die soon.

❋ 3 ❋

"D R. LAUTENS?!" ASKED the man in the red jacket.

"Yes?" Alexandre leaned in toward him, shouting to be heard over the Indians scrambling about him, collecting trunks and placing them atop turbans on their heads, shouting irritated orders to each other.

"I am Subba Rao, Mr. Adivi's personal butler. I have been sent to collect you from the train station. You will please come with me," he said, his tone infinitely polite and deferential. Subba Rao then turned toward the men handling the luggage, his countenance changed suddenly, angry and aggravated, yelling in Telugu but peppering his speech with "Idiots!" a word that seemed much sharper with the twist of an Indian accent. The luggage handlers, men who waited in front of the first-class compartments for the descent of wealthy passengers, were not so well dressed, and wore short pants and shirtsleeves in military greens, dust and dirt on their hands and their bare feet, shawls wrapped about their heads to create a platform for the luggage they balanced there so effortlessly. They moved out of the airy stone train station, with all its chaos of passengers and beggars and vendors and station workers—thousands of people, it seemed, monkeys in the rafters, swiping bananas and bread from the food stalls, pigeons fluttering about, and to the surprise of Alexandre's amused eyes, an actual snake charmer. He was an old man, dressed in filthy rags of white, sitting cross-legged, playing a sort of flute-like instrument of wood, in front of him a hemp sack from which emerged a regal cobra. The snake's neck was engorged, moving with the man's flute, immune to the sounds of barefoot street children, and it astonished foreigners, from whom the old man solicited coins after each short song.

And the children. Subba Rao, with the same tone he had used earlier with the luggage handlers, tried to protect Alexandre from the tens of children who flocked around Alexandre, palms out.

"Mister, money, please mister."

"Englishman coins please Sir."

"Sir money please."

"Just one coin Englishman!"

"Sahib, please sahib!"

Again Subba Rao fired off in his mother tongue with the colorful addition of English scolding and insults, pushing them away from him, yelling over his shoulder, again in polite deference, "So very sorry, Dr. Lautens. My most sincere apologies, Sir. The carriage is quite near, Sir." Lautens felt a violent, frightened sympathy for these children, with their large, dark, sunken eyes, their scrawny wrists and hands thrust toward him, or tugging at his clothes: "Where do they go home?" he thought. "Who will watch over them, these small children?"

He sighed with relief when Subba Rao pushed them away. And Alexandre turned and saw them behind them, a cluster of browns and reds and grasping hands.

The coach was beautiful, of an old European style with handsome, large horses strapped to it, the carriage wooden and plush with red cushions and silk curtains.

"You please sit inside and rest Sir, while we load the trunks," Subba Rao said, his arm extended toward Alexandre to help him into the body of the coach. Alexandre sat there while the men loaded his belongings, and admired the station from the outside. The children had caught up with them, surrounding the carriage, their hands pushing through the curtains, Subba Rao yelling at them. When the luggage was loaded, and the driver swatted at the lead horses' muscular rumps with a leather whip, the children ran after them for a few yards before the horses picked up speed. Subba Rao saw Alexandre looking backward at the children with naive sympathy.

Waltair had strong Dutch tones, as per its history, and was lined with palm trees, which gave it an air both stately and exotic. The coach made its way through Waltair and Alexandre fished in his breast pocket for his cigarettes. The red, white and blue flag of the Vereenigde Oostindische Compagnie had been taken down some one hundred years prior, when the British had annexed all the Dutch settlements in India. The VOC flag was replaced by the red flag of British India. Near the flagpole on Waltair's Dolphin's Nose—so called because that bit of land jutted out into the sea in the shape of a porpoise's snout—was the Dutch-built lighthouse and fort.

From Bombay to Waltair, Alexandre had been privy to so much impressive foreign architecture of late that he took in the fort in calm, studying the grandness of the place through swirls of cigarette smoke. Nearby, there was a cemetery. Thirteen Dutchmen who had lost their lives two thousand miles from the nation of their birth were buried on a hill overlooking the indifferent ocean that had brought them to India. Alexandre looked out upon the hill of Christian graves, deserted but peaceful, high above the city.

He had sweated through his clothes and the cool sea wind felt good on his skin. Below the hill, on the beach, the washerwomen who wore their saris cinched around their knees were laying out sheets over the sand to dry. With the arrival of the British, the Dutch left Waltair, and the presence of the French in the surrounding areas had dissolved into small, disconnected pockets—Pondichéry, Karaikal and Yanam on the east coast, and Mahé on the west.

The heat was more agonizing than any he'd felt in Bombay or the stops in between, and though the air was salty and the ocean near, the breeze did little to comfort him. The town, from first glance, was a medley of golds and reds, drier than Bombay, and dusty. The buildings were often beautiful and sometimes sat next to the straw and grass huts of the poor. Unlike the neighborhoods of Europe, poverty and wealth lived next to each other in India. The town's structures were a riot of pastels, whites and ivories. Buffalo, goats, pigs, chickens, horse-drawn coaches, pedestrians, cyclists all convened on the roads of Waltair, together, like a great mass of mottled humanity and beasts great and small, all converging in the light of a late afternoon upon some point in the horizon.

❋ 4 ❋

ALEXANDRE HAD BEEN in England the year before the last, doing research in the libraries of Cambridge in summer and early fall, and while there met with English philologists, many of whom were at the forefront of Indian language studies, having at their disposal the conveniences of colony. Silk-bound copies of Schleicher's maps of the Tarim basin, a handwritten note from William Jones. Love and life forgotten in that library to the comfort of a beloved and solitary labor of sound, word, syntax, grammar. The quiet comfort of study, half-empty cups of tea, hours of his life spent behind endless shelves of books. His stay in England was one of stately buildings, their medieval style so familiar to him, wildflowers, riots of yellow leaves in autumn, quiet reading rooms, outside their windows damp green grass, the sweet smell of rain in the air. His Cambridge colleagues, many of whom by virtue of their studies in religion, anthropology, history and of course linguistics had friends in this part of the world, had helped him fix his stay in India. It had taken three months of letters between Paris, Cambridge and Waltair to make the arrangements.

Alexandre, the most promising professor in the Sorbonne's philology department, was given a paid research sabbatical. His department had commissioned him to continue his interest in Dravidian studies, to write a grammar of Telugu.

The world grew smaller through the reach of empire, and Alexandre was told that Indians were nothing if not hospitable.

HIS KURTA DIRTY with the city dust, Alexandre arrived at the sprawling residence of the family of Shiva Adivi. Adivi was a man that Alexandre had been told was an aristocrat sympathetic to Europeans, a man with family money in fields of wheat and coffee, rice and fabric mills. And to own rice in south India was to own gold. It was the common starch of the land, and everyone, from street beggars to those with royal blood, sat down twice or thrice daily to a meal centered around a steamed vat of white rice.

The home was a grand one of the old fashion with an inner court.

It was from the coach that he descended, on the occasion of his thirty-fourth birthday, into the place where he planned to stay until he had a viable manuscript for his Parisian textbook publisher.

When Lautens arrived at the daunting mansion—cut in white marble and with guarded steel gates—he was at once impressed and comforted. Subba Rao shooed beggars from the gates of the home as the striking white guest took in the house. Servants in red waistcoats and spotless white cummerbunds welcomed him and waited for instructions from Subba Rao before moving, then took his cases and called the family. His trunks being taken to what was to be his room, he sat on a stone bench in the garden to wait for Adivi and his family. Bougainvilleas climbed the pillars supporting the house in explosions of orange and pink. There were lime and guava trees, and tomato vines heavy with orange and red fruit. Organized squares of rose beds and jasmine were separated with concrete pathways that met at a semicircle of marble where stood a wrought-iron gate outside of which Alexandre could see the city.

From some near corridor, Alexandre heard Subba Rao shouting commands in Telugu. Alexandre was gratified that he understood the order for coffee, and the female voice answering back in equal irritation. Alexandre rose when he saw the family.

Adivi was a handsome man, with refined features and a strong nose and the full mustache preferred by the men—or was it the women?—of India, large piercing eyes with heavy lashes and a neat, stern mouth. He, too, was wearing a kurta, though his was much finer than Alexandre's, cut from silk. Some varieties of silk here were so fine that they ruffled under the gentle touch of a woman's hand.

Behind Adivi, equally regal, stood four women: one old, in a simple white sari of cotton, with a look of benevolence and world-weariness upon her handsome face; the next, likely Adivi's wife, a lovely woman in purple and blue, with a refined and womanly bearing and a long, aquiline nose; and lastly, two females not yet women, no longer girls—in those few, tender years after childhood. The first of these was a young woman of a beauty so intense that upon seeing her, Alexandre caught his breath. Her sister had the shadow of her father's strong features though they did not suit a woman—she had an intelligent and suspicious air and was leaning her weight heavily on a cane.

"Dr. Lautens, I presume." Adivi held his hands up together in the customary Hindu greeting, his English refined with British tones.

Alexandre mimicked the gesture, to which he too had become accustomed, and bowed slightly to the women. Then Adivi smiled widely and offered Alexandre his hand. Their palms met in a hearty shake. Behind them, near the gates, the servants continued unloading his cases from the coach. Subba Rao stood at the entrance of the garden, and Adivi told him to caution the other servants to be extra careful with Alexandre's books. Bowing, Subba Rao left the garden area and walked toward the gates of the home. Adivi turned to his family, introducing him.

"A great man of letters, Dr. Alexandre Lautens. Dr. Lautens, this is my mother—"

"My name is Kanakadurga," the old woman interjected. She smiled, proudly, broadly. Her English was fluent and deliberate. Hers was a bright and astonishingly open face, and Alexandre smiled, boyishly and unguardedly, as he looked at her.

Adivi continued, "She is our daughters' *nainaamma*, grandmother; it literally means 'father's mother'—we have this distinction that doesn't exist in English." Adivi chuckled, "In some matters we Indians are superior." The old woman smiled sweetly and pressed her hands together. Alexandre had been told old women were referred to in Telugu as *amma garru*, "respected mother."

"Welcome, Dr. Lautens," Kanakadurga smiled, and she walked toward Alexandre and took his smooth white hands in hers, which were wrinkled and the color of cocoa. "It is our family's great fortune to have you here," she continued as Alexandre blushed.

"My wife, Lalita, and these are my daughters," Adivi continued. Now closer than at his first inspection, he took in the beautiful girl's face—the perfect gold skin, the large, dark eyes and delicate nose and mouth. About her face were thick knotted plaits of deep, inky black. "This," Adivi cupped the girl's face in his hands, his eyes warm with paternal pride, "is Mohini, my younger daughter . . . and this," he continued, still holding his younger daughter's face and motioning with his chin, "is my elder daughter, Anjali." The women all pressed their hands together once more, and he stepped back. "Oh and this," Adivi pointed to a sleeping sheepdog in the shadow of a tree, "is Byron." Adivi's mouth pursed as he heard harried clanging in the kitchen. "I apologize for the noise, Dr. Lautens, one of the peasant families nearby has had a death in the family, and my mother," he gave a sidelong glance at Kanakadurga, "has asked the cook to send over some rice and milk."

Adivi came eye to eye with Alexandre and smiled deeply and warmly. "My home is your home, Dr. Lautens, my family is your family. Your presence here is a very high honor for us. The servants will show you to your quarters, and after you have rested, you will please join us for our evening meal.

"Prithu!" Adivi called, and a boy servant answered from the outer corridor. The little boy listened to Adivi's instructions in wide-eyed, emotionless silence.

Prithu showed Alexandre to his room—it was splendid and simple, with a bed and dresser and desk made of teak, a deep and intricate rug in colors of burgundy and brown on the floor. The walls were left blank, which gave the room a light and spacious feeling. Alexandre lay down on the bed, stretching his tall body for a few moments. He was grateful at last to have some moments of his own, and he splashed cool water from the stainless steel bowl on the desk onto his face and changed into a suit, unsure of what dress was expected of him and wanting to err on the side of formality.

The servant child was waiting outside his room. Prithu's eyes were large and dark and he seemed younger than Matthieu. He led Alexandre in silence to the dining hall.

From the interior, the home was even more exquisite. The marble was cool to the touch and swirled in whites, creams, pinks and blues. It was wide and airy, the outside and inside not as distinct as in European homes. Still lizards clung to the walls. Rose and wisteria vines crept up the outer walls, palm trees yielding bananas and coconuts lined the property. The gardens were lush and fragrant. The home was furnished in a way that was at once minimal and decadent: all the pieces were exquisite, and so well fit their purpose as to leave need for little else. Mahogany and silk, a marble birdbath, the quiet and dutiful meandering of stewards and maids, some as young as Prithu, some as old as Kanakadurga . . . as dusk fell, the maids went about the estate lighting small candles in terra-cotta cups and swept small swells of dust off the marble floors and out into the garden with little, straw brooms held together with twine.

The long dining room opened to the inner garden on one end, the kitchen on the other. It was manned by more red-suited servants, all of whom seemed to be under the authority of a white-clad chef in the European costume. The family was standing, waiting for him, the elder daughter leaning forward on her chair for support. Silver dishes from which emanated rich scents sat covered on a cart, over which the chef stood guard, waiting, Lautens presumed, for him to take his place at the end of the table opposite Adivi.

When he stood there, Adivi said congenially, "May this be the first of many meals in which my humble family is graced by your presence, Dr. Lautens." And with a sweep of his arm, Adivi motioned them all to sit. Immediately upon sitting, Lalita hissed short words at one of the dining stewards, who quickly returned with a gleaming tray of silver-ware and made a quick turn around the table, hastily setting a fork, knife and spoon alongside the dinner plates. Lalita smiled at Lautens apologetically, "You must excuse us, Dr. Lautens. No matter how many times you instruct these servants, they can't seem to remember simple directions."

Alexandre colored, "Please! Don't apologize."

Adivi took up his knife and fork and with that everyone else took their cue also to begin eating. The food was served formally; Adivi and Alexandre were served larger portions of rice and meat. There was a stew of lamb, eggplants stuffed with dry spices, pickled mango in hot oil, puffed breads, lentils and spinach, a clear, red soup of oil and onions eaten with rice.

For the briefest second, Adivi's eyes widened, aghast, as his mother ignored the silver utensils in front of her and began eating with her right hand.

"Amma!" he said, in a barely audible hushed whisper.

Adivi's mother looked at him with a look so sharp that Lautens looked down into his plate in a feeble attempt to exclude himself from the tension.

He noted that the food was markedly milder than the food of the train, and wondered if this had been done in polite concession to his foreign taste buds. The water was poured from stainless steel jugs and its cold, metallic taste reminded Alexandre of sucking on icicles when he was a boy.

The servant came around with the ghee, warm, clarified butter, ladling small spoonfuls into each diner's plate, over the rice and curries. Not wanting to appear rude but warned by his friends in Cambridge against the rich excesses of Indian cuisine, Alexandre smiled and waved the servant away as he hovered over Alexandre's shoulder with a full spoon.

"What is that?" Kanakadurga asked with bemused confusion.

Alexandre colored, "I'm terribly sorry. It's just that I've been told to eat lightly while I'm here; you see, my system isn't yet much accustomed to Indian food."

"What nonsense!" Kanakadurga smiled and turned to the servant, waving her left hand animatedly as she directed in Telugu: "Go, go on. Give him some ghee."

Alexandre laughed nervously, resigned. The servant put a small amount of butter on his food.

"My goodness what is this! Put it properly. Must I get up and do it?" She leaned back as if to rise from her chair.

"Amma!" Adivi admonished his mother under his breath.

She addressed the servant again. "Put it properly," and then, as the servant ladled out two round spoonfuls of the fragrant butter over his food, "yes, that is it; yes like that."

"Dr. Lautens, how was your trip? You must be rather exhausted," Lalita said, her voice gentle and maternal.

"It was rather long, yes, but I do want to thank your family for your generosity and kindness, I feel rather refreshed, having rested in my room a bit."

"Oh, good."

"Dr. Lautens," Kanakadurga began, "my son tells me you have terribly good taste." She smiled, and Alexandre cocked his head. "You are studying our beautiful language? Telugu? How did this come to pass?" Alexandre smiled, glad the tension was broken. Kanakadurga resumed eating, sighing happily as she ate.

All the attention was on Alexandre, and he was courteously questioned on the nature of his academic pursuits and his family.

"Well, in university I decided to start studying philology, and I did my early studies with a focus on Greek and Latin." Alexandre mixed some creamed, spiced spinach with the rice and took a careful bite, chewing for a moment before he continued, "and then I started reading about the similarities scholars were analyzing among Greek and Latin and Sanskrit . . . and from there, my natural curiosity led me to the other languages of India. But I think that the moment it happened, the real moment I decided to study Telugu, was when I came across some French translations of the poet Vemana." He quickly eyed Kanakadurga; though the idea of eating with one's hands had initially startled his sensibilities, since being in India it had surprised him how neat a practice it could be. She ate using only the tips of her right hand; occasionally she would poke a hole in the pile of rice on her plate and motion for the servant to pour ghee in it. Alexandre cleared his throat, " . . . yes, I still remember the first poem of his I read, you must pardon my pronunciation," he smiled, *"Inumu virigeneni irumaaru mummaaru/ kaachi yatakavachu kramamu gaanu/ manasu virigeneni mari chercharaadaya . . . "* Iron, if broken, can be joined together, twice or thrice, but a heart once broken can never be put together again.

Adivi broke into a wide grin and clapped, "Bravo, Dr. Lautens! Bravo."

The Adivis were intelligent and curious, and verbosity in women seemed to be tolerated—even celebrated—but only when they attained a certain age. Neither of the girls spoke much, but Mohini looked at Alexandre when he spoke with wide eyes and a mischievous smile, asking him if he'd seen the Eiffel Tower, or what his favorite painting was in the Louvre; Anjali, however, seemed less taken with him, and mostly looked down. The attention of women was something he had long grown used to—he was charming and eloquent, but also beautiful, a characteristic that he relied on and was embarrassed by equally.

Alexandre smiled, his eyes wide and blue, "Yes, so I am here to write a grammar—a sort of description of Telugu for language students.

It is utterly foreign to European students, and I hope my book will serve as a sort of primer on Telugu. I wrote an outline on the train, and I'm hoping to get started right away . . . first by describing the pronoun system and then your incredibly rich and subtle verbal system." Out of the corner of his eye, Alexandre could see Mohini smiling, and he continued, "If I might impose now and again upon your family," he turned now to Mohini, coloring, "there is no better source than a native speaker." For so long, he hadn't had access to any real speakers—in fact he learned the language the best he could with the works of C.P. Brown, and a Bible written in rudimentary Telugu by French missionaries fifty years before. He knew a good amount of Sanksrit, and so he recognized many of the lexical elements of Telugu, but all the rest of the language presented constant challenges for him.

"But of course, Dr. Lautens," Kanakadurga answered, quickly. "We would all be happy to assist you in whatever ways we can."

"It will be my first major work of scholarship since I completed my doctorate," Alexandre said the last words to Anjali and caught himself; he was a scholar and did not need to prove himself to this girl.

Kanakadurga smiled, "Last night, my husband came to me in my dreams. Whenever he returns to me, it is an omen of blessings to come. You must be a good luck charm for our family, Dr. Lautens. I wonder what good things you will bring to us while you are here?" She had finished her meal and was now eating a banana.

Both Kanakadurga, with the well-honed wit of the elderly, and Lalita, articulate and intelligent, contributed as much as he and Adivi to the general conversation. Alexandre noticed Adivi's soft and affectionate glances at his wife. Between them was some sort of sparkling energy, like a shared secret, a happy one—though they listened to him with generosity and politeness, their attention was on each other. When the dishes were cleared, and a milky white dessert of mild cheese and syrup was served with rich coffee, Adivi said, "Dr. Lautens, it is with great honor that I announce, in your presence, that my daughter Mohini," he smiled toward his younger daughter, "is to be wed next month. We are very happy that you are here to share with us this most joyous and auspicious occasion."

Alexandre broke into a wide smile but then saw Lalita and Anjali. Lalita caught her older child's glance and looked down; Anjali's mouth tightened into a line; Alexandre noted the awkward exchange but offered congratulations to Adivi. The room fell silent, Adivi's face the picture of a sort of forced, tense exuberance. Alexandre saw out of the sides of his eyes that the announcement seemed to have moved Anjali to a sort of stunned silence, and the girl stared at her empty coffee cup and dessert dish. Her grandmother too said nothing but smiled, looking downward.

Adivi smiled widely, his eyes crinkling with joy. He slapped the table happily and said, "Champagne! We must have a toast." He turned to the servants and rattled off some instructions.

Two servants Alexandre estimated to be his own age returned with a Languedoc champagne bottle and crystal glasses. The glasses were passed out and filled in the peculiar silence that had descended.

Adivi raised his glass, and the others followed him, "To my daughter Mohini, and her future husband, Varun. May your marriage bring us all great happiness, and may it give myself and your mother many grandchildren."

After they finished the toast, Adivi turned to Anjali. "Anjali, perhaps you can recite some *ghazals* for our guest."

The girl looked down and sighed as if resigned. She stood, leaning against the table.

"Whose words tonight, darling?" Kanakadurga asked.

She looked hard at the table and began, in a soft voice, her gaze downward: "Mirza Ghalib," and then she started, *"Allah Allah aik woh log hain jo teen teen dafah iss qaid say chhoot chu-kain hain aur aik hum hain keh aik ag-lay pachas baras say jo phansi ka phanda ga-lay mein parha hai to nah phanda hi tut-ta hai nah dum hi nikalta hai."* When she finished she was looking not at but through her father, as if she could see the cold wall behind him.

Kanakadurga sighed softly and said the girl's name under her breath in a tone of gentle reprimand.

Lalita closed her eyes, as if she could block out the moment. It was not that she was simply angry. But she alone knew that family happiness was an altogether unlikely and fragile thing, and she protected it fiercely. She saw her husband's jaw clench and reflexively touched Anjali's elbow.

The quiet admonition about the table seemed to strengthen Anjali's resolve, and she followed in English, still looking, it seemed, at the wall behind her father, though her eyes now were soft: "God, God, there are some among us who have been freed from the prison three times and I have for the past fifty years this rope around my neck . . . neither this rope breaks nor it takes my life." She had memorized much of Ghalib, her father's favorite poet; she did it at first to please her father but did it now to spite him. To take from him something he thought was beautiful and to know it better and more deeply than he could.

And her father glared at her, as he often did, his face an expression of hate that masked the horror of his enraged and broken heart.

LALITA WAS EXHAUSTED. She smoothed out the pleats of her sari over her shoulder, pulling the long swath of silk around her waist and tucking it into her petticoat. Today was the culmination of a long preparation for Dr. Lautens; in the last few months, through postal messages and many-times passed-down messages across the Eurasian landmass, the Adivis had received notice as to his plans and needs. She hoped they had done enough to accommodate him. There were things to be done when one had a guest like Dr. Lautens. Lalita thought that with this type of guest, one must make one's life out to be not merely what it is in fact but what is should be: clean, moral, an exercise in good form, a well-set and generous table, intelligent conversation and social graces.

In the brief hours since he had been in the Adivi home, Lalita found him gentle and sophisticated; she did not look upon the Europeans as kindly as her husband did, and often found them boorish and superior. Due to obligations of status and class, the Adivis were regularly in European company, and too often she found herself desperate for the time when they could at long last part ways and return to the comfortable confines of their home. She had spent the last week overseeing the preparation of the home for their guest, and by night her feet ached and she would fall asleep quickly and deeply. She had all the bedclothes in all the rooms changed, the curtains and windows washed, the floors scrubbed and the hallways swept. Lalita sent the butler out to purchase extra soaps, toothpastes and powders. Two cooks were sent out to the import stores for liquors, wine, chocolate and candy and to the marketplace to stock the kitchen fully with all the basics: onions, garlic and ginger, Orissa salt, lentils, tea and coffee, nuts, oil, tomatoes and curry vegetables—the meat and fish would have to be bought on a daily basis when they were fresh, troublesome as that was.

Lalita knew Europeans ate meat every day and felt it would be impolite not to provide this for Dr. Lautens, distasteful though she found it. The food would have to be cooked in a more mild fashion for Dr. Lautens, but her mother-in-law would insist on fully spiced curries and Lalita worried that for the next several months she'd have to supervise two full sets of meals; the cook, she knew, would put up a fuss and Lalita hated arguing with the servants. Just thinking about it made her anxious; houseguests, as often as the Adivis had them, always posed extra work for her, but since this guest was European, the work was redoubled—otherwise she wouldn't need to concern herself with silverware and washcloths, table settings and flower arrangements. That sense of self-consciousness that caused her to clean the house from floor to ceiling was stronger around foreigners, and knowing that this would be an extensive stay made her sigh periodically in anxious anticipation as the servants ran about the house carrying buckets of soapy water, bundles of freshly laundered linens or baskets full of potatoes.

She sent to Bombay too for a French-English dictionary, in case one of his needs were lost in translation; her husband told her that Dr. Lautens spoke fluent English, and good Hindi, but Lalita believed that one can master other languages but the only one he'll ever really know is his mother tongue.

Despite how tired she was, there was that singularly pleasing feeling of overseeing the folding of linens or the assembly of the silverware drawer, that wave of satisfaction from completing a wifely and self-sacrificing task, that exhaustion that came from cooking and cleaning that so reaffirmed her. She was the woman of this house. It was a series of small tasks: leaving a room spotless, anticipating her husband's need for more rice and mango pickle before he asked for it, keeping the pantry stocked with her mother-in-law's favorite brand of biscuits, making the whole ordeal of wifely duty—to perform all these tasks and a thousand others all while wearing a clean sari scented with talcum powder, her hair in a neat bun, always ready to graciously receive last-minute guests, to make all of this look effortless was what filled Lalita with her quiet, womanly pride. It was a part of her very femininity that, through repeated and constant show, she had attempted to pass down to her daughters—successfully to Mohini but to which Anjali seemed immune. Her elder daughter's cold superiority had alienated Lalita more and more as Anjali grew out of girlhood.

AT THE TIME of Lalita's marriage, the 1891 harvest of mangoes began with such a boon of perfect sunshine and rich soil that her father had to hire extra farmhands to collect all of the fruit in the great wicker baskets that when full shone like pots of gold. However, at the height of the season in late June, while she and her mother were being visited daily by silk vendors with wedding saris in their trunks, a plague of fungus started on the mango trees, and as quickly as her father had hired the farmhands, they were let go. She could still remember, as she looked out from the sitting room onto the verandah, her noble father, offering up poor explanations to emaciated, sinuous young men promised a summer of work. They—brown boys with bare feet and dirt embedded in their hands—left with less than they had hoped for but slightly more than they had actually yet earned.

The mango grove, for the rest of summer, smelled of rot; flies swarmed it, and birds pecked at the blackening fruit. Nevertheless, by August the home was festooned in red and saffron curtains, and the maids dusted auspicious *kolam* patterns in white chalk on the home's doorsteps. She had met Shiva once before the wedding. In a kurta of cream silk with silver thread embroidery, he had arrived with his parents, a butler and the driver of their coach.

She was taken first by his handsome face. But later in the meeting too by his swift and arrogant manner, tinged by tenderness and humor. So decisive a young man—Shiva was three years older than she—and in whom the corporal so perfectly manifested his personality: robust, broad, with light touches of the feminine in long eyelashes and lips curved into the shape of a warrior's bow. To that first meeting, she wore a sari of pink, thinking it innocent, feminine and virtuous. Her mother had dressed her hair, braided in a single rope with jasmines. Lalita lined her eyes with soot-colored *kajal*. Foreign aid of this sort was rarely resorted to—Lalita's beauty was well-known among those of their community and wanted for little. But this occasion was pivotal to her whole life, and she without shame would admit that when she stole a glance at herself that day in the mirror she was surprised, proud and elated at her loveliness. Though there was some relative difference in the family's wealth, and though Shiva was known to be a bachelor of infinite eligibility—handsome, rich and from a good family—her beauty gave her family the upper hand. He would want for no one else. Shiva's father was like his son: tall and proud; his mother was deeply maternal, her body already heavy, her brow sympathetic and intelligent.

Both of their families had retained ownership of the land through the permanent settlement licenses reached between the East India Company and authorities of the Princely States a hundred years before. Part of the contract ensured that their families, and others in a group of then nascent landed gentry, would continue to grow not only food crops but also indigo and tea. The ever-increasing tax on a presumed crop had forced many families to sell their land, but the Adivis through their close connections with the English had made a success of the treaty.

FOR ANJALI, HAVING guests was always painful; to each new person who saw her she knew she inspired a new pity, or shame or disgust. Each felt she was a source of ridicule or pain. Frequent though guests were in their home, she never stopped feeling the intrusion. Her father would often receive business associates, aunts, uncles, cousins and distant relatives. Of the relatives she had her favorites, but most it seemed reserved their smiles for her sister, who would flutter into the receiving room with a tray of filled teacups. The formality of manners required in the presence of strangers made home less homelike, and the putting on of formal airs, especially in the presence of Europeans, exhausted her. In the company of her father's Indian friends, a "namaste" and a smile were usually enough; sometimes they would ask her how she was, but nothing much more. Around Europeans she was required to answer questions too. With white guests, she was expected to talk about the weather and her studies and interests, all with a rather feigned deference to their station and race, and more often than not, the fact that they were men alienated her further; few white women called upon her parents, as many of the wives of the Englishmen remained at home in cold, stony England, or at the very least passed most of the year with their children in the hill stations, where the weather and climate were said to be more suitable for European ladies.

HERE, AS NIGHT fell, the garden's night bloomers opened like shy children, surreptitiously, and the scent of flowers fell over the home like a velvet curtain. The floor, the walls, even the sheets emanated the long-held heat of day, like an angry woman opening a tightly clenched fist. Kanakadurga had gone to bed; Adivi and Anjali were reading the paper, Lalita was overseeing the servants as they completed their nightly chores, Mohini was embroidering handkerchiefs. Adivi had offered him an after-dinner drink, but Alexandre made his excuses and declined, too tired. "You girls get ready for bed!" Lalita shouted at no one in particular. "Go! Anjali! Mohini! Get up, go! Anjali! What did I say?!"

Lalita took a softer tone than her husband with Anjali, and Alexandre imagined it difficult for Lalita to see a daughter with an old woman's gait, who walked with a cane and sighed when she bent to sit or rose to stand. From a distance, she seemed a brightly dressed elderly lady, taking her afternoon tea, and sometimes Alexandre was surprised when she would turn her head and he would see the profile of a girl.

AS THE SKY was blanketed in midnight blue, and the stars pushed from within it, bright like bits of glass, Alexandre took out the journal he had kept on the train, filled with notes on Telugu etymology and syntax, interesting idioms and sayings. Describing languages was like pinning down a butterfly; just at the moment it was caught, it fluttered its wings, already escaping. Elegant translations, for the complex words, for the higher concepts, were few and often cumbersome. Alexandre saw a moth buzzing about the kerosene lamp and inhaled deeply of the oily, addictive smell.

He knew what drew him to this discipline of linguistics. He supposed it was, in some ways, only his interest in all things, all aspects of learning—but language was the most fundamental. His colleagues in mathematics would disagree with him. His children, waiting for bed-time stories, would not. He found that to understand language, like philosophy or religion, but unlike physics or biology, was to understand something profoundly human and close to the heart.

He felt that there was no place more right in this world to study the profound and sacred than India. He feared that France too soon would loose her foothold in here; but before that, he would have his speech samples, his lists of Dravidian family trees, his register of sounds.

To an observer, he was sure he seemed less a scientist than a scribe: a glorified gossip, an eavesdropper. But still he thought there was art in it; there was affection and care administered to the languages he worked with. He strived to describe the full richness of their sounds, the complexity of the meanings of the words, the modes in which they were acquired, their ways for describing time and space, for setting the world into sense.

He would start with the basics, addressing the linguistic structure of the Telugu family, and began to write:

FAMILY TERMS IN TELUGU

Bharta	Husband
Bharya	Wife
Naanna	Father
Amma	Mother
Koduku	Son
Kutaru	Daughter
Annayya	Older brother, also older paternal male cousin
Akka	Older sister, also older maternal female cousin
Thammadu	Younger brother

Chelli	Younger sister
Mamayya	Maternal uncle, also father-in-law
Attamma	Paternal aunt, also mother-in-law
Pethnaanna	Older paternal uncle (lit. "older father")
Chinnananna	Younger paternal uncle (lit. "younger father")
Peddamma	Older maternal aunt (lit. "older mother")
Pinni	Younger maternal aunt
Tata	Grandfather
Nainamma	Father's mother
Ammamma	Mother's mother
Manavaralu	Granddaughter
Manavadu	Grandson
Menalludu	Nephew
Menakodalu	Niece
Bava	Older brother-in-law
Maridi	Younger brother-in-law
Vadina	Older sister-in-law
Maradalu	Younger sister-in-law
Alludu	Son-in-law
Kodalu	Daughter-in-law

HIS STOMACH FELT full but not overly so, and Alexandre felt good and languorous, tired but glad, knowing he would sleep well tonight. He felt easy in his body for the first time since getting to India—finally, he was done traveling. At least, for the time being. He set his pen down and leaned back. Alexandre could feel the weight of muscles and bones. He felt again planted in his body, he felt human again reconstituted all the way to his fingertips and toes and even the tips of his ears.

He reached for the pictures in his pocket of Matthieu and Catherine in their white baptism dresses and began to fall asleep in the safety of knowing that his children were succumbing to sleep as they too gazed upon the same rotund and pearly moon. Alas. He blew out the oil lamps by which he read. He was tired now and needed sleep.

There is no sleep like that of the weary traveler—all the muscles succumb, the heart slows its pace, there is no need for a comfortable bed or fine linens—though he had both. And so he slept, deaf to all noise, blind to the nightly movements of the heavenly bodies, dreamless, half expecting to wake up next to his wife in his bed in Paris.

IN PARIS HIS family lived in the fifth arrondissement, near the university, and he walked to his office in an old medieval building. The architects of those buildings could scarcely have imagined the languages taught and studied in them now. Early in the day the sun poured down over the imposing, grey structures and they seemed briefly less serious than they otherwise did. The mornings had always been his—in Paris he woke early and walked to the small café on the corner, arriving with the first-shift waitstaff, who greeted him with the strange mix of gentle good humor and aloof familiarity. The cold metal of the chairs, the smooth tables of finished wood, ink stains on his fingers from an unwieldy newspaper—how great the quotidian and daily gift of morning. He could scarcely understand why anyone would choose sleep over sunrise, over an endless violet sky. But as he so dearly loved coffee in silent solitude, he was glad so many did.

He chose the day and the sun.

❧ 5 ❧

A LEXANDRE WOKE UP, feeling still dizzy and not entirely sure where he was; his body felt like a leaden weight and he tentatively stretched his fingers. The sun was out and he couldn't tell what time it was, and though he knew he was in a home, when he closed his eyes he could still feel the rocking of the train. He heard wrestling in the trees and the sound of clinking dishes and footsteps. He smiled for a moment, feeling very anxious, understanding he was not at home, not his home anyway; he blinked away a haze of confusion and realized he was in India, in Adivi's house, and he reached for his silver cigarette case and lighter. He sat up in bed and smoked, wondering if anyone else was awake, and if so, how exactly he should enter the main house. He looked through swirls of smoke, wondering exactly how to make his entrance, and wearily eyed his bags. After a few moments, he slowly stood up, his legs trembling slightly as he found his balance. He stood, realizing that he had a pounding headache like those he sometimes got from oversleeping. Touching his temples, he kneeled by his luggage, carefully loosening the buckles and zippers and pulling out a white shirt and dark trousers. He splashed his face in a basin of cool water left by his bedside; he undressed and noticed on his white chest and arms a few angry red mosquito bites. He dressed and raked back his dark hair with a wet comb. He grimaced: his stomach ached dully from all the travel.

Alexandre put out his cigarette and blinked into the mirror. He looked older than the last time he'd had a moment to examine his face.

The little lines around his eyes and mouth looked deeper. He had taken his beauty for granted most of his life. But as he disliked vanity in men, he tried not to pause in front of mirrors too often. Standing in front of the mirror, he felt embarrassed that he noticed his aging and even more so that it bothered him, making a small vague feeling of panic in his chest. Alexandre sighed and wondered if he should put on shoes—the family went barefoot in the home, but it made him feel awkward and informal to walk around that way. After a few moments' consideration, Alexandre chose to defer to the native custom. Alexandre, feeling oddly vulnerable and childish in his bare feet, tentatively opened the door of his room.

In the courtyard, two female servants, with their tattered saris tied between their legs, swept the stones with twine brooms and soapy water, their bright white teeth gleaming in contrast with their sun-blackened faces, their cracked heels and spaced-out, almost simian toes. They chatted with each other, laughing, telling vulgar jokes and the gossip from the nearby villages they were from. The thin hair of one was coiled into a bun; the other wore a large, silver nose ring. They had a look about them, as if they smiled a lot. Seeing them, Alexandre hesitated for a moment, at once aware of the superiority of his station with regard to theirs and yet feeling like an invader. Noticing him, the servants turned and smiled silently; Alexandre smiled, feeling strange, and looked down at his hands. His eyes darted around, looking for any of the Adivis, until one of the maids pointed at the dining room and said, "Mr. Adivi."

Alexandre nodded his thanks and smiled, relieved. He had long prided himself on his manners and his ability to say and do the right things, even at times when others didn't, and he realized how irritated he was in that strange moment. His education and comportment failed him—he wondered if the maids thought him a fool. But they—uneducated and lower class as they were—had no standing to judge him. He shrugged it off.

THAT MORNING, ALEXANDRE had Subba Rao go into town to a store where last month's European papers were sold. Adivi had put the servants at Alexandre's disposal, and they catered to him while the house busied itself, not just with the normal daily tasks but with wedding preparations. The cook was preparing to go to the market and shyly addressed him in her lower-class Telugu, "Sir, Miss Mohini has asked for shrimp for dinner and Miss Anjali has asked for squash. Is there anything you would like?"

Alexandre smiled and told her he'd be happy with whatever she bought.

He read the newspapers in the evening: there was a September issue of *Le Journal*. On the cover was another story about Hiram Bingham's discovery of that ancient South American town thousands of feet above sea level. Lautens closed his eyes, sipping coffee.

BINGHAM HAD, BETWEEN schooling at Yale and a research post in Bolivia, heard of Vilcabamba—a mythic town of the South Americas— mentioned in the yellowing originals of the first European diaries written on that southern continent. It was said to be the last foothold of the old empire, at once so vast it had had in its hold all that is Ecuador, Peru, Chile . . . it ended only when the sea began. Pizarro's men had killed in a fraction of an hour all Emperor Atahualpa's mightiest men— men whose bodies had generations before adapted to the place's thin air and could, without great effort, run the endless, rugged coastline of the empire. Atahualpa crushed underfoot the Bible offered him by Pizarro. He and his men would not convert even under threat of Spanish swords. He cried, "I am no man's tributary!" and moments later, his men around him dead and dying, the weary emperor was imprisoned by the Spaniards and bargained for the mercy of strangulation with roomfuls of gold and silver. The last of his few living soldiers raced up the treacherous South American hills carrying their wives and children where European legs could not go. They went to Vilcabamba, and there lived out the last years of empire unmolested and undiscovered by Pizarro's men.

Bingham's colleagues in Incan and Mayan studies in North America had humored him, had heard the name in passing. But they were men of science, and the quest for this South American Atlantis was of little interest to them. Years passed, but Bingham soon found himself again in Bolivia and Peru. Wandering the ancient Bolivian back roads, short of breath for the sheer altitude of the place, he saw it, shrouded in grass and vines, as if nature had conspired to hide it. He and his men were eight thousand feet above sea level and in front of his eyes was a seamless meeting of the red earth and blue sky. Vilcabamba—Machu Picchu, as it would be called. The city in the sky. Bingham and his team hacked at plants. But before doing so marveled at the patience of grass—how the tenacious growth of hundreds of years could conceal all the glory of man's great achievement of the city. Monuments of stone and cement emerged—the stubborn vines clinging to them like jealous lovers, the sun showing on buildings it hadn't touched in hundreds of years. The buildings were so austere, as if no humans had ever inhabited them. There were none of the human signs—no bones, no tools or etchings on walls. The sky was so clear, like only a mirror that may shatter and fall into the ancient city.

Bingham had family money and a European education; he had seen the ruins of Greece and Italy, the Taj Mahal, the Great Pyramids of Giza. And yet, under the vast blue sky, gasping for breath in the under-oxygenated air, sweating under the South American heat, Bingham was at a loss for words, and, mouth agape, he took in the marvel in silence, his European eyes the first in four hundred years to set sight upon the great old metropolis.

Alexandre wondered: how many lost cities were there, nations buried or sunken? How many languages died up there in the mountains of Peru, or drowned under the torrents of terrestrial tide, our ancestors ill equipped against the sudden crashing down of water walls?

ADIVI ASKED THE cook to make some coffee and later remarked that he would like to have *gulab jamun* for dessert. Dinner was Adivi's favorite meal, a time for him to assert that paternal force as the head of the family that he felt his due and right. He liked the ritual of it, and the formality—that the whole family ate together, unlike the casual and scattered breakfasts and lunches. He liked the line made by his daughters and wife and mother from his position at the head of the table. He sat smiling at the table, calling to the cook to ensure that she was able to get good shrimp at the fish market. The cook called back, assuring him she had gotten to the market early and had gotten the best pick.

"Good," said Adivi, contentedly waiting for his family as he skimmed through the paper.

The familiar feeling of his heart being squeezed set in when Adivi saw his daughter Anjali. The feelings of pity and fear aroused in him by his daughter's sickness and that absurd limp and the lack of beauty had his paternal love in a clawed grip. He tried to approach her again and again with love, after feeling awash in the guilt that his disgust aroused, but it always failed. His love was aroused always by pride, the kind of pride he felt in his wife's grace and elegance or in Mohini's beauty and that virtue that wore itself so proudly on her person. He felt it not vain but honorable that his clothes and family should all reflect a sort of virtuous propriety, and though he couldn't fault Anjali for her deformity, any disruption in that appearance grieved him deeply, and this was an affliction he could not rid himself of, not even for his daughter.

And Alexandre felt ashamed of Adivi, because Adivi reminded him of himself. Because when his daughter was a baby, she too had been very sick, and Alexandre had that thought that horrible thought that he was sure might keep him from heaven: when it was quite uncertain that Catherine would live, he thought simply, "We could still have another baby." And he felt such shame that he had thought his baby replaceable. He might be able to have another child, and perhaps even another daughter, but if she had died, he'd never have Catherine back.

ALEXANDRE CONTINUED TO write about Telugu nouns with a quick guide on forming the possessive:

POSSESSIVE FORMS IN TELUGU

My tiger	Naa pulli
Your tiger	Nee pulli
Your (pl) tiger	Mee pulli
Our (incl) tiger	Mana pulli
Our (excl) tiger	Maa pulli

Their tiger	Vari pulli
His tiger	Athani pulli
Her tiger	Aame pulli

AT NIGHT, THE home was like an island. From the outside in, it seemed as if it might have been the last salvation of a dying race, a sort of Hindu-Mughal Noah's Ark; lights and guards with lamps illuminated it, a floating Atlantis in a sea of the dark roads and unlit alleys that surrounded it. Inside, it was safe. The marble floors cooled in the evening, the stucco walls remained warm, fireflies flickered in the garden.

Weak with grief, it was through these corridors that Anjali raced in her awkward, aided gait, the skirts of her nightdress skimming the floor, toward her grandmother's bedroom. Alexandre wasn't meant to have seen her, of course. He woke, refreshed by a deathlike sleep; his body was still confused by the long journey, and it was the small hours of the morning. Alexandre walked through the house like a pale apparition, feeling invisible. He had meant only to fetch some drinking water from the clay pot in the kitchen. Weak grey light was only beginning to enter the home, the house full of shadows. He rose from bed, his body infantile in its first attempts to walk after so deep a rest. Disoriented and groggy, he moved about the home, enjoying its nocturnal stillness.

And that was when he saw her, from the shadows of an adjacent hallway. With one hand covering her sorrow-contorted face, she pushed her grandmother's bedroom door open. Though he knew it was bad form, Alexandre followed Anjali at a distance, and in the lamplight of the hallway, he saw her sink to the floor beside her grandmother's sleeping body.

How she wailed for her grandmother in the semi-darkness.

"Nainamma!" She cried, shaking the old woman awake, holding her by the arm. "Nainamma!" She sobbed for her again and again, until wearily Kanakadurga woke, and seeing the child sat up.

"My dear . . . my dear," she said, and Anjali crawled into her grandmother's bed and took solace in her arms as tenderly Kanakadurga stroked the girl's hair. She seemed already to know the source of the girl's misery. And clutching the old body of this woman who, it seemed, had with such sweetness loved her her whole life, she wept until exhausted and fell asleep.

Kanakadurga, holding her granddaughter, looked up and saw the fast movement of a shadow retreating in the hallway.

❋ 6 ❋

A S IT HAPPENED, and to Alexandre's slight annoyance, it seemed he and Anjali shared a habit of waking up early. Every morning she would say, "Mary, bring some coffee," and Anjali's voice was cold, her eyes not even lifting to the servant woman's. Despite her handicap, Anjali was able to convey a profound degree of an icy sense of superiority. Though the color of her eyes was a rich, dark brown, they were set with a look of glacial calm, a masculine hardness that Alexandre found unnerving in a girl.

And every morning Mary would reply, "Yes, Miss Anjali," and scuttle back from her mistress, her plump, pleasant bovine face lowered in submission.

Mornings in the Adivi household started early. By daylight he could hear the sounds of the servants gathering water and readying the day's food preparations and feeding the dogs. Occasionally, he would find Adivi up reading the paper in his white nightshirt and dhoti, but the women of the house never left their rooms without having bathed and dressed first. He had never seen Lalita look so much as slightly disheveled. When she made her entrance, she would head straight for the kitchen and oversee making breakfast. Kanakadurga performed her morning *puja* after a bath each morning and Alexandre would sometimes hear her repeated Sanskrit mantras or hear her ringing a prayer bell as he made his way out to the garden.

Alexandre took a cue from Adivi and allowed himself a degree of casualness in his morning appearance. Time was important, as he hoped to salvage an hour before breakfast for work. Walking to the garden that morning, Alexandre was surprised to see that Anjali was already there, sipping coffee and reading the newspaper, her hair freshly washed in a wet braid and wearing a sari. She did not look any worse after her sorrowful night.

Byron was curled on the cement, in the shadow of a guava tree. He greeted everyone with the same expression of total indifference—a single eye raised, followed usually by a tongue-stretching yawn. He barked only at monkeys and in his most extreme shows of athleticism would put his forepaws on the trunks of monkey-inhabited trees and bark, relenting only when his master called his name.

Alexandre smoothed his hand over the page in front of him:

NOMINATIVE DECLENSIONS IN TELUGU

Ill(u)-nunchi	from the home
Ill(u)-ki	for the home/to the house
Ill(u)-kosam	for the benefit of the home
Ill(u)-paina	on top of the house
Ill(u)-krinda	below the house
Ill(u)-waraku	until the house
Ill(u)-lo	in the house
Ill(u)-mundu	in front of the house
Ill(u)-venuka	behind the house
Ill(u)-ledu	without a house
Ill(u)-tho	with the house
Ill(u)-gurinchi	concerning the house
Ill(u)-prakkana	next to the house
Ill(u)-meeda	on the house

PERHAPS HE WOULD have Anjali check it over for accuracy.

Alexandre stared blankly at the stones, making shapes—that one there looked like an ear and then one over there like a palm frond. His feet were tanned in weird stripes made by his Indian sandals. His face, neck and forearms were also more golden than when he had arrived.

"Good morning Anjali," he said, quietly announcing his presence so as not to startle her.

"Good morning, Dr. Lautens," she replied, reaching for her cane to stand.

"No Anjali, please, don't get up; I hope you don't mind if I join you?"

"Not at all."

He sat down, saying nothing of the night before. She spoke about an interest in learning French, how she thought it was a beautiful language and dreamed of one day looking down on the city of Paris from the top of the Eiffel Tower.

Alexandre nodded at the paper in her lap. "What are you reading?"

She smiled shyly. "This . . . oh, it is called *Maratha*, it is a left-wing paper . . . this man named Tilak, he's a nationalist . . . he owns the paper. He's a bit of an extremist . . . but he has good ideas and he's very charismatic . . . people listen to him."

"He's an extremist?"

"Well, a few years ago he came to the defense of some Indian boys who accidentally killed some women when they threw a bomb at the Calcutta Presidency magistrate." She smiled, folding the paper, "I got the paper last week, but Daddy doesn't want me to read these, so I had to wait for some privacy."

Alexandre smiled. "Well, I won't tell." He was impressed. "So, you don't believe in 'by any means necessary'?"

"I don't believe in killing people."

"Why did they want to kill the magistrate?"

"He sentenced a boy who had hit a police officer to be caned. The boy almost died."

"Hmm . . . freedom always has its causalities, Anjali," he said, flatly. "Well, when I was young, there was a scandal, in the French army, which we now call the Dreyfus Affair."

Anjali leaned into Alexandre. Alexandre's entrée into scholarly life left little time for concern about politics and the things of public life, and recalling his impassioned youth made his eyes sparkle. He liked telling her stories. He continued. "A Jewish officer in the French army, his name was Dreyfus—he was convicted of treason for spying for the Germans. He was taken into the public square and the badges of rank on his jacket were torn off and his military sword was broken and he was shipped off to be exiled to a penal colony in South America."

"My goodness . . . " She wanted to show him she was listening.

"Well, so, a few years after he was exiled, these papers came to light, which exonerated Dreyfus, but you see, there was at the time, and still now, this very strong anti-Jewish feeling in France, and the army covered up the new evidence." Alexandre smiled, recalling his youth. "I remember protesting the government with other students and professors. We called ourselves the *dreyfusards*." Alexandre smiled to himself, remembering the moments of fraternal solidarity with his fellow dissidents. "I haven't thought about that time in my life for rather a long time." He smiled warmly. "Anyway . . . it is always good to see young people interested in political life."

Alexandre and Anjali shared a moment in silence. Though they were both facing forward, he thought he saw her eyes, out of the corner of his, darting toward him.

Though perhaps rude, or too soon in their acquaintance, he was curious as to her peculiar physical condition.

"Anjali . . . may I ask why you use a cane? Of course, it is none of my business . . . "

She did not seem taken aback or offended at his asking; he was the most handsome man she had ever seen, and she felt glad that he had taken an interest in her. Rather, she smiled indulgently at him, in the manner of an adult to a child, and began her story.

"Not at all, Dr. Lautens. I had polio as a child," she answered.

He took the girl in. Her body seemed to be cut from some very strange piece of wood, twisted. Anjali was plain, and it had never existed in the realm of possibility for any charm of face, hair or body to have compensated for that mangled leg. There was, in fact, little in her countenance suggestive of her patrician blood; proof lay, perhaps exclusively if at all, in her straight and pointed nose. Perhaps, from a great distance, some generous daydreamer, seeing the girl in profile, could fancy her a princess or an empress, a lesser maharani. But from his point of vantage, she was a plain woman-child, clearly a victim of the darker side of fortune.

"I do not look at my leg often," Anjali said.

That hardness, that startling gruff quality in Anjali was one she had purposely cultivated. After she fell ill, Anjali, even then, even as a little girl, realized that she brought out in others a saccharine pity, one not rooted in sympathy but in quiet gratitude: their pity was fueled by the guilt they felt for being supremely thankful that her fate—her illness—wasn't theirs. And so it came to Anjali, how sickening it was, to be at once crippled and sweet natured, how they would coo sadly at Lalita, "Ooh what a pity! Such a sweet girl." They would nod their heads, sighing, or click their tongues sympathetically at Lalita, as if she were the one who were sick. As if she had been the one who had once feverishly courted death. Anjali took on, at first with great effort and then suddenly one day, with none at all, that stoic quality of stone.

It was only to her grandmother that her true self was ever revealed: on the day she decided to hide her real nature, she sat to tea with her grandmother, but, indeed, her grandmother's stern, loving nature met Anjali's put-on coldness with such determined warmth that Anjali's resolve at once melted away. Her parents, weary with concern and soft words for their sick child, took almost with delight to this new, hardened girl whose stoniness they could at long last meet with anger, anger they felt at the gods for causing such pain and such embarrassment to their proud family. Lalita and Adivi could even yell at or ignore that girl who answered them with aloof gestures, or by rolling her eyes, the way they never could at that sickly, ailing little girl. It was so much easier to court the world's anger than its false sympathies; Anjali felt so less diminished by this new reaction from others. But to her grandmother, she was passionate, vulnerable and brilliant, and, far beyond the concerns of her disfigured body, excruciatingly fragile. That day, stirring her tea, Anjali had answered her grandmother's question of "How are you feeling today?" with a shrug, her mouth a flat line of indifference. Kanakadurga was resolute, shaking at once with anger and love, "I have seen, Anjali, this new attitude of yours. Shrug your shoulders at the whole world. Dismiss everyone else with your hand. But my darling, do not dare ever, ever, act this way with me."

And then with Anjali looking up, her eyes wet, her lips trembling, her grandmother smiled, seeing once again that little girl, the little girl who, since her husband, Anil, had died, was her one true love.

And Adivi became harder too, as if Anjali's illness had shown him in cruel starkness the limits of his power as a father: that his protection didn't extend so far as he thought. And that disappointment, and yes, he couldn't lie, seeing his daughter look *that* way, so contrary to anything he understood as feminine, caused his daughter to see in her father's eyes, from year to year, day to day, profound, heartbreaking disappointment.

ANJALI RECOUNTED TO Alexandre the day that it had happened, like an elegy, an old funeral poem that she recited as if she weren't the object of it:

Mohini and Anjali sat patiently at her feet that morning as their maid, Meha, oiled their hair and put it up in braids; Anjali was seven then and Mohini only two. Meha dusted their faces with talcum powder and rubbed oil onto their lips. The girls waited inside the coach as the horses were brushed and their father instructed the servants which cases to put where within the cabin. Anjali remembered, as they entered their train car that trip, seeing the shabby train cars of the poor ahead of them. Scolding Anjali, Meha ushered her past the leering faces of the masses as the peasants took in the opulent sight of the Adivi family. Lalita in her rich silk saris, Mohini and Anjali in lacy dresses cut in the style of English girls.

An extra coach was hired to carry their grandfather's body; Adivi's father, Anil, had died the morning before. He had been outside sitting on his favorite swinging bench, watching his beloved birds in the trees.

Bird-watching had become a late-life pleasure of Anil's. He was a sort of would-be ornithologist. He loved birds and would not only sketch them but also take notes on the habits of his favorites: their plumage and their song, what kind of feed the seemed to prefer. Age had so softened the heart of the very man that had in youth hunted the great tigers of Bengal, that when his once-hunting companion and lifelong friend John Stanford, an English aristocrat, had advised Anil to create a sort of aviary in the home, he refused, the thought of caging the animals in any way playing heavily upon his old heart. He told his granddaughters that violence and ferocity were young men's indulgences, a defense against the restlessness of youth. He would weep when he told Anjali tales of hunting, cornering the wild and beautiful beasts, their great eyes wide with terror in the face of so many English shotguns, village boys surrounding them, crying excitedly "Sher! sher!" Their horrible, snarled mouths, wide with jagged teeth like knives. Like great soldiers shot down, when wounded the tigers would not cry out but roar: such an indignation against their majesty. Hearing the guns, the birds, unseen moments before, would lift in a cacophony of feathers flapping and startled cries, and fly off in numbers that exceeded the thousands. The tigers' heavy bodies would sway when shot, all their muscles taut, their necks twisted as their rage-wrought growling continued until their last hot breaths would escape from their mouths, vaporous in the humid forests, ruby-colored blood pooling beneath them. Their roars would echo against the trees, until at last all the jungle would become pristinely quiet for some moments. The lower-class Englishmen without schooling at Eton and Cambridge and Oxford, the ones with the accents reminiscent of the East End—they would, in teams of five or six with Indian village boys, lift the carcasses of the great cats and throw them on counts of three onto the backs of the carriages.

Anil would sometimes recount the nightmares of his youth to his inquisitive little granddaughter, the one with lacquered, ribboned braids who would sit with him and count the birds: in his sleep, he was visited by the image of the great and fierce goddess Kali, a beautiful woman mounted on a tiger, who at turns would turn medusan in her hideousness, charging her tiger upon him, his torn and tattered body in its mouth, the goddess terrible and victorious. By the time he had grandchildren, Anil never ate meat. And rather than caging any spirit, through his copious note-taking he had discovered the feeding preferences of his favorite birds. Thus, in those years, the garden in the back of the Adivi home became a riot of bird feeders filled with sugar, seeds, water and grains. In his own hands, each morning Anil would bring out saucers filled with honey from the kitchen.

Stanford's son had, from London, at his father's request, sent Anil a pair of binoculars. Anjali could still remember what was inscribed on the brass rims of the eyepiece: J. TOZER, OPTICIAN, 70 FLEET STREET, TORQUAY. Anil died on that bench, the leather strap of his binoculars entwined among the dry, long fingers of his right hand. Unknowing, the birds chirped on merrily, feeding at the sugar water and honey that he had provided them, looking from beyond the death mask at the lovely Eden-like scene of blue, green and yellow birds among the trees of his garden . . . scarlet minivets, robins, ringed plovers, the mynas, of course—with whom he would speak—fantail flycatchers, ioras . . .

In Anjali's bedroom, she kept a sketchbook from those days, when she would sit with her grandfather and draw the birds in the trees in their garden. Under her childish handwriting naming the birds in English, Anil would write in an elegant hand the Latin names.

SHIVA WAS ANIL'S only son. It was the eldest son's duty to light the funeral pyre; the ashes were collected in great urns.

On horse-drawn carriages and in train cars, Shiva, his mouth a taut line strained with duty, took Anil's ashes to Benares. Those binoculars, from a street near a wharf that he had never been to and could scarcely imagine, were set afloat upon a lotus-laden Ganges with the ashes. A burning corpse drifted a small distance away.

Weary with grief and the exhaustion of a two-day-long journey north, the Adivis rose the next morning and Meha, who had traveled that long way up with the family, took Mohini and Anjali to bathe in the holy waters of the river. Shiva and Lalita were still sleeping. They stayed with a distant relative, a cousin of Shiva's. Meha, taken up with the religious fervor common among the poor, dressed both of the girls and called the house butler to summon the carriage. Irritable in the manner of children, Mohini and Anjali whined to Meha, drowsy and unaccustomed to traveling without their parents for even short distances.

Lit in the early morning gold light, the city of Benares was beautiful. A thousand temples. Spires like spears of gold in the sky. There, in the river, farm boys bathed cattle and buffalo. The faithful, cut from the same ilk as Meha, offered up prayers in waist-deep water to the silent witnesses of floating blossoms and empty fishing boats. The tired moans of two girls were no match for Meha's religious fervor, and she carried the girls into the river, bathing them in its mythic water.

Anjali turned to Alexandre. Her eyes were heavy, pedagogical; in another world, she may have been a scholar as well. Anjali was afraid that her airs of erudition did not have the dignity of choice, that the life of books was the only choice she had had. She couldn't indulge in feminine frivolities for fear of making herself ridiculous. And now, in the face of Alexandre's real scholarship, she was afraid that her dilettantism would become apparent, and again she would seem absurd. Still, she ventured forth. "Did you know that there are blind dolphins in the Ganges? The English think they discovered them some hundred years ago, but the Indians have known about them for ages; they are shy, strange-looking animals. Beautiful in their own way . . . the Hindu belief is that they proclaimed the arrival of Ganga from the skies; the emperor Ashoka so loved them, he made it a crime to kill one." She turned away from Alexandre, her mind drifting.

Relatives from all over came to the funeral. Stoic men, wailing women, beating their bosoms in grief. Confused children. They ate no meat for weeks, and Shiva shaved his mustache and hair. Days later, without the aid of a second carriage, they left Benares. On the train Anjali held her grandmother's hand and curled into the warm comfort of her body, drifting in and out of sleep until she woke on her own bed back in Waltair.

The home was quiet for days, but on the ninth night after returning, in her clean white sheets, a fever overwhelmed her body, and it did not abate for days. Thinking at first this was only an expression of grief, Lalita and Kanakadurga at first applied ministrations of turmeric and lime juice and cool cloths. By morning the fever had still not gone down, and Lalita called Dr. Ranganathan, the man who seven years earlier had delivered her.

"He sat next to me, on the bed; Mummy and Nainamma waited, worried, behind me. Dr. Ranganathan stuck a silver thermometer under my tongue. I remember him saying 'Good girl' when he took a couple of vials' worth of blood from my arm." Anjali reflexively touched her right bicep. "I cried when he stuck a needle in my arm and filled two vials with my blood. And then he looked at Mummy and said, 'I'll have to do a few tests, Madam.'"

Two days later, with his briefcase of medical tools—vials, needles, bandages and medicines—he arrived. Passing by her bedside, he touched Anjali's face in a gentle and paternal way before disappearing into the parlor with Lalita and Shiva.

Anjali heard Lalita wail and then Dr. Ranganathan and Shiva's voices comforting her. The diagnosis was polio. Certainly not, by any means, an uncommon one among children, but unexpected for someone of their class, for whom cleanliness, sanitation and hygiene were so important. The Adivis boiled all water for drinking and bathing. Even the house dogs were bathed in water that had first boiled for a quarter of an hour.

In the course of the following weeks the gardens grew quiet. The birds, no longer provided with small plates of sugar and honey, did not visit their home for any longer than fleeting moments. They abandoned their nests, gradually, and soon Anjali could scarcely remember how the garden looked when it was a sort of aviary.

Later that year, distraught with guilt, Meha renounced Hinduism in violent sobs, was baptized in a pool of water and emerged from it renamed Mary.

Over the following years, spells of seemingly perfect health were interrupted by the onslaught of a deep ache in Anjali's muscles, so severe that she would resort to bed rest. Her left hip and knee would throb painfully, and at times it seemed she had less control over this leg than the other. By the time she was twelve, she could no longer walk without the aid of a cane. She told these details to Alexandre matter-of-factly, without emotion. Her left leg became deformed, and she lost feeling in it gradually, until she one day realized she had no awareness of it and could feel nothing there at all. The muscles withered. It was smaller than her right leg and misshapen.

Now she smiled, lifting her head. "Sometimes, in my dreams, I am swimming in the sea, or in a river. I haven't been in water since that day—my parents forbid it; and in my dream I feel weightless and even though I am sleeping I can actually feel the lightness . . . feel the nothingness of floating . . . and the waves, the motion of the sea. I think someday, when I'm older, I may be able to go to the ocean, but not now . . . "

She looked at him, for a moment, and then looked down. She thought that perhaps there was no place in this world she loved more than the seashore—the long sprawl of sand, in whites and then browns, as one gets closer to the waterline, darker and ever more so as it melts into a never-ending, fathomlessly deep ocean; within, the beginnings of life, great beasts, plants that sway in the arms of the tide, schools of fish in colors she could not and would never imagine. In her dreams she swam, and there she felt the waters rise up and hold her body up; there she had not one but two perfectly formed and shapely legs. In her dreams her body was weightless. In her dreams the water rushed up about her legs, enveloping her body, so much a release, nearly like drowning or death.

Alexandre thought it must be terrible for her, in the mornings here, when the air smelled of sea salt.

Anjali's story made him think too about his own body—how it had never betrayed him; he had always been able to trust that tall and well-formed mass of bone and muscle that even now had retained its youthful strength and dexterity; it had always been a faithful vehicle of utility and pleasure, his skin the color of white marble. When he was a child, he used to sprint through the neighborhood with that winged fleetness unique of little boys, his book bag flapping against his hip, just so he could hear the blood pumping in his ears.

LATER THAT DAY, Anjali approached one of the household servants, Peter, who had been her father's servant since they were both boys. When Adivi was in grammar school, Peter would sneak his master's schoolbooks and read them while his young charge slept.

"Peter," Anjali asked.

"Yes, Miss Anjali."

Anjali handed the butler a list and some money. "Can you go into town and purchase these books for me? They will be in one of the English-language bookshops."

"Yes, Miss," he answered. Peter eyed the list and looked skeptically at the titles: *Candide, The Social Contract, Madame Bovary*. "May I ask why you have this sudden interest in *these* books, Miss Anjali?"

Anjali pushed her weight down on her cane and pivoted suddenly, squaring her eyes on Peter. "No you may not," she hissed.

TO ALEXANDRE'S VIEW, to be rich in India was unrivaled by what it was to be rich in Europe. How wealth here was a buffer against all the cruelties, all the vulgarities of life. Every peasant had his price. Servants watched children. They cooked, cleaned, minded the horses, fed and washed the family pets, tended the gardens, washed the clothes, brought tea, summoned cars and coaches, shopped for vegetables and meat and fish and sweets and fruit; there seemed in India no task of daily life not able to be delegated to some servant for a small price.

It did not surprise Alexandre if even very private matters could have been handed out to some particularly wretched person of the lower classes. He needed scarcely lift his brow to any one of the female servants—at all times on the grounds—before his empty coffee cup was whisked away and another was brought out: fresh, sweet and milky. It was strange how quickly he grew accustomed to the absurdity of his every need being catered to. He now grew irritated if he was made to wait more than a few minutes for fresh towels to be brought to him in the morning, or if he found his room had not been swept before breakfast.

He worked every morning, and most evenings. In the morning, when he studied on the verandah, he was sometimes joined by the cooks, who, with sifters, shuffled rice endlessly back and forth to pull from it tiny stones and bits of sand and dirt. And so was his task: shuffling languages back and forth until something familiar emerged, and meaning was found.

He was falling into a nice routine: in the mornings he would take coffee and breakfast with Anjali in the garden and review what he had written the night before. Anjali critiqued—mostly helpfully—his Telugu handwriting and would help him by reviewing his translations. During the day he would go out, sometimes on foot. At other times he would ask Peter to take him out in the carriage to the market or to a school, to speak to the natives and see how well he could describe their language. He would ask them the names of things and how to describe them and interrupt conversations to learn how the natives spoke—their use of slang, their diction, their syntax, the ways in which their registers would alter dependent on the situation and the company. He would write notes as warm-hearted natives corrected him during conversation—it was *pedda kukka,* "big" before "dog," not *kukka pedda*—he liked to purposefully make simple mistakes to endear himself to the natives as a well-intentioned foreigner who needed their guidance; it made the conversation longer. Children would rally around the tall, smiling foreigner handing out chocolates and giggle as he spoke to them, correcting him: *"Caadhu babu garu,"* no Sir, you say it like this, not that. Sometimes the more confident and gregarious, barefoot and half-naked street children would scamper alongside Alexandre, following him right up to the gate, and wave at him, smiling and waving as Rajiv, the servant who stood at the entrance, always irritated by their presence, shut the gate behind them.

IN THE EARLY evenings before dinner, Kanakadurga called him for tea in her quarters. Lautens had taken quite a liking to Kanakadurga; she was wise, indulgent and protective of her flock. He had come to call her Kanakadurga Amma Garu; he was told by one of the servants that it would be the most polite way to address her. He had called her by her first name and heard one of the older servants giggling behind him, and only after an awkward confrontation did the servant correct Alexandre. Kanakadurga's maidservant brought them delicious sweets made of milk and butter and pastry, dotted generously with almonds, cashews and golden raisins. She took her tea rich and sweet, made with very little water and too much milk. The maid mixed in heaping spoonfuls of sugar and boiled the leaves with cardamom and cloves. The old woman wore widow's white and no bindi; she no longer ate meat. And though the effects of time were obvious on her face and in her posture and hands, her mind remained sharp and perceptive, with an often-indulged, biting wit. She did not shy away from making unkind but true observations about even those she loved most dearly, and was equally quick to bestow loving affection in her words or with hugs and kisses and watery, maternal looks. She often touched his cheeks and laughed at their fullness, or put her hands on his.

She invited him to her chambers before the evening meal one day. She stood at her doorway, calling Alexandre in and clicked her tongue at her granddaughters, who were gossiping in the gardens. She smiled and nodded disapprovingly at them. "These girls today! I have told them to collect jasmines for their hair, and look at them laughing and talking. Lazy girls!" She shook her finger at Anjali and Mohini, and Alexandre smiled, leaning against the doorsill. "Come, Dr. Lautens, take tea with me. These girls today—it is not even important to them to take proper care of their hair!"

In Kanakadurga's room were photographs of her granddaughters and her children—a photograph of a stern, dazed-looking Adivi with Lalita at his side sitting calmly for the photographer on the day of their wedding, and another bridal photo, this one of Kanakadurga and Anil: Anil a more slight, softer-looking man as handsome as his son, Kanakadurga as a young bride, lovely and bemused, her fingers interlaced, her hands raised to her chest, almost as if in prayer.

"You look so lovely in these photographs," Alexandre said, smiling.

Kanakadurga giggled, "I'm still lovely, Dr. Lautens!"

"This used to be my house," said Kanakadurga. "Anil was friends with some of the English officers and they would bring their boys here for tea and cards. Anil used to stay up for hours, and I would hear those young officers drinking and laughing. It used to be a bit more jolly back then, more lively. It seemed more possible back then, at once, to be friends with individual Englishmen and against English rule."

Alexandre thoughtfully examined the photographs. There was Kanakadurga with her children—four girls and Adivi—photos of some Indian boys in regimental uniform, Kanakadurga holding the hands of two of her girls. "You have a very large family," Alexandre said.

"Yes, most Indian families tend to be large."

"Ah, it must be unusual to have only two children, like your son."

"Yes . . . " Kanakadurga looked sad, and suddenly Alexandre felt embarrassed at the thought that she might feel he was prying.

"There is a reason for that; it was not by design, you see. I still remember Dr. MacKissock. He was holding my daughter-in-law's wrist, taking her pulse as his fleet of Indian nurses, who were neat women in the Western white uniforms, heads covered, no jewelry and no bindi," she recalled, "delivered Mohini. Anjali was three years old, in the next room, and clung to my legs, listening to the sounds of her mother's cries and moans. My son sat in a nearby chair, reading the newspaper. Later, I found that Mary-Meha gossiping in the servants' quarters. She had been sent to Lalita to fan her during the delivery, and she told me that there had been a lot of blood, and that Lalita's eyes had rolled into her head as Mohini was pulled from her body and out into the world. At the same moment that Lalita heard the new baby's first cries, she also heard the nurses." Kanakadurga's face was so stoic, thought Alexandre, as she continued. "They had before only been speaking in English, and then all these voices rose, and in their panic they reverted to Telugu, shouting and commanding each other. Dr. MacKissock was also agitated and started yelling 'English! Speak in bloody English!' and then, 'Jesus bloody Christ!'"

Kanakadurga stood and walked over to an armoire and took out a brown envelope of photographs and took out one of a handsome white man sitting in the garden with Adivi, the men raising glasses of whiskey to the photographer.

MacKissock was a military doctor in the second battalion of the Argyllshire Highlanders, a Scottish regiment from Glasgow, and he had never delivered a baby before. Most of his experience, having been acquired during times of peace, was of dealing with his men, who were maladapted to the heat and water of India, or who had contracted a tropical ailment. Lautens could not remember how they found themselves on the topic of Mohini's birth.

Kanakadurga pushed a small plate of sweets toward him as she showed him the old photographs. In his limited experience in India, admittedly not great, he had found Kanakadurga and Anjali to be curiously and uncharacteristically forthright for Indians, especially for women. Kanakadurga was strangely open about all the matters of family and self that were usually kept in confidence and guarded as a matter of decorum in both the East and West. "Shiva met Dr. MacKissock some weeks earlier at some English social event, to which he wore a Brooks Brothers suit. I remember that suit; he went to such lengths to procure it. He thought it would be advantageous to have his child delivered by one of the men he referred to as 'the queen's own doctors,' and he promptly dismissed Dr. Ranganathan, the Tamilian who had been seeing along Lalita's pregnancy until that point. After Mohini was born—it could have been hours or minutes—Dr. MacKissock came out, his white coat was now bloodstained, and he pushed open the double doors, his nurses shaken. My God they all looked like they were emerging from a war zone; and Dr. MacKissock was apologetic and said, 'You have a daughter, Mr. Adivi. The girl is healthy and well. I do not believe, however, that your wife will be able to bear any more children.'

"Later the next day, from a window on the second story of our home, I saw Mary scrubbing with soap bloodstained white sheets and then beating them on a rock next to the stream that ran up the back of our property. Dear God it was so terrible!

"Lalita and Mohini, after she had recovered for a week here, went to Lalita's natal home and stayed there for a few months to be with her mother. Anjali stayed here with myself and Anil and Shiva. She and Shiva would visit them, and I would send them sweets—it's meant to be good for mother and baby. After learning she was now barren, my daughter-in-law, she wept endlessly, and her mother was afraid that Mohini would take in all that sadness from her mother's breast. Subbamma, the maid that had taken care of Lalita as a girl, and who was now an old woman, would rub Lalita's swollen feet with coconut oil and make her cool lime juice from baby limes and sugar cane.

"When she came back to our home, I remember how Anjali would sing familiar lullabies to Mohini, the ones I had taught her. Mohini was a gorgeous baby with lovely, large eyes and long eyelashes and fat, tightly clenched baby fists. Anjali would always push her fingers into the baby's fist. At first, understandably, Anjali was jealous. But soon enough, the sense of being displaced in the family dissipated, and she loved Mohini in a sweet, sisterly way. Anjali loved to hold her, and to brush her baby curls.

"Oh Dr. Lautens! I am so sorry, so sorry to go on like this! I'm an old, lonely woman, you must excuse me!"

"No Kanakadurg Amma Garu, not at all, I treasure the time we spend together," said Alexandre, blushing.

The sun early in the afternoon was white over the estate, blanching everything. In the garden the flowers were still half-closed, lazily opening under the impending brightness of day. The family's Shetland sheepdog was brought to them, Adivi once told Alexandre proudly, from a regal line of loyal work dogs in Scotland by Dr. MacKissock some years before. Byron raised his eyes warily in the morning, before suddenly springing into full life. Adivi named him Byron after the English poet; when Dr. MacKissock found this out, he jokingly chastised Adivi for naming the dog not after a great Scottish warrior but instead after an "English dandy." The indulgence of conversation and sweets in Kanakadurga's quiet, airy room was now interrupted when he and Kanakadurga heard the servants and cooks in the kitchen clanking brass pots together as they prepared the afternoon meal.

"It sounds like they are busy preparing a feast!" Alexandre laughed.

Alexandre and Kanakadurga settled into deep cushions decorating her chambers and Kanakadurga summoned the maid to bring them more tea. She looked thoughtful and calculating that afternoon. "Dr. Lautens," she began, "you do not speak often of your family. I am very curious about them. More than one week already you have been here and we know nothing of you." Unlike the many other times that they'd taken tea together, and delighted in lazy and gossip-filled talk, today she seemed to have a distinct purpose.

He did not often speak of his family as he had been in this country so long as to feel like a single man here and scarcely thought of himself as a husband or father any longer. Things here were different.

"Ah. . . . Well, Kanakadurga Amma Garu," he started, his disarming smile fading "there is not much to tell, I suppose. I have a wife, Madeline. We met in a library when I was in university. I have two children—Matthieu and Catherine. Matthieu is, well, let me see . . . Matthieu will now be three years old. That would make Catherine five."

"Do you have photographs, Dr. Lautens?" Kanakadurga asked.

"Yes, I do . . . indeed, I have them with me," he said, reaching inside his jacket. As this discord of feeling like bachelor grew, he thought it wise to have these photographs of them with him at all times to serve as a reminder of the life waiting for him back in Paris. He withdrew the few snapshots he had of Madeline and the children.

"Your wife is lovely," Kanakadurga said, looking carefully at the photos, "very different from our women . . . she is very tall . . . very . . . lean," she said, smiling mysteriously. "Ah! It never fails to amuse me how short European women keep their hair," she laughed. "Your children! What beauties! Your son looks very much like you, Dr. Lautens." She looked up playfully, "He is sure to be a very handsome man. And your daughter . . . she is going to one day be quite a beauty. Lovely children," she said, and smiling sweetly handed the pictures back to him. He folded them back into the recesses of his jacket.

"But surely there is more to your family, Dr. Lautens? In India the family does not stop at the wife and children—your parents, sisters, brothers, grandparents?"

"Well," he began, and felt immediately exhausted by the prospect of recounting so much history, of telling the facts of his life that had never interested him. "Yes, my mother and father are still living. They live in Switzerland—that is where I was born, so properly I am not French, I suppose, but Swiss. We moved to Paris when I was a young boy, when Maman was pregnant with my brother and Papa was tired of her complaining about Geneva."

The heat made him verbose. And leaning back, he closed his eyes and let himself start at the beginning.

"I was not meant to be an academic. My father, Maurice," Alexandre remembered his father's stern countenance, "had taken on the family trade of banking, and he was known in the financial circles of Switzerland to be fair and exact in all things—repayment, punctuality . . . "

"Banking is your family business? I can scarcely imagine you as a banker!"

Alexandre told Kanakadurga how the inexactitude of words proved too often troublesome for Maurice, and that Alexandre's mother filled the silent void with her singsong voice and her penchant for detailed storytelling, her love of myth and folklore. Agathe Lautens, née Sauvageot, wove tales of her trip that day to the fishmonger, or the fruit vendor, how the tailor made a pass at her when fitting her for a new dress, or the baker threw in an extra roll, telling her she had a pretty smile.

"I, sometime around the age of nine, came to realize that this dear woman, my favorite woman, indeed, in all the world!" Alexandre nearly shouted, "she lived the vast part of her day inside her own head, concocting tales half the time and relishing their telling the other half. I did not dismiss her—the world being what it is, I found it not a wholly unintelligent plan to take leave of it almost completely. And that was my childhood . . . in a fashionable quarter of Geneva, with a woman with too many stories and a man with none at all."

About him, a cacophony of French, German and Italian, and above them all—for his father's word (once it was found) was to be the last in all matters—Maurice's beloved numbers, making the world at once more pure and somehow less beautiful than his mother's description. At mealtimes hers was often the lone voice—describing the preparation of the meal, and her favorite bits of it, answering her own questions before husband or son would have a chance to reply, and inevitably afterward Maurice would disappear behind a newspaper, offering her only sympathetic grunts or monosyllabic sounds to show that he was listening, though he in fact heard nothing of what she said.

"I look like my Papa. We are similar in coloring and features, but he was a bit shorter." Maurice dressed conservatively and well, in dark suits and well-kept hats. "My height I inherited from my mother's side of the family. My uncles are like trees . . . " He smiled to himself.

"What are you thinking of Alexandre?"

"I was just thinking of my mother putting on her lipstick. I was remembering her red, red mouth.

"Her eyes were cornflower blue. Her nose was sloped and was Maman's own favorite feature, an affection she showed by complaining too often and too much about it."

He mimicked her high voice, "'Ah! But my little Alex! Look at Maman's little nose! Too small, *n'est ce pas?*' And she would stoop low and tilt her head this way and that for me to admire—I was only to the height of her waist." Recalling this he laughed, as did Kanakadurga. "And when, as would happen often, walking down the street hand in hand with my mother, some man would smile or whistle at Maman, she would bat her eyelashes and say, 'Perhaps that man is looking at Maman's funny nose! Your poor Maman with her silly little nose!'"

Alexandre would hear his mother's murmurs through the wall his bedroom shared in common with his parents' those nights. The next morning, with a full pocketbook, Agathe would let loose upon the shopping districts of Geneva and come home with tissue-wrapped parcels of feminine indulgences: a new scent, a silk scarf, a tin of expensive tea sprinkled throughout with the lush lavender of the French countryside.

In her rare moments of quite rumination, Agathe would recline in her favorite chair, full wine glass in hand, and bemoan her life, sprawled out languorously across the seat, her long legs bare to the wind coming through the open window, her face an expression of sensuality as if she had been seduced by the poetic tragedy of her own plight: that such a pretty and young woman should end up in this soulless business town, that she, Agathe Sauvageot, who as a girl had collected admirers like her girlfriends had collected seashells at the shore, should end up a banker's wife, like so many other banker's wives, in Geneva, with all its darkness and lifelessness, none of the Parisian glamour, or the Roman soul she felt her due and destiny. That she was forced to make extra money by sewing and darning the neighbors' clothes—taking garments in if they were loose or making them larger if someone had gained weight, darning socks and repairing tears and rips in jackets—this could not be her life. Alexandre would, when the steam ran out of her oft-vocalized sadness and her eyelids would droop, cover her with the blankets he would pull from his parents' bed, and would remove the wine glass from her hand carefully so as not to disturb her. Always that puckered red stain at the bottom, like a woman's kiss fallen into the glass.

And then he would go to bed, kneeling first at the bedside with his hands clasped in prayer as his mother taught him.

Other times, he would see her praying, her small, female voice like a shooting star aiming at the ears of the mother of God. A grown woman clicking rosary beads by her bedside, her elbows pushed down deep into the bed, her knees on the bare floor. That tiny, silvery voice freighted with warmth and intimacy and always beseeching, beseeching, her cries no more sophisticated than a child on her father's knee.

Alexandre, for his part, stopped praying, stopped falling to his knees before sleep by the time he turned ten. Rather, he would watch the night fall into his window, and from his bed, reach his hand out and gaze outside, holding the moon in the curve of his then-small hands, letting the silver light filter through his fingers and bear witness to his free fall into sleep.

He sipped tea, and Kanakadurga pushed a plate of sweets toward him. She had a quality of sincerity that made Alexandre like her more and trust her, despite their young friendship. This had caught him off guard—he was always wary of others, often preferring his own company.

"She was a much happier woman when she had more children. She is one of those people who needs the noise and the excitement of a full house. I have one brother and two sisters. My brother's name is Matthieu; my son is named after him. He is five years younger than me; I am the eldest; Matthieu and the girls are much closer in age. All of my siblings live in Paris. My brother is a banker. He took over the family business when Papa died. After Matthieu is my sister Anne, and then Claudine: she is the baby of the family."

"My sister Anne, she married a journalist. They have two children, twins actually, my nephews—Henri and Philipe. My other sister, Claudine—she is the beauty of the family. She just was wed last year to a stupid but handsome brute. He is a construction worker—our parents nearly fainted when they heard she was engaged. They eloped without notice one day, and Papa and Maman received a letter from Claudine announcing that she was now, in fact, married. This man she married, he says that one day he should like to start his own business building homes, but of course this will not happen . . .

"My mother cried for two days. She locked herself in her room and said she wouldn't get out until Claudine broke the engagement; but Claudine is headstrong, like Papa, and wouldn't do it. I saw Claudine a few days before I left for India. She had come to me bringing some sweets Maman had sent, as Claudine had been to Switzerland the week before. I realized then why she had gotten married to that idiot—she was nearly bursting—she was at least seven months pregnant."

He saw Kanakadurga's eyebrows lift frightfully high on her head out of the corner of his eye.

"I was angry but didn't say anything—a woman no longer belongs to her father or brothers once she takes a husband, no? What was I to say? It was too late . . .

"My parents moved back to Switzerland after Anne's wedding: they had always planned to, after Papa retired. They said they were happy; they wouldn't miss Paris. France did not have the beauty, the quaintness of Switzerland, they said. Paris was becoming a den of sin, so much filth, so hedonistic; they were happy to leave. Maman had so loved living in Paris, but even she had tired of it by the time we were adults."

A servant came in to clear empty teacups from Kanakadurga's room.

"They had raised Parisians, despite their best intentions," Alexandre laughed.

Having revealed so much of himself, he felt now weary, and waited some moments in silence.

At long last, he felt he was now allowed to ask some questions of Kanakadurga. "Kanakadurga Amma Garu, is it common in India for a younger daughter to wed before her older sister?"

The old woman's face grew pained. She looked down and started speaking slowly only after many pregnant moments. "No, my dear Alexandre, it is not done. As you can see, Anjali . . . she has a problem with her leg. She had polio as a child . . . "

"Yes, she told me the other morning . . . "

"Yes . . . well. For this reason, however, my son has decided he would not seek a groom for Anjali. He does not believe he would be able to find any suitable man willing to marry a girl with such a disfigurement. Until Mohini's marriage was announced, however, Anjali and I had kept up the hope—it was silly of course—that perhaps things would . . . " the old woman searched for words, "well . . . take a different course . . . one that would see Anjali in a happy marriage to a nice boy." She sighed. "It was a silly wish . . . my son and I, we have something of a difficult relationship when it comes to matters regarding Anjali. But of course, he is only doing what is practical. The years of my marriage were wonderful, Alexandre. We had become one heart. But I've lived too long to conflate marriage and happiness . . . I can't help but feel that Anjali has been at once sacrificed and saved.

"I will not lie: I have always paid special attention to my granddaughter Anjali since she took ill. She is a sweet girl; she is far too quick and keen for her own good. It is a better thing, the ways of the world being what they are, for a girl to be beautiful, like Mohini. But my Anjali's fast wit makes her good company for an old woman." Kanakadurga smiled and put her head down. She took Alexandre's hand. "You must be tired, Alexandre."

❋ 7 ❋

OUTSIDE, THE FEMALE servants were cleaning the concrete pathways of the garden. The ends of their tattered saris were tucked up high into their waists, leaving their dark, ashen legs exposed below the knee; they held big, stainless steel jugs of water and brushed the concrete with coarse bunches of bundled straw and would then throw water on it, rinsing it clean. Peasants pushed their hands through the gates, their cupped palms outreached as they asked the servants for rice and milk. The gardener was watering the rose bushes and another servant was picking tomatoes and limes. The servants responded to the beggars with irritation. Though on the periphery of the household, the servants were protective of the propriety and the resources of their masters' home. Because, perhaps, Lautens thought, while the difference in station between them—the servants and the peasants—was not so great, the difference was of such apparent importance to the servants that they looked upon those outside the gates with familiar disdain.

Alexandre stood in the corridor, looking out, a notebook under his arm and the copy of *L'Inde (Sans les Anglais)* that Madeline had given him. He had passed by Anjali's room the other day, looking for her, and even though she was not in the house, he saw that her room was full of books and he thought she might be interested in this one. It would also serve as an introduction to French and she had expressed interest in learning his language. But now he could not find her. He watched the women working, the way they bent from the waist. It seemed to him such a severe posture.

"Go! Get out!" Adivi strode past the gate, angrily dismissing the beggars with a wave of his hand. Their penury was highly distasteful to him, he who had no problem with the charity of churches but found repulsive their dirty hands and shamelessness and most of all the sense of entitlement that seemed so terribly apparent when they left the gates empty-handed and angry. Poverty was no excuse for poor manners, in Adivi's mind, and perhaps indeed poor manners and their tasteless display were the cause of it. No, Adivi, like others of his class, had no problem with charity, but to his mind there was a time and a place, and Adivi cared only for those charitable actions that could be considered great. It was only a question of taste.

"Dr. Lautens!" Adivi greeted him, walking down the corridor. "I'm sorry—I should have mentioned your work space would be disturbed this morning—the garden cleaning should be finished in a bit. What with the wedding soon, there is much extra work to do."

Alexandre smiled. "Not at all! I can work in my room."

"No! Please, use the dining room? It is a bit cooler in there. I'll have Mary bring you some tea? Actually I shall join you soon for tiffin."

"Thank you, Shiva, I will see you shortly then."

"Wonderful."

Adivi shouted at one of the servants in the garden to tell Mary to prepare some tea. Alexandre was happy to find that the language was becoming easier and easier for him to understand. He watched as a dispirited young woman with a missing front tooth made her way through the back of the garden to the servants' quarters adjacent to the kitchen in search of Mary.

IT COULD HAVE been a trick of light, a quick, odd look that meant nothing, that moment that Mohini saw herself from the side, walking past a mirror. She turned and faced the mirror, face forward, her shoulders back and brave, and the stab she felt subsided—she was beautiful again, and turned her chin this way and that, and thanked God she could not quite get sight again of that girl she had seen a moment earlier, what could not be and she would never let happen, becoming a less than remarkable girl.

WHEN ALEXANDRE ENTERED the dining room, a cup of tea had already been set out for him, alongside some biscuits. He could hear the sounds of cooking coming from the kitchen. He set out his notebook and began writing. Alexandre ran his hand over the clean white sheet of paper before him and wrote "Adjectives" across the top. Looking for a moment at the page with a wavering pen, he softly put the pen down and put his head in his hands and sighed.

He heard a giggle. "It can't be all that difficult, Dr. Lautens." Mohini stood across the room from him, a white plate holding a cut-open fruit in her hands. She smiled at him.

Alexandre felt the blood rise to his ears. She was wearing what he had come to learn was a *lengha-oorni*, a half sari: a floor-length pleated skirt, a sari blouse and a chiffon scarf wrapped around her waist and thrown over one shoulder. The girl was dressed in greens and blues and a trim of gold. She looked like a siren luring sailors off course. And that moment, Mohini misread his blushing embarrassment as irritation.

Mohini, when men were angry with her, felt that it was as much a failure of her beauty as a failure of action. Hers was an existence of a glowing halo of goodness, of loving smiles offered, a quiet, sweet disposition—that kind of floating-skirt female presence that betrayed an air of gracious submission to the needs of those around her. And it was an air that was met with a steady commentary on that perfect confluence of her beauty and sweetness, that willing submission that was understood as a loving nature among her relatives and the family friends. That it was as much an impression created with silk and jewels as with kindness was of no concern to Mohini, who understood her beauty to be a manifestation of that intrinsic goodness that she knew she embodied by the way others praised her. "Manam Mahasundari!" her aunts and uncles would say, pinching her cheeks, "our great beauty!" Her parents too saw her beauty as a radiant expression of their daughter's virtue. Mohini never went by unnoticed, though she tried to give the impression that she didn't much care if she was; her father's particular kind of disposition, slightly ostentatious, was fine for a man but distasteful in a woman. And Mohini sought above all else to be a girl of good taste. That she flattered her parents so well was an added pleasure, as lovely as a dusting of gold on the family crest.

"Daddy told me you were studying in here." She began to walk toward him. "I thought I'd bring you some fruit."

"Oh thank you, how kind," Alexandre stood, his fingertips brushing hers as he took the plate from her. Tuberoses were tucked into the joints of her braid, and when she stood close the fragrance hung over them both like a sweet nostalgic veil, and all together, that moment, with the beautiful butter-colored girl and the scent of hot silk and coconut oil and white flowers radiating from her, was so heady it nearly brought tears to his eyes.

Alexandre looked down at the fruit. "What kind of fruit is this?" The curious fruit's green shell held black seeds covered in creamy, sweet, white flesh.

"*Sitaphalam*—in English you call it . . . " She looked up, thinking, "custard apple."

"*Sitaphalam* . . . Sita's fruit?"

"Yes . . . after Sita in the Ramayana, though I don't know why exactly it is called that . . . What are you working on, Dr. Lautens?"

"My chapter on adjectives in Telugu."

"Ah . . . can I help you?"

Alexandre touched the page of his notebook, accusatory in its blankness. He smiled, amused and surprised by her candid offer. Though consultation with Anjali had become the norm, he'd never thought to ask Mohini.

"Well, yes, of course . . . "

She raised her eyebrows. Alexandre looked at her briefly. He noticed her lower lip was fuller than the top one, which gave her a look of perpetual petulance and innocence. There was such purity in her expression—as if she had no inner machinations. But rather than having the effect of disarming him, Alexandre felt more uneasy around her.

"Very well . . . then, well, in the previous chapter, I discussed the nominal system, basically how nouns operate in Telugu, and well," Alexandre sat down and continued. He motioned to the plate of fruit on the table, "so that the reader could construct the phrase, 'the custard apple,' and basically, this chapter is so that they can start to construct more complicated strings, like . . . "

". . . the green custard apple . . . *aku pacca sitaphalam*," Mohini offered.

"Yes, or the . . . sour custard apple."

Alexandre looked hard at the girl, in a way that made her feel searched, and she looked down. He continued to look at her face, and he breathed in the dizzying, soporific tuberose. "Will you join me? I couldn't possibly eat this all by myself." His arm reached toward her, an alabaster limb with pale blue veins, that naked arm that had held in its embrace many girls, years ago, when he ran through the streets of Paris, a feckless boy Adonis with broad shoulders, dark curls and blue eyes like small planets the color of the sea. Those days, he would lie in repose on a strange bed and watch a pretty girl dress and was never sad to see her go; he loved women and the way they stretched his sensual imagination—their smell and skin, but he had always been a boy who was secretly lonely in his soul, always feeling guilty for making any closer association than his pretty, friendless mother.

Now, Alexandre's hand wavered near Mohini's hair, the tip of his finger brushing the edge of a white petal. "*Rajanigandha*," he pronounced carefully. "The perfume of the night." He had heard the sadhus say that unmarried girls were meant to avoid its scent. The flowers smelled like night closing in, like an evening in a hot, restless city, like diesel and brave women, and Alexandre wondered for a moment why this posy of a girl would wear something so ruinous in her hair.

Mohini smiled, a slight nervousness coloring her expression, and Alexandre realized suddenly how forward he was being. He colored and withdrew his hand. She opened her mouth to speak when her parents walked in, Lalita a few paces behind her husband, and Mohini rushed toward Shiva and lovingly threw her arms around her father, her bosom lowering as she exhaled.

"I was just bringing Dr. Lautens some fruit, Daddy," she said as Adivi cupped her face, kissing her forehead.

Adivi always smiled when he saw his younger daughter. Hers was that ephemeral, bright quality of girlhood, her ever-hopeful countenance like a pretty mermaid breaking murky sea waves. Hers was, in that house, a uniquely cheerful presence that broke through the somber air like a singular beam of levity.

Lalita passed through the room, greeting Alexandre, her smile a tense line on her face. She worried for Mohini, seeing things a mother sees, that a woman's virtue is something that must ever be guarded—even the slightest hint of ill repute and she may never be able to recover. A man could not understand this, not even a father. Once a girl's reputation is damaged, it is ruined forever and Lalita thought: "In India, we never let a woman forget how she has failed."

Mohini's effect on her father was one that was easily visible to Alexandre, like a square of light moving over a dark corridor. Under her influence, Adivi seemed a handsome young father, his face proud and bright with the hope of an irresistibly normal life. And Alexandre, his heart aching, felt sympathy for that father, who, saddled with the tragedy of his older daughter's plight, chose instead of a derailing affection that happy, easy love and that glowing light of his younger girl's beauty and promise.

She entered the room as light as a songbird, such a thing apart from her sister's heavy, lumbering gait. And mesmerized too by her girlish flight, Alexandre could almost understand why Adivi preferred his younger daughter for the easy joy he found in her rather than that surely endless free fall into sympathy and sorrow provoked by Anjali. But then again, Alexandre thought, "Who asked Adivi to choose?" As a father, Alexandre felt that the love he felt for one child did not make smaller the love he felt for the other.

As a child, frightened by that occasional sound and light show outside his window, the thunder, the flashes of lightening coming from some faraway point in the horizon, silver and green trees dancing violently in the storm in hastily emptied Geneva streets, the rain and leaves thrown against his bedroom window, Alexandre recalled running to the arms of his preternaturally calm father, Maurice's hand on his head, his ear pressed to his father's chest, listening to his steady and reassuring heartbeat, and for that memory alone Alexandre could not imagine without extreme sorrow any child being denied her father's love. He wondered if Adivi was a man without compassion, or if, rather, he was one with such an extreme capacity for it that it was a source of embarrassment. It seemed to Alexandre that the only way a man like Adivi would handle embarrassment—handsome, perfectly mannered, neatly dressed, controlled Adivi—was through anger.

As if to compensate, Alexandre doted on Anjali, smiling indulgently at her when she joined him for coffee or tea, but he feared his attentions came from that repugnant place of pity, and if so, he wondered if this was apparent to the girl. It was like the enraging pity he felt for paupers in the streets of Paris or those child beggars in Bombay, all of them so shameless in their need, those unpolished personifications of modernity's failings—none of the gloss or sophistication of society—instead writhing and trembling with outstretched hands like pitiful savages before God. And there was Anjali, that constant reminder to Adivi of human fragility, and Alexandre at that moment felt for Adivi, that strong, modern man, more pity than he could ever summon for the man's eldest daughter.

"Oh, where is Mary? I asked her to see that Dr. Lautens was comfortable." Adivi frowned. "She's weeping for that . . . that Clough." Adivi turned apologetically at Alexandre. "I'm so sorry Dr. Lautens, these servants . . . you see, her minister is sick—no, that isn't correct— he is dying, and Mary's son works for him as a preacher. She's been weeping for him all morning," he said, irritated.

Alexandre had heard about the American missionary John Clough, the so-called Apostle to the Telugu, who worked in the area with the untouchables and had baptized his first Telugu person sixty years earlier, but he had no idea that Mary had any family other than the one she worked for.

Adivi sighed and turned to Mohini, "Run along dearest."

Adivi pulled a chair out for himself and shouted for Mary to bring in lunch. Alexandre sucked the sweet, white meat of the custard apple off a black seed and looked up to see Mohini smile at him before she left the room.

"WHAT BECOMES OF unmarried girls, Kanakadurga Amma Garu?" Alexandre asked.

The old woman smiled, her expression rueful and weary. "She will inherit half of her father's money, Dr. Lautens. Half the land, half our family jewelry. Her sister will get the other half of course, but Anjali will also get the house, so she can live here the rest of her life, taking care of her parents, and when we are all gone, the land will be passed back to Mohini's children."

"There is no hope that she can get married?"

"I love my Anjali more than anyone in the world, Dr. Lautens, but no one is going to marry a plain girl with a deformity and dark skin, not even a well-bred one with some land and money . . . " Kanakadurga paused, smiling, "My Anjali, you see. She has something special. A beam of valor. She is brave, she is intrepid. Once, when the girls were little, before Anjali became sick, I woke up one morning and I heard Mohini screaming—there was a spider on her bed. And Anjali was there—"

"And Anjali killed it?"

Kanakadurga smiled deeply, her eyes bright, "No, no. She took it in her hands and took it outside. She did not kill it. She was brave. She took it outside to the garden and released it. She let it live." The old woman laughed. "Imagine it! A little girl repatriating a spider!" And then she smiled deeply, sadly. "I hope she can find some happiness in the comfort her Shiva's wealth will afford her."

Prithu stood silently at Kanakadurga's door, holding a small, red box. "Ah, yes, the gloves!" Alexandre smiled at Prithu, who stared back at him, wide-eyed and emotionless. Taking the box, Alexandre opened it and smiled at the crisp white gloves within. He slid them on and stretched his hand out in the fine cotton. "Kanakadurga Amma Garu, I've been invited to the Waltair Club next week," he said, speaking of one of the British social clubs in town. He'd ordered the gloves from an English tailor in town. He showed his hands to Prithu, playfully. "Just the thing, eh Prithu?" But the child remained stoic in the doorway and Alexandre offered him an awkward "Thank-you."

ON A CRISP Cambridge evening, over drinks at the Eagle, one of Alexandre's Cambridge colleagues, Dr. Robertson, had given him the name of a friend in Waltair. "Please, when you are in Waltair, make arrangements to see my friend Anthony Davidson. He's an old friend of mine from Harrow, and he'd love to meet you. It's always good to have a contact with home in these parts, Alexandre. I've sent Tony a letter notifying him that you will be arriving soon. He would love to meet you."

A long lawn unrolled before Alexandre like a red carpet, leading from the road to the club's main building. Outside on the verandah, under the swinging white punkahs, English soldiers in their dress uniforms were drinking and smoking, sending up spirals of smoke in the early evening sun.

As Alexandre approached the building, an Indian waiter stopped him. "Sir, can I help you?"

"I am a guest of Dr. Davidson's. Eh . . . I have not met him before—would you please point me in his direction?"

"Certainly."

Alexandre was led in the direction of a rumpled Englishman smoking a cigar. He wore a dark red rose in his lapel. Dr. Davidson stood on the verandah of the Waltair Club; his hair was disheveled and his shirt wrinkled, but a little light of the aristocratic shined through nevertheless.

He smiled deeply as Alexandre approached, stretching out his hand. "You must be Dr. Lautens." Davidson puffed on his cigar, shaking Alexandre's hand. He laughed and, pinching Alexandre's cheek like an affectionate grandmother, said, "My goodness you are a handsome bugger." And slapping Alexandre on the back, Davidson led him into a large oak-paneled barroom. Indian barmen in white kurtas wove through the tables of Englishmen in suits with trays of scotch and whiskey. A waiter led them to an empty table by the large doors opening onto the back of the club grounds. Looking outside, Alexandre saw the palm trees swaying in the breeze around the bandstand, where a brass section was tuning its instruments.

Davidson waved off the menus offered by the waiter. "Two gin and tonics," he said.

"Yes Sir, Dr. Davidson."

Davidson took Alexandre by the shoulder, "So! Dr. Lautens, what brings you to Waltair?"

Alexandre smiled. He liked Davidson immediately. Alexandre told Davidson about his work and the book of Telugu grammar. Davidson asked Alexandre how he liked India.

"It is wonderful. It is nice, in a way, to know so few people. It is very peaceful. I've been getting a lot of work done."

"Oh, how bloody dreadful!" Davidson laughed.

When the drinks were brought, Davidson took his and raised his highball glass. "Well I'm sure as hell not toasting to work," he said, smiling. Outside, the sun was setting, painting the sky in reds and oranges. Davidson smiled, nodding toward the skyline: "To India."

"To India," Alexandre repeated, smiling. He looked at the dazzling sunset. He was beginning to feel at home. They spoke of Davidson's work for the Royal Botanical Survey.

An Indian horsekeep was pulling two chestnut Arabians, braying into their muzzles, from the stables as a friendly polo match was getting under way on the far lawn. The British boys in their riding kits assembled in front of a restless black gelding, weighing their mallets in their hands and strapping on their helmets, as a child behind them brushed the horse's mane. Davidson lingered on the scene before leaning back in his chair and taking in the view of the bar. "My goodness, I hate this place," he said, smiling.

ANJALI WAITED IN her room for her sister. She felt Mohini moving away from her and wanted dispel her fears that she was losing her. Anjali had sent out for Mohini's favorite chocolates and arranged them on a plate. Anjali was afraid her jealousy would strangle her alive.

Mohini had become more and more foreign to Anjali since the announcement of the engagement; Mohini had become that strangest of creatures—a girl betrothed. It seemed to Anjali that her little sister had become an expert in a dance she had never before performed. Mohini, as if by magic, had begun to adopt a wifely manner—helping Lalita run the household. Even her disposition had changed from childish to womanly; a new grace was evident in Mohini, and a secretive smile that spoke of membership to a private sorority. Her interest in the world of ideas and that space beyond the gates of the home had never been great but now was nonexistent.

Today, Anjali was prepared to play the part of the giddy and coquettish sister. Today she was prepared to gush about her future brother-in-law's dimpled smile and thick hair, and ready to admire the bridal trousseau, the saris and jewelry. In short, she was ready to attempt to play the part of a girl. But Mohini was nowhere to be seen, and after waiting for half an hour, the coffee cold, Anjali picked up her cane and thought to go in search of her sister, but then thought the better of it. When they were children, before the polio had withered her leg, she and Mohini, barefoot upon the often-toiled earth of Lalita's parents' home, would hide among the trees, the long white home of stucco and stone behind them in the distance. At night in search of their granddaughters, Lalita's parents made black shadows against the big house, shouting over the endless, blooming grove for the girls to come in for dinner, or settle into bed. The girls would run back to the house. In the air were perfume and fireflies, and on nights when their grandmother had energy and felt indulgent she would teach them how to embroider flowers and birds on their handkerchiefs.

As she waited for Mohini, Anjali looked in the mirror at herself and saw nearly incomprehensible hideousness; she shuddered in disgust at the image before her. She thought, "My God. How irredeemably ugly." She thought of that look of repulsion she so often caught in her father's eyes, how her mother's gaze would often escape her own, and she understood now why that was so. "I disgust them," she thought.

She sat waiting today in her room, hearing female voices echoing through the marble corridors, and didn't get up to look for her sister for half an hour more.

As ALEXANDRE SPOKE to Kanakadurga, he could see Anjali walk from her bedroom into the lavishly furnished receiving room. Her mother and sister were already there, as were other women from the village who were friends with Lalita. Anjali entered, unnoticed, watching them as they made the wedding arrangements, her dark face stoic.

"I should be there too, celebrating, but it holds no more appeal to me than attending a funeral," Kanakadurga sighed.

Anjali watched the life she could not have as closely as anyone could without actually living it. The week after the announcement of Mohini's engagement, merchants brought their best silks to the home for Lalita and the bride-to-be to choose matrimonial saris for the girl's nuptials. Kanakadurga continued, "The thing I worry about most for her, Dr. Lautens, is that she will not have love in her life . . . not the kind that comes from family, of course, but of goodwill, and affection . . . I am afraid she will remain ignorant of courtship, and of romance, of the kindness of the world . . . a girl needs those things." Kanakadurga was wrong. Anjali knew love in all its dimensions: with her mother the love that was wanting, with her father that which was unrequited, with Mohini that which had come and gone and lingered like a ghost, a moribund attachment, and with Kanakadurga, that type of love that was perfect in its equality, great in its tenderness, endless in its generosity, not to be dimmed by death. Of her love Anjali was assured. Of romance, all she knew was from books and poems, the ones she loved, by Currer Bell and Baudelaire.

The red fabrics were the most beautiful Alexandre had ever seen, and all were adorned in a full border embroidered with thread made of real gold. "Such a beautiful girl should have the most beautiful sari, Madam," one vendor said to Lalita. "Somewhat costly, yes," he continued, throwing the sari open, "but for marriage one shouldn't skimp, isn't it?"

Tears came to Lalita's eyes as she clasped Mohini in her arms.

"What a beautiful bride you will make, my darling!" Lalita exclaimed, wiping her eyes.

Each merchant spoke of his house's skills for weaving the best silks, his atelier's fame for designing the best border work. How beautiful his saris would look with Mohini's fair coloring, her perfect features.

Each merchant was right, of course, for how could anything look unbecoming on Mohini's perfect form, her lovely face, that thick rope of hair? Alexandre and Kanakadurga sat and watched from Kanakadurga's sitting room, from which a view of the receiving room was offered. Alexandre thought that Mohini, modeling her bridal saris and trying on jewelry, looked as beautiful as a temple dancer. Anjali was with the other women too and was occasionally asked to offer an opinion, or to call the servant to bring more food, tea or cool water. Lautens saw in her face her heart tightening when a merchant lifted up to the sound of a collective sigh a blood-red miracle of brushed silk and gold with a maroon border and blouse.

"Mummy, I think we should perhaps put aside some of the money for the wedding to serve a meal to the peasants—the ones we see each morning at the gate," said Anjali, her face tight and mean.

Lalita and Mohini looked at Anjali, incredulous.

"Anjali," Lalita sighed, "Anjali, please! Don't be so wicked! We are in a time of celebration. Don't make such a show of your charity."

"Mummy, all this money to celebrate one day! There are starving people right at our own gates!"

Mohini, for a moment, lost her characteristic grace and her coquettish charm. "Mummy what is this!? Why are you trying to destroy my wedding, Anjali?" Mohini narrowed her large eyes at her sister. "You are jealous! Now you want to destroy my wedding? Suddenly you care about beggars and peasants?" She wrung a silk sari in her hands.

Lalita put her hand up and shouted, "We are a generous family, but we are not inviting beggars and untouchables to your sister's wedding. It is inauspicious. Is that the kind of wedding you would want? Then why should you want that for your sister?"

KANAKADURGA CLEARED HER throat as she saw out the doorway her son approaching her and Alexandre. Alexandre turned and saw Adivi and stood.

"Please, Doctor, do not get up . . . in our caste, girls get married in their parents' home. I am sorry for the disruption to your studies Dr. Lautens, but it will be over in two weeks," said Adivi.

The servants, in hurried, distracted motions, moved about Alexandre and the Adivis with baskets full of flowers, lining up tiny clay pots with oil and wicks along the home's corridors and hallways. The kitchen servants had gone into town to buy extra oil burners and butter, raisins, cashews, saffron and basmati rice and extra-large dishes in which to cook for all the wedding guests.

"It is quite alright, Mr. Adivi. It is a privilege to be party to your daughter's wedding. It looks like it is going to be quite the event."

Adivi smiled and looked over Alexandre's shoulder at his mother. "Amma, we still cannot find your jewelry," he said in a soft but serious voice.

"I'm sorry Shiva . . . " she replied, looking down. "It must be in one of the armoires . . . "

Adivi turned and left, irritated with his mother's seeming lack of concern. Alexandre turned back to her and was met with a stern, hard look.

Anjali returned to her room, where her sister's favorite chocolates were melting on a plate and a steel urn of coffee was sitting cold on a table.

ANJALI TENSED AS she stood behind Alexandre. She cleared her throat, announcing herself. He turned and saw her, placing down a cup of coffee. He began to stand.

"No, no, please, Dr. Lautens, don't get up." She squeezed the book in her hand and lowered herself into the seat next to Alexandre. She sat with her back too straight. She looked up and said, too flatly, "I find the sympathy I have for Madame Bovary is clouded by the feeling I have that she is, somehow, pathetic." She felt glad with herself for managing to get out a sentence she had been contemplating since the day before.

Alexandre leaned back, resting his fingertips on his chin. "*Madame Bovary?*" he asked, smiling. "You've been reading Flaubert?" His eyes danced with amusement.

"Yes, and I . . . well, I feel it is rather pathetic, isn't it? This grown woman reading romance novels all day and then expecting life to live up to the plotlines of books . . . what do you think?" She had thought so much about what she meant to say, but now it came out too quickly. It did not sound right.

Alexandre smiled and raised his eyebrows. "To be honest, Anjali, I haven't read that book for a very long time . . . not since I was in school."

"Hmm." Anjali's eyebrows lifted; she turned away and sat back in her chair. "Hmm," she repeated. Anjali was intimidated by his obvious erudition; she wanted to impress him and engage him. But she found these attempts as often ended a conversation as began one. She felt a bit like a curio cabinet now more and more as she read up on the things in which she believed he too might take an interest.

Alexandre took pity and asked, "How did you become so interested in literature?"

"Daddy hired tutors for us when we were small. We studied English, mathematics, art and music and Hindi. These men cared more about being employed by Daddy than they did about teaching me and my sister. They were sycophants, all of them. Nevertheless, I enjoyed reading and studying. I still do." She smiled. "Myself and Mohini, we would wake early and have coffee and eat *idlies*. I remember that the cook hated those early hours; she was always grumpy and everything was prepared too hastily."

"So what is your favorite book?"

"I loved English literature best. We read Shakespeare in the garden in the morning." As Anjali spoke, she for the first time seemed to Alexandre to be a girl. "I like reading stories about love. Jane Eyre and Rochester. Romeo and Juliet. Why would anyone write about anything else?"

"Well my goodness," Alexandre smiled. "So love is the most important thing, then. Well, yes, of course you are right." He turned and looked out at the sky. "Tell me," he ventured tentatively, "do you believe your sister loves the man to whom she is engaged?"

"What?"

"Mohini—does she love the man to whom she's been betrothed?"

Anjali took her eyes from Alexandre and looked out onto the horizon.

"They've only met once or twice . . . I don't think she loves him. How could she? She doesn't even know him. This is how we get married in India. Marriage comes first and then, if one is lucky perhaps, love."

"Sometimes it is possible to love someone one doesn't know."

"That is absurd, Dr. Lautens," Anjali said, wincing.

"It is not. No . . . " he replied, dreamily. He turned to her, leaning forward on his knees. "Well, there was this man Jaufré Rudel; he was a troubadour—"

"What is that?"

"—a well, a sort of musician—" Alexandre turned to Anjali, looking at her, his gaze bright and penetrating: a father telling his child a bedtime story, "and he fell in love with a woman who lived across the sea, in Tripoli." Alexandre felt the warm concrete of the verandah on the soles of his feet.

Anjali sighed; she felt sad. "How did he fall in love with her?"

"She was the countess of Tripoli. Her beauty was legendary in Asia and Europe, and Jaufré joined the Crusades so he could go to Tripoli. See, he was already in love with her. Just from hearing others describe her. He traveled from the west coast of France." Alexandre took Anjali's wrist and turned over her hand, touching lightly the tip of her thumb, and glanced up at her, "all the way across the Mediterranean," he lightly skipped his finger along her open palm, "to here, Syria," he tapped the tip of her little finger and then fell back in his chair. "Well, when his ship finally arrived in Tripoli, he was so ill he had to be carried to shore, and he lay dying there while they went off in search of Hodierna." Alexandre smiled, making his eyes wide for the effect. "And just as he took his last few breaths, she came down from her castle onto the beach and held his body. She kissed him, and then he fell back in her arms and died. And he never knew her at all."

"Like Layla and Majnun . . . "

Alexandre laughed, his eyes wide. "Yes!"

From behind them came a deep laugh. Anjali turned, "Daddy . . . " she caught her breath.

Adivi crossed his arms across his chest, his expression jolly. "What silly romantic notions you Europeans have. Come, Dr. Lautens, tea is ready."

SANSKRIT IS SAID to be comprised of all the sounds of the beginnings of the universe. The world came into being, and the bells of the Sanskrit register were sounded. When it is spoken, the vibrations made in the throat are said to bring peace and joy to the speaker. The priest who occasionally made rounds in the Adivi home told Alexandre that merely speaking Sanskrit would bring him closer to God.

When they talked in the mornings, Anjali liked to hear anecdotes about linguistics, how the word for "life" in Italian was also the word for a woman's waist. That *nostalgia* meant, etymologically, the pain of yearning to return home. That the real word for "bear" in Russian was a curse, so the Russians called bears *medved*, the honey-eaters. She told him that the word in Telugu for "seven" was also the word for "cry" and that she had been born on the seventh of July.

THAT AFTERNOON, ADIVI arranged for Alexandre to visit the Simhachalam Temple, where a lion god presided over the west-facing structure. Subba Rao accompanied him, and Rajiv drove.

The rocking of the carriage lulled him to sleep, and Subba Rao gently woke him when the coach stopped on a flat landing halfway up the hill. "We must walk the rest of the way, Sir; the carriage can't go any farther." Disoriented and groggy, Alexandre started. He looked out at the throngs of pilgrims making their way up the hill to the stone temple. "Of course, Subba Rao, of course," he said, dismounting.

Feeling suddenly invigorated, he began to walk in large strides. Subba Rao, afraid of losing sight of Alexandre in the sea of people, hurried after him shouting, "Dr. Lautens, Sir, please! You mustn't rush so fast Sir!"

Laughing and enjoying the fresh air, Alexandre walked on. When he reached the top, he lit a cigarette and sat on a ledge, wide-eyed, studying the grandness of the place through swirls of smoke. The temple was tiers of stone with fearsome Hindu deities carved in infinite intricacy on every side. He had sweated through his white shirt and the cool sea wind felt good on his skin.

Subba Rao finally caught up with him, gasping for air. "Dr. Lautens! Dr. Lautens! You must be careful! This heat can be very dangerous to Europeans, Sir!" Subba Rao ran up the last few steps, catching up to Alexandre and opening the water flask and pouring out a cup of water for Alexandre.

"Thank you," Alexandre said. He drank the water, enjoying the steely taste of it. They leaned against the stone wall acting as a retainer along the cliff. Subba Rao's Brylcreemed hair didn't move in the high winds.

"Come, Dr. Lautens, let us continue on inside . . . we must get you out of this sun."

"You mustn't worry, Subba Rao, I am fine," Alexandre offered, irritated. They could hear the temple bells. As they moved closer, the astounding detail of the carvings impressed Alexandre more and more, with lotus blossoms and dancing courtesans and the lionlike avatar of Vishnu, for whom the temple was dedicated. The images were frightening with their fierce expressions of bloodlust.

Suddenly, Alexandre felt dizzy and stopped for a few minutes to collect himself. He braced himself, putting his palms on his knees, leaning forward to collect his breath. The masses pushed against Subba Rao's outstretched arms as he pushed back, trying to make room for Alexandre. The crowds would not make room for him, and Subba Rao tried, with little avail, to give Alexandre space to catch his breath; he shouted at the brown bodies crowded together, crying children clinging to saris, at the painted cows being pulled along by their owners.

Subba Rao wetted a handkerchief and held it out to Alexandre.

"Put this on your forehead, Doctor."

Alexandre struggled to make it through the crowd, shouldering his way past the outstretched hands and the masses pushing forward up the hill. Resting a hand on a tree, he leaned over and was sick, coughing and wheezing in the thin air. Subba Rao yelled at the crowd to move out of his way. Alexandre felt a hand on his back.

"Dr. Lautens, are you alright?" Subba Rao poured water out of the flask and Alexandre took it, rinsing his mouth. They pushed back through the crowds, the steep descent causing them to tumble to the coach below.

Alexandre sat back in the coach and closed his eyes; Rajiv sounded the horn, reversing the coach slowly, the horses grunting and snorting as they tried to turn around in the tight space, the angry temple goers yelling curses at them and pounding their fists on the coach.

When they returned to the Adivi home, Subba Rao quickly informed Adivi and Lalita of Alexandre's episode, and Alexandre was sent to his room immediately by Lalita to lie down, and a servant was sent in with lime water and a cold compress. Adivi upbraided an expressionless Subba Rao for letting Alexandre run ahead alone.

THE PRIEST WAS to be called in the next week to chant in the old language at the wedding. In the days before Mohini's marriage, the servants and the women in the family would string marigold blossoms, jasmine buds and roses. The jasmines and roses were local, with an earthy floral scent. The roses: Old World and red, with only a couple layers of petals, the first of their kind in the world and the scent had not been hybridized or altered and they smelled as they always had: like heaven.

There was much to do, and Anjali hung in the background as the other women gossiped gaily. She strung marigolds and roses for the wedding tent, frowning and running her finger across the tip of the threading needle.

The home buzzed, all atwitter with female happiness. Anjali remained quiet as her mother and sister and aunts and cousins gossiped gaily.

"DID YOU PUT the coconut oil?" Lalita asked Mohini. Her youngest daughter was sitting outside with her embroidery, darting a needle in and out of a pillowcase.

"Yes Mummy," she replied without looking up. Every morning as her wedding approached, Mohini was instructed by Lalita to put egg yolks and lemon juice on her face for her complexion and to saturate her hair in coconut oil.

"What are you doing? Move to the shade!" Lalita instructed Mohini, fretting over her daughter's complexion. Mohini groaned and pulled her chair into a shadier part of the garden.

The bridegroom's name was Varun. He was the only son of a family of landholders who owned two rice mills in Masulipatnam. No one had told Alexandre much about him, and he wondered what the boy was like. Alexandre knew only that he was handsome and shared Mohini's wheat-like complexion and coal black hair. The bridal saris had been purchased, and as a gift to their daughter and future son-in-law, Shiva and Lalita had been to their bank in town to arrange to give Varun the title to one hundred acres of the mango groves that Lalita's parents had passed down to their daughter for her wedding. None of the original trees were left. The new varietals were hardier against insects and fungus and the fruit was heavy and golden.

Lalita had been to town to buy Mohini's bridal jewelry, the star piece of which was a diamond necklace with stones handpicked by the bride's mother from a selection of Golconda diamonds. The Golconda mines had hundreds of years before rendered the Koh-i-Noor diamond, which had been pressed into Shah Jahan's peacock throne such that when the old shah was imprisoned by his son at Agra Fort, he could see his beloved Mumtaz's tomb reflected in the great gem. Lalita had instructed, only half in jest, that the jeweler was to create a piece that would rival the Koh-i-Noor in beauty.

Even though the stones were unmatched in brilliance and clarity, and had been placed in a singularly stunning setting, Lalita and Shiva were slightly disappointed. They had wanted to give Mohini her grandmother's jewels, which were family antiques and cut in the Mughal style, but the estate jewelry had gone missing. Kanakadurga was a widow after all, and as such no longer wore jewelry and had put the pieces away years before, and though Lalita had searched every safe, every bureau and every armoire in the home, they were not found. Alexandre had even heard Lalita and Shiva arguing about the missing jewelry behind closed doors. Lalita was suspicious of Kanakadurga and thought that for whatever reason the old woman had deliberately hidden the items and did not want to give the family jewelry to her granddaughter.

THAT NIGHT, ALEXANDRE unlatched the wooden shutters on the windows in his room and inhaled the intoxicating perfume of the tuberoses as it floated into his nostrils. He couldn't help but wonder what Mohini's groom was like. Was he intelligent, a man of character? He let the tuberose fill the room, and fell asleep as if drugged, and dreamt that night of wandering the world, the banks of the Nile, the Amazon, the Yamuna, Indus and Ganges, in search of blue lotuses to offer to a goddess-cum-woman on a tiger's back, Kali-Ma, the dark mother, the one with the wild untamed hair and dark skin, the one whose tongue was stuck out defiantly, like a flame. His white, bare feet walked endlessly, his skin muddied with clay as he searched desperately those fertile banks for a rare flower that looked as if it were lit from within, as if in its petals it held moonlight. Kali was terrifying and made Alexandre shudder in his sleep, but she was a woman after all, and she could be won over with flowers and he gathered all in sight. But despite his efforts, his scouring the world, she was not satisfied. Kali wants one more flower. In his dream, Alexandre knelt, the blue blossoms pouring from his arms and lap, 107 of them, tumbling at the goddess's golden feet, enough only to satisfy a mortal woman. Alexandre began to weep, and raised his eyes to her, and realized that his eyes, beautiful and azure blue, might do. He offered to pluck them out. Kali, holding a sword and a mace, her breasts covered in blood, softened and refused his offer.

Alexandre woke up, his heart pounding. He ran his hands through his hair, wet with perspiration. He lightly touched his eyes. He turned over in the sweat-soaked sheets, trying to calm his racing heart and fall asleep.

❋ 8 ❋

THE SOUND OF women's laughter infused a lighthearted, crystalline quality to the air; the wedding preparations were under way and friends and relatives had descended on the house. There were daily trips to the railway station to greet arriving relatives. Adivi's sisters were there, Lalita's aunts, cousins on both sides. There were bags of marigolds, roses and strings of jasmines brought to the house by specially contracted flower vendors. They had been left in burlap bags in the garden, and their heavy perfume clung to the very walls and walkways of the home.

The astrologer set the time of the wedding ceremony at 10:39 in the evening. The rooms in the house were full with the sounds of company—friends and relatives and some of Adivi's business partners. Everyone was to wear new clothes—Lalita had purchased dozens of new saris and suits for the guests.

Alexandre liked the simple logic of Telugu families. Families were conceptualized in generational lines—all of Lalita and Adivi's siblings and cousins were aunts and uncles to Mohini and Anjali; all the maternal aunts were Peddamma or Pinni—Elder Mother or Younger Mother, depending on their age in relation to Lalita's; and all the paternal uncles were Pethnaana or Chinnananna, Elder Father or Younger Father. All of their parents were grandparent to the girls—in addition to Kanakadurga, their Nainamma, there was also Vijawada Nainamma and Hyderabad Tata—all of Lalita and Adivi's aunts and uncles, and

some tens of other relationships that seemed so simple and uncompli-
cated to the Adivis' but rather the opposite to Alexandre—he had no
relationship with the in-laws of his cousins' nor with his great-uncles,
and he envied in Indians a bit these huge, seemingly warm families
in which everyone knew everyone. He found the number of people
overwhelming. Cousins, cousins of cousins, aunts, uncles, nieces, nephews and more cousins of cousins. Alexandre struggled to remember all
their names but enjoyed the energy all those relatives brought to the
house. He met Adivi's three older sisters: Usha, Bharati and Hema, all
of whom shared their brother's strong brows and commanding eyes,
his sense of humor and generosity and his coarse, curly hair.

ADIVI WAS THE youngest child of five; four girls and then him. Ten
years separated Shiva from his oldest sister, Usha. As a child, he had
always been closest to his second oldest sister, Draupati, who had been
through all his boyhood like a second mother to him, doting over him,
celebrating his achievements in school; she had been less girlish than his
other sisters, who guarded their hair ribbons and powder tins jealously.
As children they would sneak out the house in the afternoon when
everyone else was napping after lunch to play cricket, the other boys
on the pitch sworn to secrecy. No one could know that one of the Adivi
girls, in her *salwaar kameez*, was running around like a boy. She could
run faster than half the boys and bowl better than almost any of them.
Shiva would always take a special joy in seeing the incredulous look
on the faces of boys new to their game when his sister would bat. One
afternoon, they had returned home late because Adivi had bloodied the
nose of a boy who had pulled his sister's hair, and Kanakadurga was
waiting for them, her arms crossed, her eyes narrowed.

"Amma, I was having so much trouble with my Hindi lessons that Shiva walked me to the Hindi master's home for some extra help!" Draupati said, her eyes surprised—they had expected their mother to still be napping.

"Really? You bothered the Hindi master during lunchtime?"

"Yes Amma, I'm sorry, but I have an exam tomorrow!"

"Huh." Kanakadurga eyed her lying children up and down, seeing Draupati's disheveled hair and her son's look of nervous deception, and smiled. "Well, get inside then and keep studying."

"Yes, Amma," Draupati and Shiva answered, their faces beaming with gratitude at their mother's willful ignorance.

Kanakadurga and Anil were considered wildly permissive to allow their daughters to wear *salwaar kameezes*, and in truth Anil didn't wholly approve, but his wife insisted and on certain aspects of the girls' care he deferred to her judgment.

Draupati died when she was twenty-six years old. The police inspectors didn't dare tell the girl's husband, Raja, or her parents that Draupati's body had been reduced to mangled red ribbons between the train's steel tracks and its wheels. The basket of eggplant and tomatoes and squash she had carried from the market was emptied all over the tracks, the police officers sliding on the slippery flesh of crushed vegetables, their skins bruised, seeds and flesh bursting as they examined the scene. The morning was windy and grey, the sky cracking with silver as the sun tried to push through, single drops of rain falling to earth as the sky threatened to break. Had she been a peasant, the body would have been quickly cleared, allowing the next train to pass through unencumbered, but because of her parents' station and their friendship with the chief constable, Mr. Blackhall, who would sometimes stop by to have a glass of scotch with Anil, they did a complete investigation. Blackhall posted two of his officers at the perimeter of the scene to keep Draupati's frantic, utterly hysterical mother and her pale, shaking father from seeing their dead daughter, whose body he was grateful was at least partially hidden by the tall, vividly green grass that came to the knees of his men. Shards of her pale purple sari were tangled in the grass; and later they would find her black-beaded wedding necklace wrapped around a bolt on the train tracks. Raja stood nearby, his arms limp by his sides, looking rather helpless as silently he wondered, "What now?" They could still smell the grease and smoke from the train, the smell of burning steel, and ever since that scent made Kanakadurga nauseous.

"Anil, she must have simply not heard the train." Blackhall forced the Adivis, with beseeching eyes, to maintain eye contact with him, to not look over his shoulder, to not try to make sense of the scene, that low grey light, that wind in the grass so strong that Kanakadurga's hair was being whipped out of its braid, and the caps were flying from the policemen's heads.

A week later, Blackhall brought the cleaned bridal necklace with the idea of personally giving it to Kanakadurga, unfolding it before her in the white cloth he had put it in. When she saw the gleaming black beads she screamed, "No, no! Dear God, no!" as if she had seen a ghost. And every day since, Kanakadurga would think to herself at least once, "How could she have not heard the train? Why was she out alone, running a servant's errand?"

When the news of his sister's death reached Adivi at his sixth-form junior college, he went to his room, free of the company of the other boys, excused by his professors, and wept silently for the loss of his beloved Draupati, his fists shaking, and he would think, making sense not even to himself, how much he hated that vain, effeminate, spirit-less, bloody Raja. Later that week, he received a letter of admission from Trinity College, Cambridge, where he would never go, because now he could not bear the idea of leaving his other sisters.

ALL AROUND ALEXANDRE was noise—the preparation of the food, the arrangement of rooms and stringing of flowers—a joyous cacoph-ony that was at once foreign and familiar to him, as if the simple effer-vescence of human joy made this environment less exotic to him. And in a quiet corner, Anjali. She was on the periphery of a group of women in colorful saris, smiling but not participating in that merriment, the winking jokes about a life she wouldn't have: that conjugal, married, normal life.

Mohini was, as if from a storybook, a nervous, blushing bride and primarily concerned herself before her wedding with the preparation of her hair and the selection of saris and jewelry that had been decided upon by herself and her mother. That glowing halo of levity that she walked in continued, and those aunts and cousins, themselves all long before married, cooed as they kissed and squeezed the beautiful bride. It was apparent that Mohini welcomed the life that was coming to her—the marriage, the family, the children—that sweet, contented and sometimes even joyful life.

FOR HIS PART, Alexandre had been left alone out of deference for his work. He took meals with the men, as the dining had been split into two rounds: first the men and then the ladies and children. He some-times joined the men after dinner for a drink. Alexandre, for the first time, partook in that peculiarly segregated kind of Indian socializing:

the women spent most of their time in the kitchen or out in the garden, the men in the living room or the sitting room, where a bar had been assembled with Italian wines, Irish whiskeys and gin and vodka. "Customarily," Adivi began, "one doesn't drink at Hindu weddings, but certainly we can raise a glass the night before."

ANJALI SAT DOWN on her bed and held the envelope up; she rarely received mail, except around the time of her birthday, when sometimes she would receive cards from relatives who lived far away. But the handwriting on this envelope was not familiar to her; neither was the name in the return address, SMT. S. NAIDU, in Hyderabad. It was addressed to KUMARI ADIVI ANJALI. Anjali hesitated; mail for her was rare and the pleasure was to be delayed. The envelope was a simple white; a stamp bearing Queen Victoria's face in profile was affixed to the right corner. Anjali glanced up, making sure she had closed the door to her room behind her. She ran her fingertip over the seam of the envelope and slowly ran the gleaming blade of her father's envelope opener across the top, splitting the envelope open cleanly, pulling out a folded, cream-colored sheet with fine, floral handwriting on it, starting, "Dear Miss Adivi, I wanted to thank you for your article."

Anjali pushed herself back on her bed, resting her upper body against the wall, her legs up on the bed. She smiled deeply, in a way she rarely did, in a manner that revealed a warm girlishness. It was a wholly unexpected and rare thing: fan mail.

She continued to read. "I refer of course to your article 'Free Women in a Free India,' in the August 1911 issue of *Jai Hind*. What a rare and precious thing! A young woman like yourself who cares about the future of her country, with so luminous an intellect, with so clear a voice! Our country's struggle for freedom can only be fortified by young women like you, my dear, and I hope you continue to lend your mind and heart to our collective cause. Should you be able, I would love for you to attend a talk I shall be giving at the Andhra Ladies Association in Hyderabad in December, as my special guest. I hope you will be able to join me; I should love to lay eyes on the face of this young woman who speaks so passionately for the freedom of Mother India. *Vande Mataram.*"

Anjali's mouth was open in wonder; it scarcely seemed possible. Her eyes raced to the bottom of the letter; it was signed Sarojini Naidu, a name Anjali was very familiar with—the so-called Nightingale of India, the tiny female poetess who had won the Nizam's scholarship to attend Cambridge years earlier. Sometimes Anjali would listen to Sarojini recite poems on All-India Radio in her grandmother's room after the radio dramas or a concert of classical music broadcast from the Royal Albert Hall.

Without pause, Anjali took up pen and paper, copying the return address from the letter onto a fresh white envelope. She started, nearly shaking with excitement and joy: "Dear Mrs. Naidu, my gratitude for your note cannot be put into words. And I am in no small degree self-conscious of how my own humble words must seem so poor, so inadequate in comparison with your own. Alas, I cannot compare to a poet of such note as yourself. With profound thanks I accept your invitation to the Christmastime event at the University. I look so very forward to meeting you. Sincerely yours, Adivi Anjali."

"KANAKADURGA AMMA GARU, they are—excuse my language—prostitutes?"

Kanakadurga laughed, "No, dear Dr. Lautens, *devadasis* are courtesans." She leaned back, lounging in cushions, and Alexandre smiled to himself as he noticed that she looked, to his surprise, sensual, languorous. "They are artists, scholars, they write books and read poetry and learn languages. They sing and dance in the temples. They are part of kings' courts. They are married to God, Alexandre . . . and they are their own mistresses."

Alexandre smiled; he was unaccustomed to being viewed as a prude.

"*Devadasis* are servants of God," she finished, smiling.

Alexandre had been reading the English-language newspapers and their scandal-tinged coverage of the obscenity trial of Bangalore Nagarathnamma, the scholar-musician *devadasi* who had edited and published the work of her fellow *devadasi* Muddupallani called *Radhika Santwanam*.

"The authorities are claiming it is obscene. Fools! My goodness, they are perverts and fools!" Kanakadurga gestured about dramatically, her eyes bright with anger, "Muddupallani's work is—it is erotic poetry, it is about the joys of womanhood. Obscene? What ridiculousness."

Nagarathnamma's photograph was in the paper—she looked strong and intelligent and regal. Alluring though not beautiful. She boasted in the papers that she was the first woman in all of India to pay income taxes; she could play the violin and speak Sanskrit, Tamil, Telugu and English. She loved poetry. The papers wrote, "Ms. Nagarathnamma has published the work of eighteenth century fellow devadasi Muddupalani, whose work of Telugu erotic poetry, *Radhika Santwanam*, has caused an uproar and Muddhupallani and Ms.

Nagarathnamma have been called whores, prostitutes and adulteresses by the authorities, who view the book as a pornographic work. We can only quote the following lines from the book: 'She kept thinking. Tortured by love / she couldn't close her eyes.' Anyone in possession of this volume is asked to relinquish it to the local police authority under the direction of Police Chief Cunningham. Failure to do so will result in the offender being charged with a morals violation."

IN THE KITCHEN, there were great stainless steel bowls filled with sweets and puris and rice. Preparations for that evening's wedding were under way and even then, so early in the morning, there was a buzzing sense of urgency: the leisurely life of the Indian upper class temporarily suspended as an endless stream in a joyous panic. Saris were starched and ironed, jewels taken from locked cabinets, and heavy garlands of flowers were strung up in the garden where the wedding would take place. Relatives were everywhere, offering help and creating chaos— the maids interrupting the seemingly endless cooking only to make coffee or tea for the guests.

Amid all the chaos, Alexandre sought out Anjali. "I hope you wouldn't mind accompanying me this morning on an errand; I would quite enjoy your company. I was speaking to the cook this morning as she made me some coffee—I discussed this trip with her and she has assured me your father would not mind," Dr. Lautens said.

"Of course, Dr. Lautens," Anjali said. Her father would not mind, of course. His protectiveness was reserved for Mohini and it came so often to her aid that there seemed to be none of it left for Anjali. Moreover, he was busy that morning in town, making last-minute bank transferals for Mohini's dowry.

No proper Indian unmarried girl would be seen in public in the sole company of an unrelated man, but it did not occur to Anjali that she was doing anything wrong.

Nothing at all occurred to her; she was nearly trembling with joy. Lautens was perhaps the most beautiful man she had ever seen, and upon seeing him that first time she felt a great desire to know him and to be in his presence, a feeling that she had not, in the closed doors of her childhood home, ever felt before. Anjali could not contain her excitement—to be alone with the beautiful, exotic scholar. She fancied herself a person of a degree of substance, not one to be moved uniquely by the magnetic power of physical beauty, no matter how great. Only having known Dr. Lautens some few moments that first day he arrived, however, she knew little more about him to find appealing. But still, she could not then take her eyes from him. She noticed at dinner his manner was reserved. He had an air of quiet, observational seriousness, as if all of life was part of his study, and not just the character of speech. Since then, she had found that he had gentle good humor, neither a comedian nor a stoic. His manner was intelligent, his words thoughtfully chosen and carefully delivered. He did not seem given over to the arrogance so common in Europeans, and lacking this conceit, and the bravado that so often seemed to come with it, he had instead a quiet and calm self-assurance. But sometimes Anjali was confused by him—he seemed to be sympathetic to the poor outside the home's gates but also wary of them. He believed strongly in the education of women but thought they should stay in the home and leave money earning to their husbands. Perhaps most of all, greater even than the plain fact of his beauty—there was a great world in his eyes. Anjali gazed at his eyes: they were larger than solar systems and galaxies. In light of the first sensations of desire in Anjali, the assurance of impending spinsterdom seemed especially cruel.

She drank her coffee quickly, anxious to be with Dr. Lautens in the wide world. She went to her room, smiling in a way she never had before, a wild smile that she could not control. With so many guests in the home, she could move surreptitiously. She put sandalwood-scented powder on her shoulders and collarbone and pinned jasmines to her hair, thinking briefly of that time when Dr. Lautens had told her about Aimé Guerlain, who re-created the fragrance of his first love's skin and could capture the scent of a melancholy Paris twilight: he could make the smell of the silver mist in the purple sky, or the smell of wet flowers after a rain shower: that one was called Après l'Ondée. She had written the name down in her diary after he told her, and she wrote down too the story he had told her about Marie Antoinette being discovered in her coach by the French revolutionaries because the scent of her perfume had betrayed her: no one but royalty could afford the fragrance.

Anjali then went to her grandmother's room, knocking timidly in the early morning. "Nainamma! Nainamma!" she whispered, urgently. She heard a weak grunt of acknowledgment; she pushed the door through, beaming. "Nainamma! Dr. Lautens is taking me out! He wants me to go into the city with him."

"What for?" the old woman asked drowsily, her brow furrowed.

"I don't know. He says he has an errand to run—maybe to the news agents or the tailor . . . I'll be back soon." She turned to leave.

"Anjali!" the old woman said in warning, her voice raspy, grabbing the girl's wrist. But seeing so strong and rare an expression of joy on her granddaughter's face, she said only, "Be careful."

They would be beyond the confines of this estate and all its stifling, all its spying, all its gossip. As she walked out of the house, she saw her mother in the kitchen. Lalita's hair was ever-so-slightly disheveled, and she was talking to the servants about the wedding menu.

Anjali continued on, and thought twice, before turning and saying, "Mummy, Dr. Lautens has asked me to—"

Lalita turned, her face red with irritation. She put a ladle down and rubbed her eyes, "My God Anjali. Can't you see I'm very busy right now? My goodness." Lalita clutched her head, *"Naaku cheppalenantha pani undi!"* I have so much work.

Turning, Anjali ran outside to meet the doctor.

"I have called the carriage. Rajiv is waiting outside for us," Dr. Lautens said, and as they rose up, he crooked his arm toward Anjali. It was a strange gesture, and as she steadied herself upon her cane, she looked at him quizzically.

He smiled and taking the cane from her, offered her his arm. He beamed. She could see from his expression that he liked who he was in this moment.

Anjali smiled, flattered and frightened at once. She was never without her cane. But she did not want to offend him. And she did want to touch him. She rested the cane against a chair, tentatively. She clutched the chair's back as Alexandre moved nearer to her, and she imbibed the scent of musk and soap. He reached for her hand and looped her arm through his. She held to it tightly and fearfully, unstable upon her feet as she found a new balance. His arm was heavy and strong, his body warm and solid.

Alexandre nodded to the guard to unlatch the gates. Anjali clutched Alexandre's arm for life as he led her outside the great gates.

The morning guard, Peter, was a man of the darkest skin with a bushy mustache. There were cracks in the skin of his hands. He was one of the lower-caste men who had converted to Christianity when the white missionaries went through the slums of the untouchables. He nodded to them, muttering in acknowledgment, "Miss Anjali, Dr. Lautens."

As they walked outside the gates, she delighted in feeling the burn of the eyes all around them, even those of the driver, who had known her for years as a proper girl. Their unvoiced accusations angered her, but she felt a great surge of pride at feeling the embarrassment unique to women. Never before had she been able to give the suggestion of impropriety.

Outside, a thin fish vendor wearing only a *lunghi* was returning from the early morning market. Under his arm, three silvery fish wrapped in newspaper—taking home what he couldn't sell. A blond street dog was trailing him, whining and whimpering, his ribs and hips jutting out of his skin and thin coat. The fishmonger waved at the dog dismissively, shouting, "Po!" Go, get out of here. But then Anjali saw him turn around and throw a fish at the starving dog, which attacked it with his snout and teeth, laying waste to it in minutes. And Anjali felt inexplicably light, as if a heavy hand had been lifted from her chest, so glad to see such goodness.

As they sat in the carriage, Alexandre wore again his strange smile.

"I hope you enjoy what I have planned, Anjali."

"I am sure I will, Dr. Lautens."

She did not recognize the curve of the road as they wove through the streets, but she lifted her face, imbibing the salt in the air.

Before her, an expanse of blues and golds came into view, fairly sparkling. And Anjali smelled that ocean air, saw little plumes of sand rise up in the wind.

Alexandre asked the driver to wait in the carriage. He kicked his shoes off, exited the carriage and came around to her side.

Anjali followed his example and slid her sandals off. She leaned toward him and took his arm as before.

They walked along the long stretch of sand, and she felt the sand against her feet, grainy between her toes and against the dry skin of her heels. The morning was cool, but the rising sun warmed them, and she could feel it bear down on the earth. She shuddered in the early morning breeze and held Alexandre's arm as if it were more dear now.

They stood for a moment, gazing out at the great, roaring blue and green and white ocean. He sighed deeply, and for a moment, she lost his gaze and saw that his mind was far away. For a moment she could not feel the strength of his body and thought she might fall as the waterline rushed up around her ankles. She felt fear in her stomach, and in the next moment, her vision was filled with the sky. Alexandre lifted her into his arms. She screamed even though she was smiling.

He marched out swiftly in the sea. Alexandre laughed, and looking down at her exclaimed, "Anjali, today you will swim."

A cold, clear pool rose around Dr. Lautens's legs, his pant legs pooling around his body as they moved deeper and deeper into the water. Anjali closed her eyes as the water washed over her again and again. She continued to scream in fear and joy and disbelief. They moved deeper and farther into the water, and Alexandre continued to laugh with such unbridled joy, in such hysterics, that he seemed a much younger man than he was, the cool water lapping at his chest, the fishermen in their boats laughing and pointing and yelling at them.

The water was deep. It was rising up past his waist and up to his chest; he laughed, giddy from of the shock of the coldness of the water. She did too—it took her breath away and she gasped and sputtered and flailed, clutching Alexandre's body for dear life, her legs and arms flailing.

"Don't worry, Anjali," he laughed, "I'm here!" He yelled over the roar of the waves, laughing at the fear, panic and happiness in her face. "I'll hold onto you! I'll hold onto you!" She felt the warmth of his body as wave after wave crashed over them. Her skirts pooled out in the water, rising up to her knees, and she felt her skin tighten in the cold. Alexandre caught a brief glimpse of her deformed leg. Anjali's hair came loose from its bun and spread like a dark cloud around her face.

Dr. Lautens continued to hold her up. "Don't struggle against the water, relax, let your body float," he instructed her, remembering teaching his own children how to swim. "The water will support you— it will hold you up. And I am holding you also."

The gentle and amused expression on his face caused her fear to subside, and she could feel her muscles begin to relax, to move with the waves. She felt his large hands clutching her body, pressing his warmth into her through her wet clothes. She pressed down into his palms and closed her eyes and shouted and shouted again with joy. The water washed over her once and again and again, every time cleansing her as she floated as if sinless.

Alexandre's tunic clung to him, and his wet hair fell back over his head in slick, dark curls. His skin and eyelashes sparkled in the early light with drops of seawater, his eyes shimmering in amusement. He seemed to glow in the light, and she thought him never more beautiful than at that moment—alive and free in the water, his skin pale against the darkness of his hair, his body tall against the bright orange and gold of the sun moving up, steady against the horizon. He cradled her head in the crook of his arm as a groom might hold a bride or a mother her child.

She looked up at the grand stretch of blue and gold sky, having never felt more joy, at peace with life, more full of hope for all her dearest held wishes. The fishermen continued to call out to them, their bodies ebony and midnight blue against the bright sunshine, their wooden boats covered with colorful sheets and their green and black nets. They yelled out to them, laughing at the ridiculous girl, in wet clothing no less obscene to them than nudity, the strange European man with her. She felt wonderfully outrageous. She couldn't believe herself.

He did not know why he did it; he only knew that not before in his time in India had he felt more himself, more free in this stifling land with its strict codes. He held the girl in his arms. He lifted her body into the sea and for a moment imagined releasing her.

The morning sun bounced its light off their skin, and the sea and sand: everything was bright with the evanescing promises morning brings, and her skin shone gold as his did in silver, the water crackling with sun, the fishermen lifting up nets full of fish like bags of silver coins out of the generous and yielding ocean.

When the girl's hair fell out loose over the water she seemed for a moment lovely. He saw her for a moment as the girl she could have been, had circumstances and fate been different. Her expression was different, as if for the first time she had forgotten pain.

She could feel the strength in his arms, his enormous strength written across his broad chest and the taut line of his lips, she could feel the sinews and the veins in his forearms and hands, she could feel the pulsing heat of his blood under his skin washed away again and again by the cold water of the sea. She felt as light as air, utterly weightless, her body trembling with joy and she wanted to put her head under the water so she could cry for all the joy, and love she felt at that moment. She thought for a moment of drowning so as to never have to live this life as before, because she now knew what it felt like to be awake.

Dawn became morning and he carried her back to the shallows and they walked back to shore. She looked at him in his wet clothes. It was the first time she had seen the striking linear beauty of a man's body and she blushed. They squeezed the water from their clothes and hair. He shook the sand from his pant legs.

Rajiv, the driver, was leaning against the carriage smoking, wearing an expression of scorn. Alexandre turned to Anjali and raised his eyebrows mockingly. She smiled, as if they shared as secret.

He helped Anjali back into the carriage and felt sad, knowing they would soon return home. Inside the carriage, she leaned her body weight against his for a moment before retreating to her side.

Alexandre knew that soon enough, life would take him away from this place, that part of his duty of studying these languages he loved was sharing them with his fellow scholars—he would not have all his life to listen to the Indians barter at the vegetable stand in Telugu. But today he had brought a girl joy, and he would remember that. He would remember this morning, remember the exhilaration and the joy of those long, wet moments: the colors of blue and gold, and the sound of the mighty ocean, inhaling the ever-present perfume of Indian jasmine, so different from that of the Grasse jasmine his grandmother had once grown in her garden.

He watched the villages pass them by, India in browns and the pastels of the sunrise, the whites of the men's clothing.

"Dr. Lautens . . . " she gasped at last, as if she'd been holding her breath.

He turned to look at her; her skin was glowing, her hair in wet tangles over her shoulders.

She looked at him, her eyes wide with gratitude. She wanted to thank him, but could not find the right words.

They sat there in the coach, no more than a mere foot apart. His affection for her was at once fraternal and fatherly and something else; what a failure of words, he thought. In Europe, he could affectionately clasp her hand in his, with its lunar transparency. He could perhaps look into that plain, dark face and see that sister soul in her.

And yet, sitting next to her, in this stateless state, that nation without words that exists in the space between two people, how silly those things seemed: countries and maps and borders, empires and colonies, those absurd constructs of his world, that world of men, like the winnings of two boys playing a board game, moving toy trains and ships around the perimeter of a square. "My words are failing me," he thought.

"I thought it was terrible that a girl with such an affection for water should also be afraid of it; you spoke so poetically about the Ganges—the lotus flowers and the dolphins; it seemed a pity to me that it should be your only experience of being in water." He looked at her with immeasurable kindness, a sort of sweetness that made her skin warm. He touched her hand lightly. "Well, you are quite safe Anjali; and I'm sure we needn't tell your parents." He smiled, his face the radiant and warm expression of his feeling that he had just done something terribly kind.

They came to a stop, waiting for some cattle and their herd to cross the road, and Alexandre turned abruptly and took Anjali's face in his hand. He looked at her, his face full of affection. He almost kissed her forehead, but he stopped himself.

As they made their way back to the home, they spoke of the times and of the politics of the day.

They passed the British administrative bungalows, the Indian soldiers acting as guards at the gates, the railway station.

Alexandre motioned at the station halfheartedly. "Whatever you think of the English, they have given India the best railway system in the world . . . "

"There are things more important than trains," Anjali replied.

But her heart wasn't in the argument, not then. She was too consumed with the sudden beauty of everything around her, that blue sky like the cobalt of her grandmother's Krishna idol, the sun passing through the coach, shimmering through the branches and leaves of the trees that lined the roads, the pristine quality of the morning air. Anjali felt as if everything around her was blossoming. The light, the sea, the sky, the feeling of joy that was rupturing inside of her: the shimmering beauty of a new life made her heart ache—an utterly new feeling of girlish hope.

They stopped talking until Alexandre said quietly, "We are home."

Alexandre looked hard at Anjali. He thought for a moment of saying that he knew it must be hard to watch her younger sister get married. But her face was so pure with happiness that he stopped himself and thought to let her have this moment.

And Alexandre looked at Anjali and for the first time really thought about the difference between sadness as a state and sadness as a quality, and how as a quality it could change a girl and make her an old woman, make the very light shine less brightly off her skin so that she seemed to be older and less luminous than the child she actually was, and even the timbre of her voice was that grave and sometimes trembling voice of a woman who had seen at least eighty monsoons and eighty summers in this scorched-earth land that was India. For the moment she seemed like a girl.

And this isn't the way life is supposed to be, not this, this hopelessness, this girl on the outside looking in, and it broke Alexandre's heart. For Alexandre, to see someone in such a state of sorrow left him only two options: he could look away, pretending he didn't see, and allow her that privacy of heartbreak, or he could embrace her, and nearly against his will Alexandre momentarily enfolded her in his arms.

Lautens turned and saw the house, looming at the end of the road. As they pulled up, he waited a pregnant moment, expecting Rajiv to open the doors. But Rajiv leaned back heavily into his seat and, turning, looked at Alexandre sternly.

Alexandre grimaced in an expression of irony and then he smiled and released the door locks. He stepped out and reached back in for Anjali's hand, helping the girl out. "Come," he said.

He could see her cane resting on a chair in the front garden. "Let me fetch that for you," he said, and he walked over briskly to get it.

Handing it to her, he held her arm as she steadied herself.

"Dr. Lautens, thank you," Anjali smiled an easy, glittering smile. "After we bathe, I can ask Mary to bring out lunch to the verandah, if you'd like."

Alexandre felt a sudden spasm in his chest. He saw in Anjali's eyes a look he had seen so many times in his youth, before he met Madeline. Anjali's eyes were bright with love; it was the last thing he expected from her. Alexandre hung his head for a moment, before answering coldly, "Actually, Anjali, I'm rather tired. I think I need to rest." A cloud fell over Alexandre's face as he turned on his heel in the direction of his bedroom.

HE DECIDED HE would avoid her for the rest of the day, after which things could return to normal. She was a smart girl and would begin to understand things as they really were; she would shake off her infatuation. Had he been a cruel man, he might have handled things more directly.

IF SHE HAD known men better, perhaps Anjali would have registered Alexandre's look of dread. But her heart was soaring, so she took Alexandre's claim of fatigue as the truth. She thought nothing of it. Watching Alexandre retreat, Anjali smiled deeply and felt her face get hot as she looked down and began to walk to her room, calling along the way toward the servants' quarters, "Mary! Bring hot water for my bath!"

Mary's voice was caught in the echo of the marbled halls, "Yes, Miss!" Many of the guests had eaten lunch already and were taking naps; despite how full the home was, it seemed quiet for the moment.

Before she began her bath, Anjali found Prithu and gave him a few coins to go out and purchase a string of jasmines for her hair—the flower vendors were still out on the main road. Anjali had a momentary strange thought.

Mary brought in a large steel bucket of hot water. Anjali closed the door behind her and began to undress. She saw her legs only when she would catch a glimpse of them when she dressed and bathed, but these glimpses amounted to little more than a brown blur of a familiar body in motion, but today she looked at them, for suddenly they didn't seem important enough to avoid. The muscle atrophy had made the affected leg thinner, and thus it seemed longer too. It disgusted her still, but she allowed herself to skip her fingertip along the strange shape of her calf. She smiled, remembering briefly what it was like to walk without her cane that morning.

As Anjali began her bath, she felt her muscles relax and she let her mind wander. She wondered about the flower vendor—what of his family and his interests? How could he have anything real when he was on the road holding a basket of marigolds and jasmines all the time? Then she remembered the fishmonger feeding the street dog and smiled.

But for her, for Anjali that day, everything was now different. That haunting feeling of absurdity was gone. There seemed too a line tethering her to the world in a warm embrace of possession. She saw beauty now in the crystalline water of her bath and even, as she washed it, in her own unremarkable hair. After washing herself of the saltwater and sand, Anjali dressed herself in an orange sari. She took the white blossoms Prithu had left on her dresser in her hands, inhaling them deeply before pinning them into her braid.

She called Mary to bring some curries, yogurt and rice out to the garden. Anjali sat in the garden, expecting Alexandre to come out for lunch as he customarily did.

ALEXANDRE SAT ON the edge of his bed, smoking. A moment of guilt had washed over him, but it dissipated as quickly: he reminded himself of the mercurial nature of schoolgirl infatuations. He reminded himself of the simple kindness of his intentions.

❋ 9 ❋

T HAT EVENING HE joined the Adivis for dinner as he always
did and made cheerful conversation with all of the relatives in
the house. His French accent amused them and they were flattered he
was speaking their language. The women lavished him with motherly
caresses and the men kept his glass full of whiskey. He managed to
avoid being alone with Anjali and avoided her gaze too.

The evening went beautifully, just as always, as so many Andhra
evenings before in the Adivi home, and Alexandre joined the men in the
family afterward for cigars and more rounds of whiskey.

"Your daughter is too beautiful, Shiva." Adivi's uncle Anand said,
his hands gesturing like those of a poet.

Adivi's friend Abdul chimed in, "Your girl will be moving away
soon, Shiva!"

Adivi smiled. Once he had hoped to send his girls abroad to university. Mohini hadn't had the aptitude or desire; Anjali with her condition could not travel.

The home was ready for a wedding, and everywhere were flower
garlands and lanterns; the men were feeling sentimental. They relaxed
into their chairs, listening to Thyagaraja *raagas* floating out of the
gramophone; Alexandre watched Adivi and his cousins sway their
heads, eyes closed in appreciation of the rhythm. His nephew Aditya
leaned back in his chair and rested the glass of whiskey on his big belly.
Adivi's hand moved in the air to the music like a feather falling toward

the earth. Adivi talked about how beautiful Lalita looked on their wedding day, his smiling eyes becoming watery. "She still looks like that," he commented into his whiskey glass. Alexandre noticed just then how handsome Adivi was.

They asked Alexandre what Madeline was like and whether he felt European and Indian women were different. Alexandre blushed and smiled, "Women are women, isn't it?"

ALEXANDRE WOKE WITH a pounding headache owing to the whiskey he had had the night before. He went to the mirror and stared at his red-eyed self. He shaved and dressed, walked into the courtyard, and asked Mary for a strong cup of coffee.

He settled into a chair and began again to work on his manuscript. Alexandre was writing in his notebook, and as he heard her, he looked up to see Anjali settling into a chair next to his, another servant behind her holding a tray of two steaming cups of coffee and a plate of fruit. He shifted to stand up.

"No, Dr. Lautens, don't get up, please . . . you are working on your book?"

He looked at her and noticed happily that her expression had lost that sheen of hopefulness that yesterday had caused him apprehension.

He smiled but was careful to keep his expression neutral. "Yes . . . I was just starting the introduction, actually. I wanted to take a break from some of the technical elements of the language to frame a context for my readers."

"Ah . . . " she smiled, glancing over at his notebook.

"Would you like to hear some of the introduction?"

"Oh, yes, I would love that!"

He cleared his throat and smiled, "Dear Reader, I would like to begin the introduction of this grammar of Telugu by thanking you for your kind interest in this beautiful and poetic language. I trust that your interest will be well rewarded; Telugu is a difficult language for the Western mind, but knowledge of it will broaden one's understanding of human language greatly. It is not a well-known language in the West, overshadowed by some of its Northern neighbors like Hindi and Bengali. It was first recorded in Western records by Niccolò de' Conti, who remarked on Telugu's harmonious qualities, so much like his own language, calling Telugu the 'Italian of the East.' Students of Indian studies will know that Telugu is one of the major languages of the South Indian Dravidian family. The others are Malayalam, Karnataka and Tamil."

He broke for a moment to sip his coffee as Mary brought out *idlies*.

Anjali leaned forward a bit. She had the look about her of someone about to announce that she has a great gift she is about to bestow on a friend. "Where are your people from, Dr. Lautens?"

He smiled, amused, and slipped in a yellowing bookmark that read "QUI MI ADDORMENTAI. Here I fell asleep." Madeline had purchased that for him years before in Florence. He sighed and smiled, resigned. "My people are from Switzerland, Anjali. I did tell you that, no?"

"Of course I knew that, Dr. Lautens. I don't mean which country . . . I mean to say, do you realize all the things that needed to happen in the world, all the movements of history and the migrations of people to . . . and all the wars . . . trains and ships had to be invented . . . to bring you to us?" Her eyes were big and bright, as if she alone had just discovered the whole world. And though Alexndre didn't mean to, he laughed.

But Anajali, unaccustomed to masculine expression, took his laugh only as a sign of his happiness at seeing her, and continued. "For instance, if the Greeks and Egyptians had never thought to create ships, and, well, if the English never came to India, we would perhaps never have had trains, and if my ancestors, the Dravidians, hadn't built these towns and these cities . . . " He couldn't be sure, but her voice was shaking and she looked down, and he thought she might cry. She continued, "I would never have known you . . . and now that we know one another, well I can't imagine the world being any other way, though, for all the things it took in the world, all the unlikely things, Dr. Lautens, we should never have met."

Alexandre looked at the pale part in her hair, for her head was still bent down. She had never before looked away from him but always in the eye, like a man, as if greeting all the world in preparation for a battle, in that particularly put on way, like a young infantryman, afraid of everything and so fixing his gaze to appear afraid of nothing.

He said nothing, only listening to the light breeze move the trees and the leaves of the garden; he looked up and saw the rose blossoms tremble.

"Do you know, I'm not terribly hungry," he said softly, "I think I need to do some more reading. I'll share the rest of the introduction with you later." And he stood and left.

BY LATE AFTERNOON, the house was spotless, cleaned to a sparkling shine; and when Alexandre awoke from a long nap, the servants were all attending to last-minute duties. Water was already being heated for Mohini's bridal bath. Anjali stood behind her sister, holding safety pins and hair clips as Lalita pinned flowers to Mohini's head. Mohini shrieked when Lalita stuck her scalp with a pin, the trembling orange flowers in danger of being crushed by Mohini's hands as she reflexively grabbed her mother's. "Mummy!" she screamed.

"Mohini stay still!" Lalita commanded through gritted teeth, holding bobby pins in her mouth. "Anjali, hold these," she said to her older daughter, looking at her in the mirror as she unpinned a coiled loop of strung jasmine blossoms and threw them to Anjali. "Oh for goodness sake!" Lalita cried, irritably, as two servant women arranged the pleats on Mohini's sari. "Go! Get out!" she yelled at them in Telugu, removing Mohini's sari altogether and starting from scratch as her younger daughter, in her blouse and petticoat, stared angrily at her mother.

ALEXANDRE FELT IT easy to disappear in the midst of the commotion. There was to be a prayer before the groom's family arrived, and flowers and fruit were gathered in the *puja* room, which was full of pictures and sandalwood idols of many-limbed gods; ghee lanterns ready for *aarti*, that part of a Hindu prayer that Alexandre found particularly lovely, when mortals would beseechingly fan that divine flame toward themselves, letting the heat of that fire wash over them like a smoke baptism.

The dark night fell upon the wedding evening like a cloak, and the air smelled of kerosene and flowers and food. The guests assembled in their silks and bejeweled finery around a low stage upon which Mohini and Varun sat with the bare-chested Brahmin priest. Adivi called out to Alexandre, "Come! Dr. Lautens! Come, sit!" Adivi grabbed Alexandre's arm and brought him over to sit with his cousin Aditya on the floor, cross-legged. Alexandre sat with some difficulty. Alexandre sat back on his hips, trying to find some comfort and looked around. He saw Adivi's sisters and Anjali sitting with Kanakadurga, the small children of various relatives in fancy kurtas and *lenghas*. They were allowed to run about freely. Old men from the village chatted among themselves, smoking, as the ceremony was under way.

MOHINI LOOKED NOT unlike Lalita, in the wedding photo Alexandre had seen in Kanakadurga's room. Mohini also had that wide-eyed, gazelle-like wonder, that glint of expectancy in the face, as if to say, "So this is what life is." Hers was the expression of a girl throwing herself to the spinning joyous urgency of life. Lalita, her features now softened by age and motherhood, but her beauty no less intense, now wore on her face a look of sweet nostalgia; she was thinking of her wedding day as she watched Mohini undergo those rites under the golden glimmer of this perfect, auspicious night. This is how it was supposed to be, she felt. Lalita thought: "This is right, all of it is right." She remembered how she was too young, too innocent then, on her wedding day, to even be afraid. That it somehow hadn't occurred to her until the moment it happened that she would be pulled from the safety of her mother's bosom and her father's loving protection; she had worried only about which colors to wear, wondered only why everyone around her seemed so sad, so melancholy; why her mother would fold the saris in the bridal trousseau in that distracted way, as if thinking of something she'd lost many years ago. On her wedding day, when they'd pulled back the curtain, she nearly didn't recognize Shiva from their prior meeting, his characteristic and charming arrogance absent and in its place a stern expression of boyish fear tempered with a manly desire to appear proper in the face of tradition. It was if someone had warned him that on this day he was to act like a man, to leave the mischievous expressions of boyhood behind.

For the first time since Mohini's wedding date was set, the joy in Lalita's heart gave way to loss.

The wedding began with the bride and groom separated by a silk curtain, and Lalita and Adivi rose to wash the groom's feet in a brass bowl. The priest began to recite *śloka* in a low, meditative song, almost a rhythmic chant that reminded Alexandre of the Catholic priests reciting Latin prayers in the churches of his youth. Mohini was resplendent, a bride whose skin glowed in the light of the oil lamps. Older women took plates of rice and turmeric and lit candles, and the curtain separating Mohini and her groom was removed.

Anjali saw Alexandre looking at Mohini—she was the bride after all, breathtaking in her brilliant sari and jewels. But Alexandre's gaze was steady and serious, violently intense. Gone was that merry expression of the afternoon. His eyes shone in the light of the oil lamps, piercing the darkness like two intrepid stars. Anjali felt the heat of his gaze though it was not directed at her. She felt her own muscles tense though her sister was in her own revelry and did not seem to notice the handsome man taking her in like a last meal. Anjali did not know how Mohini could not feel his gaze, how the waves emanating from his body did not force her to turn around, silence everyone, stop all the mouths and cause their bodies to freeze in mid-gesture, why the maids did not drop their pitchers of water, and the leaves stop rustling in the trees, and the lizards on the sides of the home did not stop crawling. Anjali thought the oceans should have turned to ice with that gaze. Yet Mohini beatifically looked out onto the crowd of loved ones and well-wishers and oblivious, beautiful in her innocence, Alexandre consuming her with his eyes, Anjali unable to look away from him.

Had anyone been looking at Anjali, he would have seen the blood rise in her face, into her ears, lamplight making her wet eyes shine. He would have seen that her whole body was made of fire and that she could incinerate everything.

The groom, preternaturally stoic, took a black-beaded necklace and fastened it behind Mohini's long neck, his fingertips never making contact with her skin. Then both Mohini and her groom placed heavy garlands of marigold and jasmine and rose on each other's neck, Mohini never lifting her eyes to the slim boy across from her. Kanakadurga had told Alexandre that in the Hindu ceremony, the bride and groom are thought to become, however briefly, avatars of the divine—she Lakshmi, he Vishnu. They became, in front of the ghee-soaked *aarti*, in front of the pans of turmeric and brown sugar, in front of their families, glowing gods.

The priest invited everyone to come up and bless the couple by pouring grains of turmeric rice and flower petals over their graciously bowed heads. Mohini's aunts walked up, loving and jovial as they spilled forth blessings from their open hands, Mohini smiling up at them affectionately.

Anjali, saffron rice in one hand, the handle of her cane in the other, stood in front of the seated couple. She bent forward, her hand tensing on the handle of her cane as her weight shifted, and Mohini looked up to see her sister hovering over her, Anjali's rice-filled hand poised over her sister's head, and each sister looked at the other in a pause as long as the blink of an eye, each looking at the other as one might look into a clouded or broken mirror, eyes narrowed as if to see something familiar that had been obscured—a singular beam of sisterly light passed between the two girls, each looking like half of Fortuna, and then, just as quickly, that light between them was gone, as surely as a candle blown out. And then Mohini looked back at her sister, recoiling, like someone walking through a dark house and thinking she has seen an apparition among the shadows.

After the last of the guests had blessed them, the new couple rose, Mohini's sari tied to her groom's dhoti, and mechanically, almost as if she'd practiced it many times before, she followed him around a small fire, and upon sitting, Varun pushed silver rings onto Mohini's chubby toes. They were married.

Alexandre closed his eyes as the wedding celebrations danced on, the entertainers and musicians still joyful in their arts, the mood of celebration moving steadily on into the night and bursting out onto the streets of the village. The servants came out, arranging a huge and delicious meal. Despite the absence of alcohol, he felt dizzy and drunk on the perfume of cigarettes and pipes, the incense still burning from the *puja*. There was dust clinging to the sweat on his skin: the Adivis had bought him a silk kurta for the event and it was starched and heavy. Heat emanated from his hands; everything felt hot. He could feel his heart and head pounding to the percussive thumping of the musicians; his muscles felt powerful but relaxed. He felt the dancers spinning as if they were moving inside his body. He smiled as he looked at their painted faces. He felt euphoric. It seemed like a dream and it was nearly morning before he thought of bed. The lights of the festivities flickered merrily against the night sky as he walked at long last to his bedroom, the smell of burning oil, of silk, spices and burned sugar, smells he had come to greatly love, filled up the air, and he slept, his pale, bare chest rising and falling in the troubled but deep sleep of the unjust.

AFTER THE WEDDING, Mohini had gone to her new husband's home with a small entourage of her mother's cousin, as it was custom for the girl to be taken to her new home by a maternal aunt. The servants slept very little and were awake and working by the time Alexandre rose in the late morning. There were charred spots on the garden floor where lanterns had burned all night; flower petals, grains of rice and teacups everywhere; a hundred banana leaves that had been dinner plates the night before in a pile ready for the rubbish fire. The morning light made mundane what had been a grand party the night before. He sat down in the garden and lit a cigarette. He saw a servant and with a single glance made it understood that he wanted coffee. He opened his notebook and reread the introduction to his book. He saw Anjali coming toward him and inwardly sighed—he was too tired for company, especially hers. He smiled, nevertheless, and motioned to a chair nearby. A servant came by with a cup of coffee, and upon seeing Anjali scurried back to the kitchen to fetch another cup.

"You promised me you'd read the rest of your introduction to me, Dr. Lautens."

"Yes, I suppose I did," he said sleepily. If he were not a polite man, he'd have asked for some peace, some time alone this morning. "Where were we?" He ran a lazy fingertip over the open page of his notebook, cleared his throat and pushed his hair out of his eyes, "While Telugu speakers share many religious and cultural similarities with North Indians, Dravidian languages are indeed distinct and do not share a common source with Sanskritic languages like the aforementioned Hindi.

"As I will demonstrate later, Telugu has a rich case system. This type of system will be familiar to students who have studied languages like German, but Telugu expands this system and you will find it quite intricate.

"It may not be of utmost importance to the average student to learn to read Telugu. Nevertheless, I will briefly expound on the written language later—"

"ANJALI!"

Anjali started, spilling coffee onto the floor, Alexandre stood up, the maids dropped plates of food. They all looked over to see Shiva standing in front of the garden. Despite her legs, Anjali leapt to her feet and, grabbing her cane, hobbled over to her father.

"Daddy, what is it?"

"Come here." The coldness in his voice made her shiver.

Alexandre jumped and ran to her as Shiva's palm landed hard on the girl's cheek.

"Shiva!" Alexandre shouted, forgetting himself, "What is this?!"

"You stay out! This is a family matter, and you are a foreigner. You have caused enough trouble for my family! My God! Even the bloody fish vendors are talking about me!"

"Adivi please, what is happening?"

Anjali cowered, her face in her hands, weeping.

Shiva glowered at Lautens. "Taking her out of this house with you, like she were a common whore, which," Shiva breathed shakily, "evidently she is!"

"Adivi, please," Alexandre felt the blood drain from his face, "please, let me explain . . . it was nothing." Alexandre and Shiva turned to see Lalita and Kanakadurga approaching, Anjali running into her grandmother's open arms, the old woman's eyes horrified and confused. Tired relatives, hearing the commotion, began to wander into the garden.

"Shiva, what is this? What is happening?" Lalita looked at her husband and daughter and the pale European in her home, each of their contorted faces like Greek masks of tragedy; Mohini followed her mother, her eyes wide, startled by the commotion.

"This whore," Shiva pointed at his eldest daughter, "decided to disgrace our family by going out to with this foreigner yesterday, bathing in the ocean practically nude!"

Alexandre pressed his hands together, pleading, "Adivi, Lalita, please, listen, it was nothing . . . she merely accompanied me yesterday morning as I ran errands."

"LIAR!" Shiva boomed. "Do you know, Dr. Lautens, how I found out this morning? I heard the servants gossiping. My servants. Gossiping. About me. Made to look a fool in my own home. Only Subba Rao had the decency to tell me outright." Shiva caught his breath, "Dr. Lautens, I am afraid I must ask you to go. You are no longer welcome in my home. I cannot believe you had the nerve to disgrace me in this way! And in front of our whole family! You have until the morning to gather your belongings and leave. If I find you cavorting again with anyone in my family, making an ass of me the way you did yesterday," he hissed, "I shall report you to the police for your . . . indecencies with my daughter."

"Indecencies! Adivi, have you gone mad? I took the girl to the beach yesterday morning. That is all! We went into the water, fully clothed! I beg you to calm down and collect your senses." The female guests in their nightgowns all looked at the goings-on with expressions of open-mouthed horror, clutching crying babies.

Seeing her husband shaking with rage, Lalita stepped between the two men, pressing her hands on her husband's chest, restraining him only with the help of one of his cousins. "Shiva, please," she whispered. Over her shoulder she looked at Alexandre, "Dr. Lautens, I am sorry, but it is best if you leave. I will have Prithu help you pack your belongings."

Dumbfounded, Alexandre turned to Kanakadurga, who was bent over her sobbing granddaughter. Kanakadurga, sensing his eyes on her, looked up, her eyes watery and brown, her leathery hands holding Anjali tight.

Alexandre looked at her and lightly touched his right palm over his heart. He looked into the old woman's eyes and said in a voice that was barely audible, "Kanakadurga Amma Garu, I am sorry."

HE WALKED TO his room, astounded, the soft taps of his footsteps echoing in the lonely silence. And then he heard a small voice—something that slipped through the air like a whip of wind, so lightly sounded he wasn't sure he'd heard it until he turned reflexively and saw the last syllable still on her lips, her eyes wet and darker than ever before. "Alexandre . . . " Anjali said. He turned and looked at her, her deformed body folded into a corner of the hallway, and she seemed frozen like a statue, her arms raised in a poetic gesture, as if she might catch his name back in her long, graceful fingers. The word lifted off her mouth and sailed toward him. "Had she said that?" he wondered. Had she dared say his Christian name? Alexandre felt the blood rush to his face. He almost shouted in fury but turned away instead and marched to his room.

"Alexandre! Alexandre!" They always said it, all of them. The time Claudine had taken out his bicycle without his permission and fallen, and Alexandre, then still smooth faced, carried Claudine through the neighborhood streets like a little bride, his dented bicycle lying in the street near the wall into which she'd driven. The neck of his shirt was open and his book bag flapped against his leg. He cleaned the cuts on his sister's face. "Alexandre!" from his mother, whose need for sympathy could never ever be satiated. "Alexandre" from Madeline, whether in irritation or lust, always that calling; he wished to banish those syllables so they would none of them know by which name to call him.

Did Anjali call out to him in desire? Was it that helpless cry like Catherine? A childlike sob for help or a sisterly plea? He could no longer tell. All those voices converged like a rope around his neck and Alexandre, closing the door on his room, as he had never done before, pulled angrily at his hair like a widow in mourning.

❊ 10 ❊

PRITHU WAS CURLED like a small animal on the floor near the room that Alexandre had come to feel was his own. The boy jumped up and wiped his eyes with the back of his hand.

Alexandre felt weary and without any fight left in his spirit. "It is alright Prithu, you can rest." Alexandre frowned as the boy, clearly drowsy, remained standing. His eyes were red, but his back upright, like a toy soldier.

Though he was trembling inside, Alexandre steadied his hands and found the corporal strength to arrange his things. Alexandre first took his notes down from a shelf, collecting them in his leather case. He'd kept extensive lists. All the etymological bases, the verbal systems, and the mythology, too, that Kanakadurga had told him; it hadn't been immediately relevant to his work but it fascinated him. He found it funny that so many of his favorite memories from the Adivi home had been the times he'd spent a languorous afternoon with an old woman.

Prithu, not accustomed to handling Western clothes, clumsily tried to help Alexandre fold his suits into his suitcase. Alexandre touched the boy's head lightly. "Good boy," he said, softly, pressing the crease of a pair of trousers under his chin as he folded them against his chest.

Alexandre assembled his books and looked through his notebooks for Anthony Davidson's calling card.

HOURS LATER, HIS belongings nearly all packed away, there was soft knocking on the door, and Alexandre opened it slowly, unsure of what or whom to expect. Kanakadurga stood in the doorway, in her hands two stainless steel tiffin boxes. "You can't leave without some food, Alexandre," her voice was hushed.

She walked into his room and put the tiffin boxes on his desk. "I had them loaded with snacks and sweets. These will keep well so you can pack these now. In the morning, Mary will bring you some curries and rice." She spoke in Telugu to Prithu, her voice soft but stern; the boy left the room. Kanakadurga walked past the bed and the wooden armoire in the room and opened the doors to the balcony. Alexandre was surprised to see the sun setting, realizing how much time he must have been alone in his room, preparing to leave. Kanakadurga took his arm, and walked him out onto the balcony.

The old woman pointed. "Dr. Lautens," she said, eyeing the sky and the great birds circling overhead, "do you have the ossifrage in France?" She pointed at the purple-plumed vultures. "The bone-breaker. It captures the little turtles off the ground and lifts them up into the sky— higher than they have ever been before, and the turtles gaze at the large world that they have never known the majesty and vastness of. There it is—the whole world: the turtle sees the land and the blue ocean, the forests, the towns—then the ossifrage finds a bed of rocks upon which to drop the turtle, to break his bones and eat his meat.

"It is ironic, isn't it? The turtles only see the world they are part of right before dying," she said.

The birds shrieked. Their cries were terrible, like the horrified sobs of the dying, echoing off rocks and rooftops. Alexandre looked hard at the sky, watching them circle.

"No, I've never seen them before," he said sadly. He turned to her, "Kanakadurga Amma Garu, I want to thank you for your frien—"

She put up her hand, stopping him. "Dr. Lautens, let us not cheapen our friendship by speaking of it," she looked him in the eye, "you must go now."

ANTHONY DAVIDSON WAS a jolly man; he welcomed Alexandre with open arms. As a member of the Royal Botanical Survey, his home was filled with hundreds of plants. Alexandre was left at the front of his house by Adivi's driver, Rajiv. Rajiv snorted as he jerked the carriage to a stop in front of Davidson's comfortable but modest home and left Alexandre to unload his own trunks. "Bastard," Alexandre muttered under his breath.

After all the formality of the Adivi household, Alexandre found himself happy in the relative bohemia of Davidson's home. Anthony catalogued plants and was attempting to hybridize native vegetable and fruit breeds to make them heartier, resistant to pests and fungus. The home was full of lush, verdant flowers, fruits and herbs. Vines grew on the walls of Anthony's study. Some, Anthony was hoping to be able to cultivate in England soon. Alexandre was deeply grateful for his hospitality. He arrived at Anthony's home tired and unsure how or even if he would be received, and Anthony proved to be a sympathetic audience. Anthony had a wife back in Manchester, to whom he would send money and drawings of roses, and an Indian mistress named Madhuri who did the cooking and brought Alexandre and Anthony Scotch in the evening.

"Beautiful girl, isn't she?" Anthony watched her leave the room, his eyes lingering.

"Yes, very." "Girl," Alexandre thought. Anthony looked to be about fifty, and Madhuri looked half his age. But then Alexandre caught himself. He scolded himself. Who was he to judge? If the last week had proved nothing, he did not understand this place. And Anthony and Madhuri looked happy together. He thought of Madeline and the various women he had courted before her and wondered if ever he had looked as happy as Anthony did now.

Alexandre told Anthony after arriving at the Englishman's home how Adivi had thrown him out, how he had slapped his own daughter. "All of this because of a swimming lesson!"

Anthony blew smoke rings and smiled, listening. He grinned deeply, "My dear Doctor. India is a wonderful place. It is fascinating. Mother India," he said, almost purring, taking a long drag from his cigarette. "Cobras! Tigers! Monkeys! Peacocks! My God, what a place. Every bloody village has its own language, its own gods, its own cuisine. Alexandre, buy diamonds and silk here for your wife! Study the languages and while you are at it, the religion and the culture and yes," he let his hand fall back, pointing at a rose in a vase on the table, "the plants. Travel the whole subcontinent, go see the Taj Mahal and play blackjack in the clubs in Calcutta . . . " Madhuri came in to pour the men more Scotch, and Anthony grabbed her hand and kissed it impetuously and she giggled. "Take a mistress. Yes, definitely do that. Eat the food, especially the mangos—you'll miss those—believe me. But for God's sake, man. Do not get involved with the Indians like that. I've been here for many years, Alexandre. Thank God you were only caught swimming!" He chuckled, "Otherwise her father and uncles would have likely scalped you!

"Believe me, that kind of intermingling never ends well. We British have been here for what? One hundred and fifty years? And we still cannot make heads or tails of these people. Cut your losses, Doctor. Trust me, it is for the best."

Alexandre colored, knitting his eyebrows.

Seeing Alexandre's troubled expression, Anthony lurched forward in his chair and slapped his knee. "Alex! Come outside with me. I'd like to show you something."

The men walked out into the garden. The front was mostly taken over by vegetable plants, and the stems hung low with ripe tomatoes, cucumbers, aubergine, okra and green beans. Some of the vegetables Alexandre didn't recognize. The back of the garden was full of rose plants and heavy with the scent of so many blossoms.

"Come, come . . . " Anthony gestured, bending low near a rose-bush. Its flowers were white at their hearts, but the petals' tips were tinged with pink, as if they had been dusted with women's rouge. "You see these roses, Doctor? Come here, smell these."

Alexandre stooped and inhaled the blushing blossom; the scent was at once green and animalic, like a fresh floral musk caught in spring rain. "It is beautiful, Anthony . . . very nice . . . "

"Yes, thank you. I cultivated this rose a few years ago. I call her Madhuri. She is a blend of two varieties, a white tea rose called Glory and a red Old World variety named First Love. The problem is that if one overly cross-pollinates, and hybridizes the two too much, we lose the scent. But, if I dare say so myself, the first generation of Madhuri is simply brilliant." Anthony plucked one of the roses and stood and placed it in Alexandre's breast pocket. "I'm not one for subtlety Alex. You get my meaning, I'm sure. You must remember this, Alexandre.

Enjoy yourself in India—find yourself a pretty nut-colored girl to keep you company while you are here and get fat on lamb curry and *pala-kova*. Just don't get too involved."

ALEXANDRE ASKED THE rickshaw driver to park on the main road: "*Ikkade undo.*" You must wait here. He walked into the small alley, past the peasants cooking over fires, their tiny hovels, searching the buildings for a sign of the Saraswati Grandhalayam. Some dusky, bare-foot children ran alongside him, begging for coins, but he was rid of them after only a few yards; he'd learned how disengage with beggars, how to look straight ahead as if he couldn't hear them.

Alexandre had seen a tiny advertisement for it on the last page of a local Telugu newspaper: "Rare books. Ask for Mr. R. Pantulu. Open between hrs. 1400 and 1800, Mondays and Thursdays."

There was no sign, only a small painting of Saraswati on the door, a placid, full-lipped, plump-faced goddess holding a veena, flanked by a regal peacock. Alexandre knocked on the mint green door and waited. A few minutes passed until finally a white-bearded old man in a dhoti unlocked the door, peering outside. Alexandre could see only his long beard and one watery hazel eye, a cynical bushy, grey eyebrow lifted.

"You sell books, Sir?"

The bearded man frowned and made a gesture Alexandre had come to understand as "I don't know" or "I don't understand" among Indians—his fingers were extended in the shape of a flower, and he shook his hand near his ear, frowning.

Alexandre fished the newspaper advertisement from his pocket and unfolded it, offering it to the bearded man, and this time asking in Telugu, "*Meeru pusthakamalu amatharu?*"

The man looked at the advertisement and then again at Alexandre, eyeing him warily for a minute before opening the door.

Alexandre stepped in before the man stopped him and pointed at Alexandre's feet. *"Daya chesi cheppulu gummam mundu vadhalandi."* Kindly remove your shoes before entering.

Alexandre backed out of the store, removed his shoes and left them outside, thinking he would never get used to walking into an establishment barefoot. He pushed open the green door and walked into a small musty room stacked from floor to ceiling with hundreds of dusty books. There were red cushions on the floor on top of an old, Oriental carpet. The bearded man pointed at Alexandre. "English," he said matter-of-factly.

"No, I'm not English. I'm French," Alexandre said, his voice more belligerent than he had intended.

"Ahh, French. Victor Hugo!"

Alexandre smiled, his shoulders relaxed. "Yes. Like Victor Hugo."

"You want French books?" The bearded man began to pull books from the stacks. "I have Hugo. I have Voltaire," he smiled, his teeth shiny and yellow, as if stained by *paan.*

"No, no. I'm looking for a book called *Radhika Santwanam.*"

The bearded man smiled, "You are not English?"

"No."

"You know that book has been banned. All the copies have been seized by Chief Cunningham and burned. I'm sure you know that."

"I do." Alexandre smiled.

"So what do you expect me to do?"

"My friend, Kanakadurga Garu, told me that you could help me."

The bearded man smiled and turned, shouting in the direction of some curtains that separated the bookstore from what Alexandre imagined was the old man's house. *"Chandini! Coffee cheyyi!"* He motioned Alexandre to sit down on one of the plush cushions, and he too sat.

Alexandre lowered himself uneasily to the floor and sat cross-legged and smiled at the man, and they sat staring at each other, Alexandre feeling awkward, the bearded man in quiet placid contentment. "Frenchman," he said, nodding. "France!" He lifted his hand in a grand gesture, as if reciting poetry, *"Liberté! Egalité! Fraternité!"* He laughed from his belly, his eyes jolly.

A small girl with a thick, oiled braid walked in carrying a tray with two cups of coffee. Her skirts didn't quite reach her ankles and she had pink ribbons in her hair. She kneeled next to Alexandre and offered the tray to him. Alexandre lifted one of the tiny, chipped porcelain cups, and the bearded man took the other. She left the small tray near them.

"I am Ramakrishna Pantulu," he said in slow, carefully articulated Telugu, clapping his right hand over his heart. He savored the hot coffee, resting the small cup on his belly between sips.

"My name is Alexandre Lautens. I'm a linguist from France. I am a guest of the Adivis. I am a professor at the Sorbonne. I am here to study Telugu."

"Ah! *Sumdara telumgil paatisaitu!*" he said, again gesturing like a poet.

It sounded somewhat like Telugu but wasn't. "Sundaram . . . ?"

"*Sumdara telumgil paatisaitu;* they are the words of a Tamil poet. He says: Let us sing in sweet Telugu."

Alexandre smiled, finishing his coffee with a satisfied exhalation.

Pantulu motioned for Alexandre to put the cup down on the tray. He cleared his throat and stood. Alexandre too started to stand, only for Pantulu to shake his palm, saying, *"Coorcho Babu."* Sit down. Pantulu looked at the endless stacks of books and then gathered into his arms a stack of some twenty books and cleared away several more stacks, displacing some hundred books before removing from a dark corner a small, silk-covered book. He handed the book to Alexandre and sat down, his back straight and his arm extended before his chest as if in oratory: "Her braided hair was black and long like Rahu, the sky snake / Come to devour the full moon of her face that outshone it."

Alexandre smiled. He ran his fingertip over the binding. "Thank you so much. I can't tell you how much I appreciate it."

Pantulu smiled and nodded.

"How much?" Alexandre asked, reaching for his wallet.

"My dear Frenchman, how can you pay for a book that doesn't exist?"

ALEXANDRE FOUND HIS cigarettes on a bedside table and sat down on the bed. The room in Davidson's house that he was given was smaller than his in the Adivi home, but comfortable. Pulling his legs up, he sat at the head of the bed and leaned back against the pale yellow stucco wall, his feet flat on the sheets, one wrist on his knee, taking a deep pull from his cigarette. His body felt restless; he watched the Indian night through the bedroom window and listened to the crickets.

Once, a few years earlier, he had seen a Sorbonne colleague, Marc Beauvais, at the Café Deux Magots outside the university's campus. Marc, an economist, was middle aged and had never married. Marc was in a corner, a pink-cheeked student with him. Alexandre watched as Marc laughed and put his hand on the boy's leg. He leaned in and pressed such a full kiss upon the boy's cheek that although the gesture was seemingly innocent, to Alexandre it dripped with something sinister. Seeing Alexandre, Marc abruptly stood up and cleared his throat. He threw bills down on the table, saying good-bye to the student and to Alexandre, who nodded in acknowledgement through a haze of cigarette smoke and diners and service staff. He watched Marc put his overcoat on, pulling up his collar, his fingers nervously fiddling with his buttons as he walked out, his eyes as anxious as a thief's. Alexandre looked back at the dark-haired boy, alone at the table. His lips were red like cherries and they were pursed as he counted the money left by the professor, placing some back down on the table and pocketing the rest. Alexandre got the attention of the waitress. She was flushed from running from table to table; the girl was plain and plump, and he could make out the shape of her body through her blouse and skirt. There was something unfinished about her, like a flower that hadn't fully bloomed yet: her hair was done neatly but she had no makeup on. She smiled at him generously, the way plain girls do. He smiled back at her, in the restrained way handsome men do, like a favor or a gift.

That evening when he returned home, he found Madeline at the stove cooking. He approached her from behind and clutched a handful of her hair. He thought of the waitress's hips and bent and bit Madeline's neck, inhaling the scent of her perfume. She pulled away abruptly, startled. He'd scared her. Alexandre, seeing her frightened face, frowned and walked away. He prized his wife's beauty, but sometimes it stifled his desire. He liked sometimes the profanity of an ugly girl. He envied Marc his secrets. This surprised him. He had always been aware of the utter fragility of the middle-class happiness he had built with Madeline; he was ashamed of bringing home the vulgarities of his public life in the café. Madeline wasn't like him; she was a girl from the country. She hadn't been raised in city life. Alexandre had always felt a protective impulse to keep in their home the tone of a simple, rural home life. Had it not been for him, she'd have gone back to the countryside after a few years of working in the city. She'd left the countryside for him, and he felt the need to preserve a bit of that in the home.

Sitting on that small bed in Anthony's house, thinking of that time, Alexandre's body flinched with need. His thoughts turned back to the plain waitress. He sucked his teeth, tasting tobacco in his gums and on his tongue. He felt his muscles tense as suddenly it seemed that all the banked desire of his many months here overcame him. He stood, walking about the room.

He felt now the guilt of harboring a secret but was unsure what it was. In France, his wife and his children knew him, and the neighbors and his colleagues and friends. He knew the streets and where they would lead and the shops that lined them and for once since coming to India, Alexandre was unsure he wanted to go back to Paris. But then he wondered if he *should* just go home—if he should forget the book and India and go back home. After all, who would this grammar help? Whose life would it change? What good would it bring to the world? Was he writing it only for his own vanity?

He had just met Anthony, and though the man was friendly and gregarious to a fault, Alexandre still did not know him well. And Alexandre, alone that night in that room in a country more foreign than he had estimated, clasped his hands in prayer as he had not for more than twenty-five years, and spoke not to his mother's silently listening Virgin in blue but rather to some warm-spirited conjuring of his very own, a fatherly figure who would intercede on Alexandre's behalf to speak to those from whom Alexandre had been banished and whom he would never see again. His hands together, Alexandre knelt, in that manner of his childhood, and prayed—a prayer that was not his custom; all alone, Alexandre attempted to convene with the divine.

Two weeks after leaving the Adivis, Kanakadurga sent Prithu to Anthony's home with a letter from Madeline that had come in the mail for Alexandre. Seeing Prithu, Alexandre smiled and went to greet the boy, but the child greeted him with the same fear and formality that Alexandre had felt from him the day they met. Excited, Alexandre didn't think to dismiss the boy and tore open the note.

He hoped that Madeline had sent him pictures of his children, but was disappointed to find only a short note. She told him she missed him and that the children were sad to be celebrating Christmas without him. His sister Claudine had had her baby, a wrinkled, pink little girl named Celine. Madeline asked for a silk shawl if it wouldn't be too much trouble, and the children wanted Indian toys. She asked him when he would be coming back.

He sighed and folded the letter again. Alexandre missed his children, not for the ways in which they were changing and growing without him, but in spite of this. He missed his children as younger children, as toddlers and swaddled infants. He missed this most in Matthieu; the world would allow for some softness in girls. But he feared his dear boy, the sweetest boy, was already becoming hardened in response to the world—that horrible machine. His little, weird, inquisitive blond boy, his shy baby, how Alexandre missed him. He missed Catherine also, his tiny girl with curls who would brush his cheeks with a whisper of love beyond articulation. There were times when, watching her play, he could swear his daughter was made of flowers. Daffodil hands and a miniature rose mouth. Hair of snapdragons and skin of tuberose and lilies and bluebell eyes. Her growing was like petals falling through his hands.

He asked Prithu in Telugu how Kanakadurga and Anjali were. The boy answered that Kanakadurga was well and that Anjali was no longer in the home. Alexandre asked him where she had gone, but Prithu simply shook his head, *"Teeledhu babu garu."* He didn't know.

THERE IS A town named Rumigny on the French side of the Franco-Belgian border, in the Champagne-Ardennes region, where wheat and rapeseed are grown and in the dry season one can find pale yellow bales of hay in great desolate fields. Rumigny was where the never-ordained Abbey Nicholas de la Caille was born in 1713. Thirty-eight years later he washed up on the South African shores of the cape and catalogued nearly ten thousand stars between Capricorn and the South Pole and made the case for fifteen new constellations; he wrote the calendar for eighteen hundred years of eclipses. The Cape of Good Hope was named as such by John the Second, a Portuguese king, who thought the rocky tip of Africa portended great things, like a sea route to India and China. The Cabo da Boa Esperança, despite its rocky shores, was in truth a trying, African Ithaca. When Alexandre was a child, a biography of de la Caille was always on his father's desk. A small tattered paperback. Every now and then, his father would wearily thumb the pages of the book and glance sidelong at his sons, saying sternly, "This man did real work. He served mankind with his discovery."

Had Maurice Lautens, the father of Alexandre—Alexandre, who would become an important figure in the disciplines of comparative grammar and psycholinguistics—not had the familial expectations of continuing his father's trade of banking, he would have liked to become an astronomer. He liked very much to make out constellations in the Swiss sky and would sometimes creep out of bed, not seeing Agathe's eyelids twitch, her eyes opening in the dark, looking out the window at the starlight that her husband found more alluring than her. This despite her blond pin curls and long legs. Maurice liked the quiet of the purple night sky, and not without some ambivalence would occasionally take his boys out into the garden in Geneva and later in Paris, waking them from sleep to share a truly beautiful and clear night sky.

His son Matthieu, to Maurice's chagrin, seemed to resent being woken up and made to go outside in his blue pajamas and robe, but his little Alex delighted in the interruption, holding the small, layman's telescope. Maurice would kneel behind his son, pointing out stars and bright planets, painting the heavens with mythological heroes and astrological lore. It was his time with his boys, and Matthieu and Alexandre never heard their father speak more than on those nights when he would tell his secret compendium of stories. Agathe would struggle to find sleep again, hearing the lightness in her husband's voice, the love and the laughter among him and her sons from outside. It wasn't the voice he used with her.

So Alexandre grew up with a love for the sky. He had once found Anjali sitting outside in the middle of the night, eating sweets quietly, and the girl turned to see him when she smelled amber and oak. Alexandre stooped as he bent to sit next to her. He nodded his head, acknowledging the sky, "Do you see that, Anjali, that very bright constellation? You are lucky to see it. Half of the world can't. France is part of the Northern Hemisphere, so I've had the recent joy of seeing a whole new night sky. Some of your constellations here are so rarely visible in France. The priest who comes around from time to time, Guru Hanumanth Rao, was helping me map the Indian sky. He is very good . . . very helpful. In Europe we call this one Ursa Major . . . "

Anjali had been tutored in Latin by one of her father's sycophantic hires. "Ah . . . the Great Bear. We call it Saptarishi Mandal, the constellation of the seven sages."

Alexandre's inherited knowledge of the celestial map comforted him about certain things like death and regret. Knowing that light could show from a star billions of light-years away reassured him of some sort of some divine calculus.

But moment to moment Alexandre felt small. He felt that he lacked direction in his life, and seeing the washerwomen on their way to the river or the fishmonger weighing his daily catch, he felt that the hard labor of the lower classes gave their lot a purpose that he in his intellectual sphere envied. It was not asked of him daily that he lay bricks or sweep homes or cook for some rich family. It was only asked of him that he think each day, deeply and profoundly, that he think of the questions of language and of speech and of thought itself. Even teaching was done not only to impart information as a series of facts but to inspire his students to take the discipline further than he would be able to in his own lifetime. He taught not in spite of his impending death but because of it.

And then sometimes he would think that poets and philosophers, intellectuals and artists would do well for themselves to pick up brooms and buckets and washrags and weary themselves from the sheer exhaustion of living the day rather than falling into fitful sleep, burdened by wondering if their minds were good enough, if the intelligence and inspiration that started on a paper or sculpture would be enough to carry them through to follow through on the promise.

There were things he liked to do with his hands. He liked to cook and to wash dishes. There was a satisfaction in those things because the result was so plainly seen. He liked squeezing lemons and cutting carrots and cleaning burned grease off pots and pans. It felt good to him to put his arm muscles to scrubbing in warm, soapy water and lifting a dripping and glistening dish from it.

Excluded from so many of the thinking professions, he wondered if women too contemplated the questions of life and death. He couldn't ask Madeline for fear of condescending to her, and even if she did think of those things, he imagined they did not bother her greatly because she had a way of ordering her life into small duties: washing her face, making coffee, warming bread for breakfast and dressing the children. The progress in her days could be measured by finite chores like preparing a roast. That the chore would be repeated the next day, Alexandre, suspected, did not prevent women from feeling satisfaction at each subsequent completion. He could measure Madeline's satisfaction by how it grieved her when these duties were not complete; how she would fuss and curse if she burned a pot of coffee or forgot an item on her shopping list; what a racket their morning household was if Matthieu or Catherine refused to get out of bed or comb their hair.

Sometimes Alexandre felt that he'd gladly trade her duties for his; his world consisted of languages of the Orient, hers of their home, and to his mind only hers was a manageable one, one where finishing was possible. And anyways, if he didn't write more of his book or have some sort of breakthrough in theory, a handful of specialists might be disappointed—but given the competitive climate of academia, this was unlikely—but if Madeline were to stay in bed all day, the children would go unwashed and unfed.

The problem, he supposed, was that his wasn't a great mind. It was a good one, a very good one even, but the distance between good and great was vast. He wasn't like some of his contemporaries, who could pore over a book for hours with little need for food or sleep. He'd had spells of that behavior, when he felt as if he'd pushed past some sort of mental block, but it wasn't usual for him. He liked to think about other things too, like food and women's bodies and perfume. He liked also to think of the stars and his father feeling small underneath them, not just his physical life but his life as a whole, that to live his life as a banker in a world in which planets spun in orbits and all of life lived by a rhythm of the moon and seas was a small life indeed, and Alexandre felt his father's angst too.

Alexandre thought that life was the hardest with a good mind; to be productive, he needed discipline. Had he had a great mind he would simply be a vehicle for his science, for his work. And though that kind of life seemed to be one exclusive of a woman's love or friends or children, he thought it must be easy to surrender to the demands of one's genius. A poor mind too would manage to dictate the terms of one's life easily. There was always plenty of work in the world for the physically hearty and mentally meager. Only the good but not great had to work hard to create the life their minds were capable of envisioning but not fulfilling.

There were times when Alexandre's mind would work with crystalline clarity, his thought nearly as liquid and as effortless as desire, and in those rare moments thinking seemed terribly easy, as if for a brief time all the parts of his brain were working under the direction of a single conductor. These moments weighed on him at all the other times, when his mind felt lumbering and mediocre.

IN THE EVENING, Anthony returned home from the garden of a friend he had been visiting and bicycled up the slight hill to the house. Alexandre was writing in the sitting room and saw through the hallway as Madhuri greeted Anthony with kisses. Alexandre heard her squeal with delight and then Anthony's footsteps and the *clink-clink* of her anklets as they approached the sitting room.

He held a bag of tomatoes. "These are delicious, Alexandre—fresh from my friend's garden . . . a new variety of green tomato." He held one silky skinned, heavy fruit in his hand and took a hearty bite out of the pale green flesh. He ate it with relish and handed the bag to Madhuri and asked her to use them for dinner.

"Nothing better than *russam* made with fresh tomatoes," he smiled at Alexandre. "How are we this evening, Alex?"

"Well, thank you. I received a letter from Madeline."

"Oh, lovely. Anything interesting?"

"No, not really. She asked for some things . . . she reminded me about Christmas! I had almost forgotten!"

"Ah yes . . . your first Christmas away from home?" Anthony smiled, "nothing here to remind one to have a Joyeux Noël, eh?"

"No, I'm afraid not . . . the Adivis' servant boy brought the letter over . . . he said Anjali isn't at the home anymore."

"Poor girl! Her father's probably sent her away to . . . " Anthony sat down, heavily, lighting a cigarette, "some sort of school for wayward

Hindu girls who disgrace themselves with handsome Frenchmen on the beach!" Anthony laughed and handed Alexandre a cigarette.

Alexandre smiled uncomfortably, speaking through lips pursed around the cigarette, his head inclined toward Anthony's lighter. "I hope she is alright . . . "

"Don't worry too much about her my boy . . . she's probably just been sent away to some spinster aunt until this 'scandal' blows over. Indians are gossips . . . once their neighbors and relatives have something else to talk about, you know, once some unmarried girl finds herself with child, or someone's cousin is caught drunk making a scene at the social club, her parents will call her back."

Alexandre looked out the window, expressionless.

THEY HAD DINNER that night. He, Anthony and Madhuri, and as Alexandre watched the two of them banter, and the affection and humor between them, he missed the women in his life. Anthony and Madhuri used the familiar "you" form between them, *nuvvu*, like *tu* in French. A linguistic undressing. Despite the disparity in age between them, they seemed like young sweethearts, and Alexandre felt a pang of jealousy.

After dinner, Madhuri and the maid cleared the table, and Anthony and Alexandre went to the sitting room to smoke.

"Dear Doctor, you look pensive this evening . . . you hardly spoke during dinner . . . is something on your mind?" Anthony smiled deeply, his cheeks red. "Surely you are not still worrying about that girl?"

"Oh, it is nothing, Anthony."

"Oh, come now, Alex! You've been here, what? A week? Friendships move faster in India. We are old mates now! Tell me!"

"Well . . . " Alexandre smiled slightly, "I was wondering, well, I have a question for you Anthony but it is rather untoward—"

"You were wondering how I've managed to stay so handsome all these years?" Anthony laughed from his belly.

Alexandre laughed too, and then asked, "You wife . . . Patricia, right? Does she know about Madhuri?"

Anthony laughed again. "Oh, Alex. God bless. Old Pat knows about Madhuri . . . well, of course she thinks she is only my cook. No, she doesn't know the exact nature of our relationship, no . . . Pat is a good woman; she's the mother of my boys, she laughs at all my jokes and she can drink me under the table. As long as she has a little extra money to put on the horses, and cake and cider for her knitting circle, she's happy. Me, I need whiskey and a pretty girl in my bed. Believe me, Alex, Madhuri is the best thing to happen to my marriage. Pat and I have never been happier. Come on boy, you are French! You of all people should understand!" he laughed before settling into a dry cough.

Alexandre smiled, and his eyes lifted to see Madhuri walk in, and he watched her rolling hips under her pink sari. She went to Anthony and held his face in her hands and kissed his cheek, wishing him a good night. He clasped her small brown wrists.

"Good night, my darling," Anthony replied sleepily, smiling deeply, his old eyes twinkling in the lantern light.

She turned and looked at Alexandre and said, "Good night, Dr. Lautens."

ALEXANDRE WENT TO his room and tossed a newspaper onto the desk and drew back the sheets on his bed. As he undressed, he looked at the small Ganesha idol on his desk, and he changed into cotton pajama pants. He stood bare-chested in front of the mirror and ran his fingertips lazily over the lines where his pale chest met his sun-baked forearms and throat. He sighed.

He had just read in the paper that the Nepalese had a new king, a child who was only five years of age. A little boy king photographed for the newspaper in regal, oversized robes. Alexandre fell onto the bed and looked at the ceiling, thinking about his children and their last Christmas together and why he was in India.

At the Adivis' home he would hear Kanakadurga doing private *pujas* in the prayer room across from her bedroom. She would sometimes refer to Sanskrit as *Deva Bhasha*, God's tongue. Alexandre found the room exotic and frightening. It smelled of incense and the coconuts Kanakadurga would break while she chanted, her hands pressed together, rocking. He would hear her sometimes in that room, her voice low and trancelike in prayer, "Avaneesh, Avighna, Balaganapati . . . Gaurisuta . . . Heramba . . . " In Kanakadurga's puja room, a wild-eyed idol of Kali looked at him with her tongue out. Ganesha was muted, his elephant eyes wide and serene; silver tins of turmeric and bindi were among the coconuts and fresh flowers. There were framed paintings of beautiful Lakshmi in her lotus, Saraswati holding her lute, a blue-skinned Krishna spying on nut-brown milkmaids. a gold Nataraja Shiva balanced on a dying serpent. In the center of the room was a picture of Hanuman, Rama's faithful monkey warrior, holding his chest open, Rama's name written on his ribs and blood and flesh and heart. "His love for Rama and Sita was questioned," Kanakadurga had told him once, "and in response, he tore open his chest, so all of Ayodhya could see that they were literally in his beating heart. There was also a photograph of Adivi's late father, Anil, a man whose face echoed his son's but was softer. "He wasn't as handsome as my son, but he was a kinder man . . . " Kanakadurga had said, smiling sadly, "so often beauty and cruelty seem to go together." Fresh flowers rested against Anil's photo, and there was red talcum powder dusted on his sepia forehead.

Now, in his room in Anthony's house, Alexandre got up off the bed and went to his desk and held the small marble elephant god in his hand. Like his father, he had never been religious—attending church only on Easter and Christmas. He liked the community that religion provided—the sense that he belonged to a family of man, and was not too proud to bow before a god or speak to one at night when his heart was distraught. But not for him the proscriptions on life. Not for him his mother's kneeling nightly like a child seeking a new toy or forgiveness for cheating at jacks.

Kanakadurga had given the little Ganesha to Alexandre on the morning he left. "The remover of obstacles and the patron of scholars. Sometimes, when I feel myself lost, when I feel away from myself, I sit and I say the *gaṇeśa sahasranāma*, the hundred and eight names of Ganesha. I feel the rhythm of his names in my blood. It calms my heartbeat." He smiled as she handed it to him, her kindly eyes deeply wrinkled, bright and watery. She was not one to cry, but she held his large white hand in hers, which were small and brown. She clasped his hand tightly and pressed it to her soft cheek. "My friend," she said.

His Ganesha was round and cherubic, and he held an axe and rope in two of his hands, and a lotus and a sweet in the others. Alexandre remembered Dr. Bonventre introducing him to Devanagari. Bonventre drew a slash after *deva*, "God, plus city . . . the language of the *city of God*." Bonventre whispered in quiet awe and smiled—an indulgent, sweet, unscholarly smile, like a boy dreaming. "It will take you all your life to learn Sanskrit. But you should. In the Hindu mythology, Sanskrit is made of all the sounds of the beginning of the universe. It is a most beautiful calculus."

❈ 11 ❈

WALKING WITH THOSE women, it occurred to Anjali how they were just women like the women she had always known: daughters, mothers, wives, most of them in saris. They were the respectable women of respectable men, not lawless rebels or society's rejects. And Anjali hoped that she would not find herself an outcast yet again.

THEY WERE ALL there, hundreds of them, many of them men in white khadi, like an endless army of widows, but neither somber nor funerary. This was not a military procession of strong young soldiers wearing armbands of black. Anjali turned and saw the crowd closing in on her as if suddenly rushing, all of them, and felt terrified; never in her life had she seen such a crowd. The women pushed and wailed, carrying frightened babies against their breasts, the men shoved, their hands straining forward even if separated by several feet from the door, among them all children seemingly without parents or means; Anjali thought that the English were at least a civilizing force on so miserable that swarthy mass. She saw the baby-faced white officers, their stoic faces betrayed only by that glimmer of terror in their eyes and the thin, transparent lines of sweat trickling down their temples, suggesting discomfort as they attempted to manage the crowd in the spotless uniforms of the Indian Imperial Police. Standing outside that afternoon, tentative, Anjali waited as the other women filed in, eager to hear the fiery, young freedom fighter, this woman said to rival her male counterparts in passion and intellect. And then, with her awkward gait and with that long-carried burden of solitude, pushing past a thousand onlookers, Anjali walked into the courtyard of the University of Madras. There were red paper stars fixed to the gates: the college was preparing for Christmas.

She saw from inside the gated walls of the college how they were: how deplorable, how selfish, how ruthless and how barbarous, how jealous and greedy, how small they all were, how ugly the most beautiful, how poor even the wealthiest among them, how sick even the young and robust; just human, pathetically human, a million incarnations of flawed, so fragile, each of them as volatile as fire crackers, each needing only a single, catalyzing spark to explode and explode again, in a brief shimmering display of rage and fury before that silent demise of death, disappearing into the ether of that pillaged and plundered earth.

One blond officer, whose icy blue eyes were wild with fear in the face of angry old Indian women, met Anjali's gaze. Anjali for a moment saw him, herself and those all around, not for what they had but for what they didn't, their secret stories of loneliness and fragility, of anxiety and fear. And Anjali, as quickly as she felt the repulsion, felt depthless sorrow and pity and compassion and thought how variously vulnerable they all were, how sometimes wretched. She decided then, while covered in sweat and dust, the dizzying heat bearing down upon her, to love them then, in spite of herself, in spite of those twin candles of rage and fury that burned equally brightly in her; because they were just like her, selfish and small and foolish, but trying, and in trying became godlike, to shake the shackles of human existence.

She turned to see her heroine mounting the podium. When Sarojini ascended the steps, she turned to the British flag behind her and removed it from the wall; turning it upside down, she tacked it back up. "Ladies and gentlemen, the empire is in distress."

Anjali, now in the confines of the hall, closed her eyes as she imagined the night she was banished. She was still smarting from her father's scolding as she walked out into the garden in the purple evening light. A pitying servant had quietly handed her a tray with sweets and a cup of tea, and began to pack her bags. She left in the morning.

Alexandre's face had somewhat faded from memory, but Anjali did in fleeting memories recall that hair, those eyes, that soap-scented skin and remember feelings of being illuminated from within. Love makes one present. Now, in quiet moments, she sometimes felt she had only the past.

After her father expelled her out of the family home, Anjali stayed with the Sastry family, friends of the Adivis, for a few days. At night, she kicked and screamed in silence and pulled her hair and imagined her body riddled with gunshots or hanging from a noose or drowned in a river, her clothes weighed down by rocks, and then and only then would her mind cease its endless spinning and she would kick only until the kicking stopped . . . and her fingers pulling at her hair would relax and she would dissolve into a merciful sleep and to then, to look upon her then one might think she were someone's daughter, someone's beloved and best girl.

Inside she was dying. Inside there was rotting flesh inside her living flesh, death eating her from the inside out, killing her in the world's slowest-ever murder, those thoughts that came to her mind, that she could not be loved, that she could be neither missed nor noticed, that she figured into the life of the world no more than the dirt on the road filled her heart and she believed them. She was addictively attached to the sorrow in her heart, thinking these things to feel the pain that reminded her she was living. She felt the death inside her bloom the moment her father exiled her, but in truth the death entered her at the moment love did. She who had not been made for love. Only through loving and losing was this despair made possible, and it clouded each minute of her day, all the colors in the world were bleached out. Each moment of her existence stood quiet, alone, hollow: an infinitely long and horrible moment against which she had to decide to brace herself, again and again and again. Each moment of her life was unattached to the one before or after, as if she had come to exist in a hell that could not be assuaged by the passage of time. The evenings were her favorite time of day, because she knew sleep was coming; the grey light of morning was always cruel to her, for she did not want to wake up. The sunlight painting the whole world in the façade of cheerful hope seemed a mockery to her to whom each moment was only suffering.

It soon became apparent that she was overstaying her welcome and that Dr. Sastry was concerned that his housing Adivi's disgraced daughter would cause a falling-out with his old friend. Anjali moved in with Sarojini and her husband in the city of Hyderabad, taking over a small bedroom in their home, where she did her morning *puja* and slept. Anjali, with some shame, had related her story to Sarojini and Sarojini had invited Anjali to stay with her. Under normal circumstances, Anjali would have never accepted so generous an offer, but desperate as she was, she accepted. Never particularly religious, now estranged from her family, she appealed to the divine. She took her meals with the family, and during the afternoons they would strategize as to their next move, or plan Sarojini's next public appearance, how to rally all these women for the good of their shared cause. Anjali helped Sarojini with her children and keeping up the house. That so revolutionary a woman could also be so domestic! Sarojini taught her things—how to cook and also about rhyme and meter. Anjali told Sarojini about her family life— the grandmother she missed every moment of every day. Sarojini's husband, Govinda, was like a brother-father to Anjali, always kind and gentle in his teaching. He was smitten with his wife. Sarojini tended to have that affect in some way, through the charms of her multifaceted and unabashed femininity, the force of her intellect; everyone was, just a bit, in his way taken with her.

"Therefore, I charge you," Sarojini said, "restore to your women their ancient rights, for as I have said, it is we, and not you, who are the real nation builders, and without our active cooperation at all points of progress all your congresses and conferences are in vain. Educate your women and the nation will take care of itself, for it is true today as it was yesterday and will be at the end of human life that the hand that rocks the cradle is the power that rules the world." Sarojini concluded her speech in the little college lecture hall, filled with men and women standing toe to toe, fanning themselves with leaflets. Anjali turned and saw a perspiring woman wipe her forehead with the end of her sari.

Anjali felt tears prick her eyes; she felt wildly youthful and clapped in joy, a nobody among all these strangers. It was only 1911, but Anjali felt that this woman, petite Sarojini, was already helping to unbind and unravel a system no thinking person had ever considered delicate.

The hall could contain only a fraction of the people who wanted in; a crowd spilled out into the hallway and further on into the street. But there were many who stayed, flooding the street outside the college if only to catch a glimpse of that tiny poetess. Inside the merciless afternoon sun—moving in great squares through the shapes of the windowpanes—cast Anjali's shadow long across the floor. She held tightly in her fist the personalized invitation sent to her by the Naidus.

Sarojini smiled at Anjali—a special, warm smile meant just for her. As the crowd around her cheered Anjali felt suddenly that at long last, she had shaken that specter of loneliness. All kinds of heroic images flooded her imagination. She thought: "This is where I belong. I shall start here, and end when India begins."

"MY VERY OWN Lakshmibai!" Govinda would sometimes call Sarojini, referencing Rani Lakshmibai of Jhansi, she the princess-warrior, who led her men into battle with her baby strapped to her back. It took two Englishmen to mortally wound the rani, and when they did, her soldiers removed her baby. She ascended her funeral pyre herself.

Anjali and Sarojini sat over a pile of green beans, clipping their ends. The maid, careless, had moved the cane away from Anjali and when she went to stand, Govinda held her by the arm and lifted her as the maid went scurrying for her stick. Though no touch could be more innocuous, more fraternal, Anjali started.

"He may very well be a mahatma, but I tell you Anjali he is also a maha-headache. I'm not throwing out a lifetime's collection of *kanjeevaram* saris to wear some bloody prickly white homespun." Sarojini opened her closet, pointing to shelves of neatly folded and pressed silk saris. She pointed, "These I got for my wedding, and this one," she beamed proudly, holding up a beautiful green silk, "Rabindrinath Tagore gave to me." The great poet had given it to Sarojini after she had sent him her latest manuscript. Sometimes Anjali did not always know how to react; she did not want to be seen to be a joyless person or an ungrateful one—and though seeing the feminine and domestic pride in Sarojini did spark in Anjali sadness and jealousy, she wanted to partake in her mentor's happiness. It was a strange balance of bearing she always had to strike in the presence of other women.

Even Gandhi, with his insistence on homespun khadi cloth for Indians, could not make Sarojini give up her great collection of saris. That ban on imported fabric among Indians had resulted in a great conflagration of cottons and silks in the towns and villages, whose residents had long paid dearly for the Lincolnshire craftsmanship and the British tax that accompanied it. "It is as if every woman in town is a widow," Sarojini marveled. The khadi cloth was often more expensive to weave than the ready-made Lincolnshire cottons, and some of the erstwhile most fashionable Hyderabadi women had decided on principle to choose among two or three plain white saris. Six yards of coarse, unadorned fabric. The sacrifice of beauty and glamour had been harder to stomach than some of them had imagined.

Anjali thought of her mother's own collection of saris—the expensive silks with the hand-embroidered *zari*, the blue one from her wedding trousseau, the green tussah-silk with the pink-and-silver border that she had worn as the mother-of-the-bride at Mohini's wedding.

Anjali wondered about the somber vows of marriage, about the feeling of being protected by the cloak of matrimony, about motherhood—the feeling that women spoke of: of love for their children like a love they had never believed could exist, about caring for a man and feeling safe with him. Between Sarojini and her husband there was such warmth and sense of humor as Anjali had never seen before, something like genuine goodwill.

❋ 12 ❋

THERE WERE SOME Indian sweets that, had he been able to ship them quickly enough that they would not go bad, he would have liked his children to try.

A few weeks before Christmas, Alexandre sent a box of silks for Madeline, a doll dressed in a sari for Catherine and toy wooden building blocks for Matthieu to Pondichéry. A French postal ship would be leaving from there within the week, and he wanted to send gifts home; he doubted the gifts would make it to Paris before Christmas but hoped that at least the children would receive them before the New Year.

He celebrated Christmas with Anthony and Madhuri. It wasn't like Christmases at home; Madhuri seemed unmoved but amused by the occasion, watching Alexandre and Anthony drink with paper crowns on their heads, Anthony trying to persuade Alexandre to sing with him. The three of them took a walk together after dinner, to St. Peter's Church near Hollander's Green, where the British soldiers and sailors attended services. Everyone everywhere looked at them, that odd trio—the old Englishman with his cigar, the pretty young Indian woman in her red sari and bindi and the handsome young Frenchman. Madhuri walked with her hand in Anthony's bent elbow.

"It must bother you," Alexandre murmured to Anthony, discreetly.

Anthony smiled, blowing wisps of fragrant smoke into the warm night air, obscuring the candle lights of the church and the stars. He kissed the back of Madhuri's hand, bending in a dramatic gesture like a showman and looked straight into her eyes, "They know nothing of life at all." Alexandre was not sure how much English Madhuri understood, but her face was an expression of pure compassion, of love and charity and sweet absolution. She looked radiant in the evening light, her cheap sari bright in the wind, covering her head, like a tattered Jolly Roger on the mast of an old pirate ship. Anthony then set his eyes upon Alexandre and fixed him with a stern gaze; tapping off the ash of his cigar, he reached out, squeezing Alexandre's hand, "My boy. Dear boy, who the bloody hell cares what any of them think?" And then, with long strides he led Madhuri and Alexandre forward into the church.

The church was over-full, and the open doorways were packed with worshipers standing barefoot in the sand. Some of them put their hands up toward the deity and touched their eyes as if in a temple. Others cried in delirious devotion, "Mary Matha!" Mother Mary! Over their heads, Anthony, Alexandre and Madhuri could hear them singing over the sounds of the ocean and could see the candles illuminating their dying, golden savior on the cross. He wore a garland of marigolds and roses on his thin neck, which reached the place where his feet had been nailed to the cross.

After some time, Anthony suggested they turn and walk back home in the balmy Indian night. On the way out, Madhuri cupped the heat of prayer candles in her hands and swept it up to her face, quietly performing *aarti* in the corner of the church. They walked in quiet contemplation, enjoying the cool air. Anthony stopped to buy a string of jasmines for Madhuri's hair and two newspaper cones filled with peanuts boiled in saltwater, one of which he handed Alexandre.

"I have a special treat!" Anthony announced on returning home. From his bedroom he produced a small tin box. "Christmas pudding! I had it shipped here from one of the military canteens in Madras. Cost a bloody fortune!" He laughed and merrily he instructed Madhuri to retrieve some dessert cups, and he dished out the viscous brown sweet, his nostrils filling with candied, dried fruits and brandy.

They ate in quiet reverie, and after a while Madhuri, who had left her dessert unfinished, went to bed and the men stayed up celebrating.

"Come Anthony, sing 'Silent Night' with me!" Anthony said, slurring his words, pouring himself another glass of whiskey and then topping off Alexandre's glass too.

Alexandre smiled, leaning back in his chair, letting the cool evening breeze hit his chest through his unbuttoned shirt. He was drunk too, and the whiskey warmed his body as he listened to Anthony sing half-heartedly. "Sorry Tony, I don't know any English songs."

"Well you are no fun Alex . . . oh, bloody hell I'm drunk. I should go to bed . . . " he attempted to get up but, too inebriated to stand, fell back in his chair.

The two men laughed and Alexandre stood, his own footing unsure, as he went over to help the older man from his chair. Together, Alexandre supporting Anthony, they stumbled to the bedroom Anthony shared with Madhuri.

Alexandre walked Anthony down the hallway; the bedroom door was ajar and through his stupor Alexandre saw Madhuri in bed, turned away from them. He looked at Madhuri's naked brown back, a mess of dark hair across the pillow. She didn't stir as Alexandre helped Anthony remove his jacket and get into bed. Anthony lay back heavily and cupped Alexandre's face in his meaty, pink hands and pulled it to his own and kissed Alexandre's cheek and grunted, "Good night, my boy."

DAYS AFTER CHRISTMAS, Prithu arrived again at Davidson's home. The housemaid, Sarita, greeted the boy and they spoke casually in Telugu. She called Alexandre to the sitting room, and as he came to the sitting room he saw Prithu smile for the first time as he spoke to Kumari from the doorway. Seeing Alexandre, the boy stiffened and looked at him wide-eyed. He told Alexandre he'd brought a letter from Kanakadurga. He thanked Prithu and found a few coins in his pocket, which he offered the boy. Prithu took the coins, examining them in his palm.

Alexandre took the letter to his room and sat in his bed as he read it.

Kanakadurga asked after his health and asked how his studies were going. She wished him a Merry Christmas and asked about his family. Kanakadurga told him that Mohini and her now husband had moved permanently to his family home in Bezawada. She was now expecting. "You may have heard that Shiva sent Anjali out of the home, Alexandre," she continued. "I don't want you to think it was your fault. A week after you left, Shiva found out that Anjali had sent an article to an anti-colonialist paper in America founded by some ex-patriot Indians living in San Francisco."

A short missive to some mysterious street ten thousand miles away would bring every red-faced Englishman from fifty miles of their home angrily asking Adivi what the bloody hell his gimp daughter was up to. For Adivi, it was the last straw. He and Anjali had barely spoken since Alexandre had left, and the article, entitled "Free Women in a Free

India," was as stinging an embarrassment as the morning she had spent on the beach with Alexandre. Kanakadurga was afraid it was her own fault that the girl had turned out this way; she kept nationalist newspapers in her bedroom. She had even kept in a journal some yellowed caricatures of Clive raiding Calcutta with bags of money strapped to the flanks of his horse. Some of the clippings were over fifty years old. Adivi deferred to no one, except occasionally his mother, whom he had exasperatedly tried to persuade to throw out the old papers a hundred times, but the old woman was stubborn and kept them in wax papers between her starched, folded saris.

THAT HOME, WHERE Anjali grew up, was no longer hers. The day she left her natal house, she stood outside the gates and Peter shut them behind her. She clutched her small suitcase in one hand and under her arm held a gunnysack of clothes and a few bars of soap. She stood there, not sure in which direction to turn. She had lived in that home all her life, but the city outside of it was foreign to her and the men on the streets stared at her: this woman alone and crippled but groomed and dressed in a good sari. The only women in the streets were the old women who sold fruits and strings of jasmine for women's hair. She bit her lip, she tightened her hold on her luggage and began to weep. She did not know where to go; she did not know how she would get there even if she did. Outside, alone, she was a rogue woman, no father, no family, no name. She turned back to the house and ran to the gate and looked into Peter's cold, dark eyes. They were black like stones. He had been hired the month before she was born; he had played with her and Mohini when they were children. And as Anjali stood there she thought too of all the mendicant hands over the years that had been pushed through the gates, which she had passively observed. Perhaps she should have chosen the local gesture—that quiet care of one neighbor for another—over the grand one, she thought.

"Peter, please, let me back in . . . " she pleaded.

"Mr. Adivi says you are not allowed in."

"Peter, please!" She felt ashamed by her fear.

He threw his baton against the bars, startling her.

"Peter, I order you to open these gates!" Anjali shook, her voice betraying her fear. Anjali stood outside the gates and began to cry from the very core of her being, her body convulsing with sobs as she looked from outside at the only home she'd ever known, her small hands rattling the gate as she held onto it, her hands cramping with strain. She'd only ever before looked out from there, and now was looking in. Her family, her home, all of it inside separated only by a wrought iron gate, but as impenetrable as a sea barrier or the snowy Himalayas.

"Get out! Get out before I call your father and he calls the police . . . " He muttered under his breath, "whore . . . " and sneered at her.

Kanakadurga closed the letter by saying, "I wonder if it is for the best, Alexandre. Sometimes I would weep, thinking about my granddaughter's life as the spinster daughter of aging Anglophiles, living out her days in her natal home. She'd have to live through the deaths of everyone around her: myself, her parents. And she would be apart from her only sister. What a waste. It may seem trite, Alexandre, to those who grow up free, out of doors and cages, unfenced, that she, the daughter of a rich man, never experienced a fraction of the life in the doors of her father's house that she will, now, when at long last she summoned the coach on that morning, in her briefcase the saris and the small amount of jewelry her mother would let her leave with.

There were few things in the world that were truly hers anyway. I did not want her to go and I wept. She was my grandchild, and the love of my life, but I was proud too. I knew she would live life. I knew her soul was too big for this place. I knew she would see this India that she and I were determined to see free one day. The India of buildings of brick and stone, temples, mosques, wild jasmine, the barefoot poor, the villages motley and wild beyond the kept gardens, the marble fortress that is our home. And I know that despite her body, Anjali is a soldier. My son and Lalita, they are impoverished souls. They acquiesce, gladly, to the expectations of their family and society. Appearances, money and beauty make them happy. They have no fight in them. But my Anjali does.

"I know she has gone to Hyderabad to stay with a woman named Sarojini Naidu, a poet who is also involved in the Home Rule movement.

"It has been, what? Nearly two months since Mohini married. My girls are gone, and everything is now shades of blue and grey.

"Perhaps it is my old woman's imagination gone wild, but I swear to you, Alexandre, I am an older woman each day now; I can actually see myself age. Sometimes, if I look very quickly, if I glance, I see myself as I was when I was younger, and I'll feel suddenly lighter, and then I look up and look closely and there I am: an old woman with lines around her eyes and mouth, whose skin is grey and whose hair is silver. Whose life will end soon. Whose son and daughter-in-law don't trust her, and whose granddaughters are out of her grasp. I'm thinner now, and the skin on my jaw and arms seems to hang from the muscles and bones. Sometimes I feel as though I am only a grey shadow, so close to perishing, and missing my girl so much, that I am an apparition in white saris haunting the halls of the home that used to be mine.

"Mohini came to visit the other day. It is as if the lights have gone out in her eyes; Alexandre, it is horrible. She is older too now, and wears her bridal necklace with the same sorrow a prisoner wears his shackles. She told us that her husband is cold, silent, that he can take all the warmth out of a room. She is pregnant. And the thought of her in that state, I hesitate to admit, filled me with dread. She says he almost never speaks to her, that her life has become about seeing to her mother-in-law's medical needs and making certain the servants are doing their jobs. They have money, of course, and standing, but there are things they don't have. There are things I don't want my granddaughters to know about in life, like loneliness. And now Mohini knows what loneliness is, especially that peculiar kind of loneliness that can attend a person who is not alone in a room. There is no love in that house. Now Mohini can disappear into walls.

"She asked her father if she can come back home. When Mohini asked her father, it was as if he had turned to stone. He said, 'You will go back to your husband, and live with him as his wife forever.' And I saw Mohini shiver as if a tiny earthquake had gone off inside, allowing the land to give way beneath her.

"Alexandre, I've missed you since you left. I treasure our friendship. You should know I am not well. This is not a tragedy. I am an old woman and I've lived a full life. Anyhow, Hindus don't fear death, but I would like to see the New Year in. If I don't see you again in this life, I want to thank you, not just for your friendship but for the help you've extended me. You know of what I speak. Happy Christmas, Dr. Lautens."

Alexandre folded the letter and let his head hang down. He felt an unaccountable sadness wash over him. It wasn't meant to have been like this. He felt hot tears sting his eyes and suddenly he felt tired to his bones. He decided he wanted to leave India before the New Year. He wanted to leave it all behind. It was a decision as sudden as it was absolute. He would thank Anthony and Madhuri, pack his belongings and go home; the book would have to be finished from Paris, and if it were never finished, well, that was fine, and much better than staying in India. He leapt up from his desk and began packing frantically. It no longer seemed like much of a decision but rather the only thing to do.

MADHURI LOOKED RELIEVED, as she fluttered about Alexandre in worried excitement, to hear the door open and Anthony call out, "Hello?"

"Look! Look at what he is doing!" she cried out, as Anthony walked into Alexandre's room, guided by the sound of the commotion.

"What is this? What is going on?" Anthony asked, his eyes darting around the room.

Madhuri looked like a worried mother hen, hovering over her chick. "He says he is leaving! What is this?!" she asked, gesturing at the open suitcase on the bed, the stack of neatly folded shirts.

Anthony lightly put his hand on her forearm. "Alright, alright. Darling you take care of dinner, I will take care of this," he said. Anthony closed the door after Madhuri, who walked out, tugging her hair anxiously.

"Is everything alright, Alex? This is a very sudden decision . . . " Anthony asked.

"Yes, everything is fine . . . *Benga pettukovaddu,*" he said, looking at Madhuri, "it's nothing." He squeezed her small, brown hand and looked away from her, afraid he would cry. "It is just that, well, I feel my work here is done. I've collected all the data I need to finish my book. I miss my children . . . I just feel it is a good time to go."

"Madhuri tells me the Adivis' servant came round and brought you a letter . . . has that have anything to do with it?"

"No, no . . . you've both been terribly hospitable, and I'd hate to impose any longer on your generosity. I just feel the time is right . . . perhaps I'll get home before the last snowfall in Paris," Alexandre swallowed hard and coughed to mask the falter in his voice. Alexandre looked only at the small pile of clothes on the bed, folding them impatiently.

Anthony sat silently, looking at Alexandre, waiting for the younger man to look at him. When Alexandre finally looked up, Anthony looked hard at him, his eyes narrowing in scrutiny, and for a full minute, he held Alexandre's gaze.

Alexandre faltered; his eyebrows quivered, and he looked down.

Anthony coughed, "Well, Madhuri and I have enjoyed having you, Alex. You seem to have made your mind, but if there is anything I can do to persuade you otherwise, do let me know." And he stood up.

Alexandre looked down again. He folded a pair of slacks, "Thank you Tony. But I don't think I'll change my mind."

"Very well. At the very least I can help you with your departure . . . I'll send out tomorrow morning for the passenger ship schedule. We'll have to get the train schedule to Bombay also." Anthony looked once more at Alexandre, lowered his head and left.

BEFORE HE LEFT the home, Madhuri gave Alexandre a sweet look of stern concern and kissed him on both cheeks.

"I told her that is the way the French greet people," Anthony said, laughing sadly, his hand on Madhuri's lower back.

"Thank you for your hospitality, Madhuri," Alexandre said to her in Telugu. He gave her some money to pass along to Kumari.

The train would bring him to Bombay three days before the ship was due to leave. He did not send word to Kanakadurga that he was leaving, nor did he attempt to contact Anjali. Anthony took him to the train station in Waltair in a hired coach. As usual, the train station was chaotic and full of beggars and food vendors and station attendants, and watching the blurry brown mess of an Indian station, Alexandre sighed contentedly to himself, knowing he was at long last going home.

Anthony hired coolies to load Alexandre's cases, including the tif-fin boxes Madhuri had sent along with snacks for the long journey. He had secured a sleeping birth in the first-class cabin of the East Coast Express. It was late in the day, and the golden sun was pouring into the train station and the wind was whipping everyone about. Alexandre shook Anthony's hand, smiling as his hair blew across his forehead.

"Anthony . . . I have no words to thank you enough. I could never have completed my studies here without your help . . . I couldn't have. Thank you so much," he put his hand over his tie where his heart beat.

"Don't mention it, my boy," the older man's eyes shone with watery sadness. Anthony clasped Alexandre's hand in his, pausing for a moment. "Childhood lasts forever Alexandre, and then, suddenly, you are an adult, and every year speeds by faster than the last, and soon it is all gone, and those you love turn grey and old . . . " his voice broke.

Alexandre's lips tightened, restraining some vague, melancholy feeling. He looked out onto the platform and for long moments was no longer sure there was a place for him. He thought of the gods he'd been so unsteadily faithful to. His place was not India, he knew, but he knew too that it was no longer France, because now nothing was the same. He looked at the kaleidoscopic, dizzying view of thousands of women along the stretch of the platform in colorful saris, billowing like the sails of ships. For a moment he regretted his decision to leave, thinking that Anthony's home, a home in India where Scotch whiskey was poured and English was spoken, was perhaps the only place he belonged anymore. But it was a home that wasn't his. He regretted too all he had not done, that he hadn't taken the train to Calcutta or Delhi, or spent a fortnight in a houseboat in Kashmir or gone to Benares to see holy men walk across fire or eaten fish curry on the Portuguese beaches of Goa. He wished he had befriended a maharajah and lived richly above the rules of society and in between the boundaries of nations.

He envied that Anthony would take a simple ride home and share a tasty meal with the woman he loved while he, Alexandre, would be making a journey that was nearly unbearable. The conductor called all passengers to board and Alexandre looked at Anthony, who cleared his throat and nodded in acknowledgment.

Alexandre boarded the train, and when he sat he found Anthony waiting through the grates of the open window. The train's engines had already started, and it was difficult to hear. He feared that when he turned back to look at his friend, he would see the old Englishman's eyes and everything would stop, that his sorrow would stop the people milling about the station and that the clocks on the walls should not strike another minute, that the sun should stop pouring down its happy rays over the station. Where were the soldiers in their black armbands? And the girls with baskets of chrysanthemums? Alexandre felt tears in his eyes, the words of his countryman Pierre Loti imprinted on his mind: "My God! If the Indian sages that I seek could but convince me that I might find pardon and pity too." "My God, my God, my God," Alexandre thought.

"I miss them already!" Alexandre shouted to Anthony, his knuckles white as he clenched the cold grates in his hands. His eyes were red and his jaw taut. His breath was coming in wet little gasps.

"WHAT?!" Anthony yelled back, and he walked with the train as slowly it began to pull away.

Alexandre looked at Anthony through the iron grates of his compartment window and futilely, over the engines' roar, shouted something lost to the noise of the train and the station and the crowds. Anthony cupped his ear and raised his eyebrows in question.

Anthony now ran alongside the train as it slowly lurched forward; and then, after a few moments, as the train gathered speed, Anthony could not keep up, and Alexandre craned his neck back, looking back in the distance at the old white man standing alone on the platform, red-cheeked with exertion, his right hand raised in final farewell.

And when Alexandre could no longer see his friend, he sat and faced forward, looking at the strangers in the train, and held his head in his hands and cried.

ALEXANDRE DID NOT partake of the served dinner that evening but rather ate the snacks Madhuri had packed for him. They were fried, tasty and very heavy, and Alexandre, his stomach full, soon felt drowsy. He fell asleep in his seat, upright, and didn't wake up until late the next morning. The other passengers had eaten breakfast already, and he called the dining steward to bring some coffee and fruit.

He took down his books and journals from the overhead storage and thought about how his job and Anthony's weren't terribly different; to his mind, the defining theme of the age was cataloguing: animals, fish, birds, religions, peoples, diseases, plants and languages.

The grammar was nearing completion. Every word in Telugu ends in a vowel, and for a very short time the task of acquiring the language well enough to describe it seemed to be a practice of learning music. It was an agglutinating language; a sentence could stream off like bars of an opera. A language like a song, and so very far from his own mother tongue. So many sentences in Telugu were the inverse of French sentence syntax. To his thinking, and for all his exposure to the many tongues of men, there was still no finer language than French—no language that quite so accurately conveyed the agony, the beauty, and the wonder of the human condition.

He wondered if he might be able to complete the manuscript on board the ship, and the prospect of publishing his grammar so far ahead of what he had forecasted dulled the sadness in him. In a year, Alexandre's grammar would be received with much fanfare among linguists and Indologists. It would be the first comprehensive grammar of a Dravidian language; its aim was not to teach the language so much as explain it to a European audience, for whom Telugu's structure was exotic. The vocabulary was so largely borrowed from Sanskrit that Alexandre was also invited by his editor to write a chapter, entitled "Language Contact in South India," for a textbook of historical linguistics. It would begin: "In the Dravidian language of Telugu of South India, one of the most populously spoken languages in India, we find one of the most impressive cases of language contact on record. Sanskrit, sometimes thought of as merely the liturgical language of the Hindus, is alive and well in the unrelated but equally beautiful language of Telugu."

Academic renown was in Alexandre's future, but now, on the train heading east, Alexandre found reassurance only in the rhythm of the train's movement, which soothed him as he rewrote sections of his manuscript.

On board the train Alexandre tried to shake the malaise off, that nostalgia he was horrified to be feeling, too soon and for the wrong place. He tried to convince himself that this was merely the disorienting effect of travel and fatigue. He should have considered his life less than completely lived to have never visited this mythic and strange land, located less in markers of longitude and latitude than in the psyche. We had all visited this place, he thought, in our dreams and in our longing to see humanity explode in all its permutations, all its absurdness, all its circus-like freakishness, all its glory and all its beauty. But India was not his home.

There were places like this on Earth—America, Florence, the islands of the Pacific, Egypt . . . they suggested with their beauty, with the embodiment of a great idea, something of a universal human dream.

He thought Paris was like this—with its romance, its glamour, but he knew it too for its reality, its starburst intersections, its back alleys and grand avenues, its taverns, its bars, its hidden rooms and dance halls. How many times had those roads known his familiar footfall—as a child skipping along their long stretches, with schoolyard friends, or unevenly lifted by one hand by his mother, as she bought bread and cheese and meat from the local bakers and butchers; then as a young man, with a sporting step, holding Madeline by the waist, stopping to press his lips against hers; as a father he would often walk holding Catherine's hand, or with Matthieu hoisted on his shoulders, counting trees or pigeons. Paris kept his secrets and remembered his youth, like a loyal friend.

In Waltair, the streets had revealed his isolation, his unfamiliarity, and his misgivings like an indifferent stranger, all the passersby avoiding eye contact, and he scolded himself for letting himself go so astray that he missed the place. He hadn't meant to.

ALEXANDRE WOKE TO a dream realized—he had fallen asleep dreaming of Bombay and woken up in the city's Victoria Station. Bombay was waking up, loud as always in the morning as chaos and arriving trains descended on the station. Anthony had offered to make the lodging arrangements in Bombay from Waltair by post while Alexandre made the train journey, and he was grateful that the arrangements had been squared away. He checked into the station's desk and, as expected, found an envelope from Anthony detailing his hotel arrangements.

He hired coolies and a carriage to take him to the British-owned hotel. Alexandre looked out the windows drowsily, seeing the city go by him in a blur of browns and reds and blues. He began to feel dizzy and sick and put his head in his lap, queasy. The driver jerked and weaved through the traffic. Street children and animals and vendors crowded the streets. Alexandre held his head in his hands and sat up only when he heard the driver say, "Sir, we are at your hotel."

Alexandre checked into the hotel, greeted by an elderly British woman. He was exhausted, his hair and clothes rumpled; he felt he'd been wearing those clothes forever. He ran his fingertips across his jaw. His beard was thick and rough.

"Dr. Lautens, welcome to Bombay," she said cheerily. Bellboys took his luggage, and Alexandre asked for tea to be sent up to settle his stomach. "Yes, of course Doctor," she said.

Alexandre went his room. He ran his fingertips over his unshaven beard and ran his hands through his hair, working knots loose. He washed his face, shaved and changed into pajamas; an Indian boy arrived with the tea, and Alexandre thanked him and drank it down quickly. He then lay down and fell into a deep, dreamless sleep, oblivious to the sounds of the restless, fitful city outside his room.

When he awoke, Alexandre moved his sleep-heavy body across the room and opened the shutters on the window. He sighed as he leaned outside, his bare white chest tilted forward into the Bombay night.

Alexandre walked over to the middle of the room and opened a suitcase, found a clean pair of slacks and white linen shirt and dressed quickly. He had decided to see the city, and he smiled, knowing that for the night he was anonymous.

BOMBAY GLITTERED. DARK Indian eyes shone in the nighttime streetlights. Alexandre bought food off the street and walked the foreign city alone. He moved through groups of Indian schoolboys and drunken British sailors and vendors. The dirty, barefoot street children from the slums were selling small toys and newspaper cones filled with boiled peanuts. The night air was heavy, and he could smell flowers and kerosene and the ocean. He felt as if he hadn't woken up, that he had drifted from a deep sleep to a dark night peppered with languages he couldn't understand, and despite his long rest, his mind felt unclear, as if the hot, humid air of the city had clouded him.

He walked down a small, narrow street and saw an old woman standing on a stoop, her fist on her hip. She looked like an Anglo-Indian, one of those daughters of a British official whose mother was Indian. She had pale skin and dark hair. She smiled at him deeply.

"What are you doing darling?" she called out. "A handsome boy like you shouldn't be alone in Bombay . . . "

Alexandre stopped and looked at her, smiling back. He considered her and saw that she looked friendly and harmless. Almost motherly. "What are you running there," he asked, looking at the building behind her, the windows covered in red cloth, a soft glow coming from behind them. "You have girls inside?"

"No, darling . . . well, yes, but—just come inside. You look lost. Come." She opened the door to the building and Alexandre followed her. A heavy cloud of sweet smoke hit him, a honeyed mix of tobacco and marijuana. He inhaled deeply. The old woman took his hand. "Come," she said gently. There was a coatrack near the entrance, and Alexandre saw a British army jacket hanging from it limply. She looked at his feet, "Your shoes, darling."

Alexandre removed his shoes and followed her as she pushed open saris that served as makeshift curtains. When she pulled them open, the smoke became heavier and sweeter and Alexandre felt weak and submissive. He ran his hand over a sari-curtain, enjoying the softness of the silk. He saw through one a young British soldier sleeping on a bed, a pipe lying next to him. A bare-chested Chinese man sat at the end of the bed, smoking, his eyes red, looking at Alexandre without expression. A pretty young Anglo-Indian woman walked by wearing a sari without a blouse, the end of the sari thrown loosely over her shoulder.

The older woman stopped her, "Miriam, help make this young man comfortable."

The younger woman smiled and took Alexandre's arm. They walked to a bed in the back of the room upon which lay the inert body of an old Englishman, his legs curled up to his chest. Miriam smoothed the sheets on the end of the bed and motioned for Alexandre to sit.

She gently touched his face and lifted a long pipe off the floor and lit a small brass lamp. Miriam sat at Alexandre's feet, her dark eyes flashing in the low flame of the lamp. Her hair and eyes were dark but her skin nearly as white as his. She put black opium in a small bowl at the end of the pipe and let it warm over the flame. A few moments later, Miriam placed her mouth on the pipe and inhaled deeply. Alexandre watched her collarbones emerge as she breathed in. She looked up at him, her eyes limpid and black. She lifted the pipe to his mouth and Alexandre followed her example, inhaling. They passed the pipe between them again, and Alexandre leaned back on the bed. He closed his eyes and let warmth take him over.

He looked at Miriam and saw that her eyes looked bigger and darker, her mouth pinker and fuller than before. She sat down next to him on the bed, and Alexandre felt her lips on his ear, her small hand on his chest. He looked at her and muttered, "You are very pretty." He felt tears roll down his face. He looked at her: she was like a phantasm, her alabaster limbs like vapors. He took her hand from his chest and gently placed it in her lap and woke up late the next day, curled up on the bed opposite the old Englishman he had seen there the night before. The sun pushed through the curtains and Alexandre felt blinded as he woke.

THE NATIONALIST JAMSETJI Tata had designed his hotel to face inland, her back to England, and had ordered spun iron pillars for the hotel's interior from Paris when he went to see the premiere of the Eiffel Tower some years before at the Exposition Universelle; the fair had been held to celebrate the one-hundred-year anniversary of the storming of the Bastille. Tata had seen Africans for the first time in the *village nègre*, the American sharpshooter Annie Oakley and a small number of Thomas Edison's inventions.

Alexandre, on a British passenger ship in December of 1911, days before the New Year, months after the Gateway had been completed for the Delhi Durbar, looked upon the city of Bombay as the other passengers made their way on board. His belongings had been stowed in his stateroom on the ship, and he stood on deck looking at the city. He took in the deep blue water of the bay and the Tata's Taj Mahal Hotel.

FIFTY-NINE YEARS BEFORE, in 1852, an old copy of *Blackwood's Magazine*, which an English army physician, Dr. Brydon, had crammed under his helmet, took the brunt of the blow. An Afghani soldier had thrust his sword into the surgeon's head, chopping magazine pages rather than brains. Brydon escaped the Afghani and fled, finding en route a wounded Indian soldier who lay dying. The Indian offered the young doctor his horse and pointed him in the direction of the British stronghold of Jellalabad. Of the 16,500 army men who had gone into Kabul, Brydon was the only one to survive. He followed the bugle call sounded by the Somerset Light Infantry from Jellalabad. They sounded the bugle every hour to guide those long presumed dead to safety. And on the end of the third day, Dr. Brydon arrived at Jellalabad, mounted on a horse, both he and the horse half-dead and all alone. When this news reached Queen Victoria, she rewarded the Somerset soldiers for fighting for their queen and country by having their regimental colors augmented: JELLALABAD was inscribed over a brick-laid crown.

Alexandre, in 1911, hearing the ship's horns blow, watched as he pulled away from India, and he could not have known then that the Somerset Light Infantry would march slowly in 1948, and as they did, Anjali would hold Sarojini Naidu's arm in Bombay. Alexandre did not know then that the light infantry would be the last British regiment to leave India. Anjali would cry on that last day of February 1948 as the first battalion of light infantry would move alongside their Indian escorts: the Bombay Grenadiers, the Second Sikhs, the Indian Navy, the 3/5th Gurkhas, the Mahratta Light Infantry, men with whom they would fight and die in Gibraltar, Normandy, the North West Frontier, the Japanese islands and Mesopotamia. The Indian and British soldiers would offer each other their last royal salute, and the crowd would quiet itself, somber as the band played "God Save the Queen." In the crowd, sentiment would make way for joy as the standard bearers, carrying the Union Jack and the regimental colors, led the soldiers as they passed under the Gateway of India. The *Empress of Australia* would wait in Bombay's harbor, great puffs of black smoke rising out of her funnels. The soldiers would board the steamship to "Auld Lang Syne." Anjali would bend at the waist, leaning hard on Sarojini. In the distance, with the other officiates, she would weep and would not know why.

At the center of the ceremony would be the man that Anjali revered most: Nehru would hold the arm of Major-General Whistler as his troops boarded the *Empress of Australia*. His expression would be stern, but even at that distance Anjali would make out in her hero's face a melancholy about his eyes. An attendant would hand Nehru a red box. Nehru had wanted this feeling since he was a rich boy without direction or will in Cambridge. His would tremble as he handed the box to Brigadier John Platt, who would wear a scar on his face since shards of a German Nebelwerfer had hit him when crossing the Garigliano River. Platt had shot tigers in Madras, and in the brown faces of the Indian regiments, could make out men who had served under him during the war. "We are most reluctant to leave behind so many good friends and your great country which our regiment has known and served for so long. At the same time, we are happy for you in your newfound freedom, and I take this unique opportunity of wishing you all good luck and Jai Hind." The crowd would cheer him on as he opened the box and reached in and lifted out a silver scale-model of the Gateway to India.

The wind would lift the drapes of saris like white sails, smiling women pulling the frayed ends of overworn khadi into their teeth, covering their heads as the sun bore down on them all. Men's glittering eyes would show like obsidians, and sapphires, like emeralds. Anjali would look out on the crowd; "This is what hope looks like," she would think. It looks like lightness. Hope is the fearlessness that allows one to pull up the anchors and set forth on an unknown path. She would feel nostalgia for the moment even as it was passing, as if seeing the whole scene in the beauty of a photograph, the sepia grains of white cotton cloth and a pale sky, of sand-colored people, all of them looking up; she saw it all as one might in ten years or twenty.

As ALEXANDRE WATCHED the subcontinent move away from him, as he stood on the deck of the RMS *Medina*, the world was nearing in on 1912, the last days of the last month of the year. There it was, haunting, foreign; perhaps from an Atlantic sea breeze—a cold whistle of air in his face and hair. It was hot, cruelly hot in India, but it was winter in Paris. Alexandre thought, "I'm going home. I'm going to the place they call me Alex, Papa, Darling."

INDEPENDENCE FROM THE Britain was, for India, nearly four decades away, as were the things that Anjali would come to be reconciled to, once and for all.

❧ 13 ❧

I N TIMES OF contemplation, when the worries of adult life became
too much for him, Lautens had once taken comfort in the youthful
ruckus of university life. The vigorous debate of young minds, the hope,
the joy, the romance and love of young people. No longer. Looking out
into the medieval space of the university, Lautens was saddened to see
it so quiet, so declawed in this the first year of peace after the war. So
many of the boys had died, a million and a half young men. The prices
of everything were up, without their young hands to propel the manu-
facturing industries, now in the care of men past their prime, fathers
without sons. There were so many mothers whose boys had taken their
last breath on battlefields they'd never been to before in Somme and
Ypres, Gallipoli—the Dardanelles running red and black with the blood
and guts of the dead bodies of boys. There were bits of propeller blades,
shards of skull and tibia bones, bootstraps, fragments of helmets, tattered photographs of children playing in backyards in places like Des
Moines and Detroit, a birthday party in Leeds or Dover littering the
fields and beaches of France's northern coast.

Once again, Alexandre found the truth of the matter was in the
etymology: the infantry—an army of children.

It had been seven years since he left, and Anjali had written to
him sporadically, having obtained his address through his publisher.
Shortly after he arrived back in Paris, she had written inquiring after
his safe journey home, Madeline and the children, how his work and

studies were going. She told him she had obtained a copy of his book in English through a friend who worked at the Bombay office of his London publisher. He had received others, telling him about her activities and how she lived now with a woman poet-politician named Naidu. She told him that Mohini had two daughters and a son and that her grandmother had died on the first day of 1912.

ONCE, BACK IN India, he had found Anjali reading Tolstoy in the garden and had said to her, "This is hardly relaxing reading for a young woman!"

And Anjali smiled shyly—for all her defenses, her smile was sweet and disarming—but then her face immediately fell into an affected stoicism. "I fear Tolstoy's writing is rather erudite for me, but I keep hearing that he is well regarded among the anti-colonialists."

Alexandre smiled. She always used elevated language when speaking to him. He matched her, as if speaking to his students: "I am afraid I haven't read enough of his work to offer much meaningful commentary; which of his books are you reading?"

"*The Death of Ivan Ilyich*; it is about a judge who is dying."

"Ah . . ."

"There is a French phrase that is used many times, even in the English translation: *comme il faut*, what does it mean?"

"*Comme il faut,* as it should be . . . proper."

"*Comme il faut,*" she repeated, she beamed at him brightly, "I shall use it."

He hoped that in not responding to her letters, she too would recall this conversation and remember that his silence was only proper, only the way it should be.

At the beginning, she had hoped hard and even prayed that he would write back to her. And then, after some time, she made herself stop hoping, in the hopes that by giving up hope she would trick fortune and he would write.

DR. LAUTENS DID not get news of the massacre until after the New Year, until the story of General Dyer had reached the international press and made its way to the Sorbonne-area newsstand. Dyer had ordered his ninety soldiers to fire their rifles into a crowd of Indian holiday revelers. They fired off seventeen thousand rounds.

Sarojini Naidu was reported to have been in the crowd. Years after he read the news, he would still remember that his first thought went immediately to Anjali, but he quickly corrected himself and thought of the general tragedy of the episode.

Anjali would be there, alongside her mentor. By that time, she would have been a proper woman, having shed the shadow of girlhood but unable still to run from gunfire and stampeding horses. The paper said 379 people had been killed.

The Morning Post in London, which had praised Brigadier-General Dyer's actions on the grounds that he had protected "the honor of European Women," gathered a group of thirteen women to present to Dyer a purse of eighteen thousand pounds sterling and a sword encrusted with Indian jewels and inscribed SAVIOR OF THE PUNJAB.

A hundred years prior, Dyer's father, Edward, had opened a brewery and sold Lion brand Himalayan-made beer to the English army men, whose stint in India was more parching than they had expected. An advertisement declared it "as good as back home." Edward's son Reginald, the man who was born at the hill station of Murree, who was

schooled in Shimla and Bangalore and would become the commander
of the Forty-Fifth Infantry Brigade at Jalandhar, was being sent home.

Dyer ordered ninety soldiers to fire their .303 Lee-Enfield rifles into
a crowd at the Jallinwalla Bagh, and Anjali heard a chorus of blood-
curdling cries as bodies fell. Months later she would hear that the general had ordered his soldiers to fire into the thickest part of the crowd.

Startled, Sarojini fell to her feet and pulled both girls—her daughter, Padmaja, and Anjali—to her body.

"FIRE!"

Anjali, deafened by the sounds of the guns, looked to her side. A
baby lay under her mother's motionless body, wailing. Anjali, balanc-
ing her weight on her forearms and good leg, slipped her hand around
the child's stomach and pulled the baby to her own body, crouching
over her.

"FIRE!"

Sixteen thousand more rounds fired.

She wrote to Alexandre that for nine more minutes, she cowered,
shaking under the sound of the gunfire. Anjali shook, her arms holding the baby girl so tightly that for seconds after the firing stopped she
couldn't release the child. Anjali looked up when for long minutes she
heard nothing. Sarojini and Padmaja, both trembling, looked at Anjali,
their eyes wide, their mouths open. In their eyes, horror. Anjali looked
down. Her chest was covered in blood, and then she felt it warm and
sticky on her arms. Anjali's arms relaxed, and the baby's limp body fell
away from hers.

THAT NIGHT, ANJALI, Sarojini and Padmaja stayed with the
Singhs, friends of Sarojini. The army cut the wire cables, the railroads

and the city's electricity and water. Quietly, a servant led Anjali to the washroom to clean herself. Anjali looked at herself in the mirror. The light was gone from her eyes, and she felt despair in every muscle in her body as she wrung the child's blood out of her sari. Her fingers were numb in the cold water. She looked for several moments at a plump, yellow lizard on the wall, as still as death. The servants had filled every pot in the house with water when word spread that the water would be shut off, and she had been given only a small bowl of water.

It was a beautiful night; there was no breeze. Anjali looked out the window of the washroom at the trees—their leaves outlined in silvery moonlight. The stars shone brightly; the world looked endless. And quiet. No words. No one had spoken in several hours. Anjali closed her eyes and thought happiness. She thought of floating in the sea in Alexandre's arms.

As night closed in on the home, Sarojini spoke at last to the maid. "Where is Mr. Singh?" She had not seen her friend leave.

"He is still at the garden, Madam. Helping to identify the dead."

Anjali stretched her weak body on the floor. She fantasized that night of heroism. In her mind's eye, she was an Indian Joan of Arc, and then a dark-eyed Athena with bow and arrow. She thought: "I can carry this city's sorrow. I can walk these streets, and cradle the motherless children, and bring comfort to the young widows and herd the shepherdless goats. My heart is gentle and constant." She cupped her hand outwardly, into the dark air, in a gesture of benevolence, as if bidding near her a child who was very close and incredibly dear.

But in the next moment she closed her eyes and hated herself more than ever for thinking of herself, of making a myth of herself, among such despair. She hated herself with a burning intensity she had never felt before. In the darkness she saw again her hands covered in blood and dreamt then only of oblivion, of dissolving into the earth and becoming only embers and ashes. And in the morning, for a moment, she again fancied that she could be a heroine.

RIOTS IN ALL of India continued for days afterward. Anjali saw, on a thoroughfare in Amritsar, the corpse of a calf and a pig strung up on a post and she wondered if anyone would leave the city alive. The city continued under marshal law after spotty rioting. And Dyer ordered that on the Kucha Sawarian, the street where an Englishwoman had been attacked, the natives would have to crawl on their bellies, their noses in the ground as their eyes followed the tips of the soldiers' gleaming bayonets.

ALEXANDRE CHOSE NOT to reply to Anjali's letters and wished she would stop writing, but he reread her letters, again and again, keeping them in a drawer in his office at the university.

He thought of Anjali penned into that garden, with no means of escape.

He thought of her again when reading about the Siberian cellar where the once-tsar of Russia held his son in his arms—his wife and daughters were killed first, the diamonds they had hidden in their dresses proving too solid a shield against bullets. And so the women were speared to death with bayonets, producing the unusual sound of diamonds colliding with steel.

In bed at night, Alexandre sometimes recalled Anjali's description of that day in Amritsar, and his heart beat in a slow, funerary rhythm in the quiet and dark city. He thought of her in Amritsar: Anjali, the daughter now of no one, and he tossed fitfully in bed in his Parisian flat when the last candle burned out in a lightless city. He fell to sleep thinking of that dark, far-off country, India—a country the shape of an elephant's ear, a greater distance away—in his sleep the map lines did not exist; he and Anjali and everyone else on the great Eurasian plate, and the ancient places—Bactria, Persia, the vanished kingdom of Rajaraja, the great Himalayan peaks, all moving with the spinning of a small, watery planet invisible from the rings of Uranus.

Alexandre's was a ritual sadness and would never leave him.

IT TOOK ANJALI twenty-five years to understand the rhythm of the seasons. She wasn't oblivious to the changes of season and temperature, of course, but she was a quarter century old before she saw that year to year all the patterns would be the same, that at Christmas the converted Christians and the British officers and civil servants would bring out the paper crowns and the holly wreaths that they draped on the doors and in the hallways, and that spring would start annually with at first just a sweet smell of blossoms, and that at each season she'd miss the one prior and also look forward to the one upcoming and be able to see months into the future to the next and the next season. It would always be the same; it both assured her and scared her, that the only change to be exacted upon Earth was the kind she could unleash, the change people can make.

For her associations with the likes of Gandhi, Sarojini, the Nehrus, kind-eyed Bacha Khan and his army of unarmed redshirts, and for any activity deemed seditious—every article, speech or demonstration—Anjali passed many of her days in prison. Often she would be released only to be arrested at this rally or that only a few days later. In the silence of the prison walls, she would think of Mohini and how different their lives had become, from season to season, and wonder about their parents and if they were at all proud of her or if her actions had not only been politically offensive to them but unladylike in their estimation too. In prison she could not see the flowers bloom, or the fruit grow heavy on the vine, or see the monsoons sweep through the city like an angry sea.

Her cell at the Naini Central Jail in Allahabad, where she spent many of her prison days, was a six-by-six room, grey and dank, with only a cot and a chair. Without much ventilation, it trapped humidity and heat, but the bareness of it, its cement floors and ceiling, gave way to coolness in the evening. There was a bare, flickering lightbulb on the ceiling, which flashed on and off at the will of the current. At night, swarms of mosquitos would cluster around the light and make a low buzzing sound to which Anjali would fall asleep. She had a small window, an unreachable pane of glass high up that tilted open during thunderstorms and then clamored shut, and then open again, its wooden sill splintering. Through it, at night, were constellations. Like a sailor drifting in the sea, thrown overboard, she had become adept at telling time by the shifting of heavenly bodies, enough to impress any nautical expert. There was a great fortune in her disfigurement: the men would not touch her, while the other women cowered in fear of some of the male guards.

Still, Anjali preferred her steel-bared room to Mohini's house arrest, her husband-jailor; prison imprisoned only one's body.

Some few years before, Anjali had made rounds with Sarojini from one poverty-stricken village to another, their drought-plagued fields brown and dry, scorched saplings in hundreds of neat, dizzying, infertile rows; the villagers were starving and desperate, struggling under the weight of unrelenting and unforgiving taxes. Many of the farmers had never recovered from seizure of their crops for the war effort, when the government replanted many of the fields with indigo, which left the soil barren. Sarojini was under direction to organize the villagers in protest, in a tax strike, but the work was slow. Anjali was charged with collecting endless notebooks of tedious data: how much the average annual yield was, how many plants were in each row, how many bushels of carrots or turnips were saleable, and so on until so much that in her dreams Anjali would see only numbers. The women were afraid of the men being jailed, and each family—long ignored—wanted to tell Sarojini and Anjali their stories. Sarojini was afraid that if even one family paid the tax, the whole effort would be ruined. "Everyone must be involved," she said sternly, "or else the government will just pick off families, one by one, throwing all these farmers into jail and the women and children will starve."

But when the government threatened to seize the jewelry of the women in the village, a new panic spread through the place from home to home. Anjali and Sarojini and their volunteers helped the villagers hide valuables. At the home of the Pandya family, the young, thin mother nervously served watered-down coffee without sugar to Sarojini and Anjali as Anjali helped the old woman fold a small amount of cash into her saris. It was an amount that as a girl Anjali would have kept as pocket money for candies and toys at the railway station.

Sarojini looked at an empty amber bottle on the table and glanced up, making eye contact with Mr. Pandya, who hung his head.

"They will take our land! Oh God!" Mrs. Pandya looked heavenward and clenched her fists to her breasts, her face contorted in horror. "They've seized the land of our neighbors already! I don't know what to do with my jewelry," Mrs. Pandya said. She held up a meager, ancient, marriage necklace and a small set of silver anklets. "This is all the family has left. Should my daughter get married like a beggar girl?" She held a thin, weak baby to her chest.

Sarojini looked over the room listlessly as Anjali passed through her gaze. Suddenly she looked strong and sure and moved in to face Mrs. Pandya.

"Give it to Anjali, Mrs. Pandya."

"What?"

"Give your jewelry to Anjali. They will never inspect a crippled girl."

Anjali looked nervously at Sarojini, afraid; she did not want that responsibility. Mrs. Pandya anxiously clutched her jewelry more tightly. Sarojini took the items from Mrs. Pandya's hand and thrust them at Anjali. Anjali recalled that there was a time, before, when she was small and thought jewelry would make her beautiful.

"Anjali, put these on," she instructed, "you needn't even hide them. The authorities will assume they are yours," she laughed. "They wouldn't dare."

Anjali began to fasten the thin chains around her neck, ashamed that she paused for a moment as she considered that she was putting on peasant jewelry, and then she wondered if she belonged to any society or group anymore, having no father who would claim her as his daughter. She thought how her father and mother would reproach her for this, for taking coffee with farmworkers.

THE POOR WHOSE lives she could not before imagine were now, in the jail, her neighbors. Anjali had been jailed beside pickpockets and prostitutes—women who couldn't afford blouses to wear beneath their saris, with missing teeth and thin grey braids, rashes—some suffered from syphilis. She searched her memory and could only ever remember seeing that kind of person outside the home, from the view of their family carriage or inside a train station. And then she thought of her family's servants, welcome only in that home when working, in the home but not of it; and she thought about her last image of that stately house—Peter's blocking her view of the garden, his face parsed by the iron bars of the gate.

Anjali had known Peter all her life; he was the one who would run errands to the pharmacy for medicines when she was sick with polio. She had never known anything about him. He ate his meals quietly with the other servants outside of the kitchen, and Anjali realized she had never considered him. She had no idea what he thought about. Indeed, she'd never even considered that he did think about much; his was the realm of duty to her family, and she did not know about his family or where he came from. She wondered if he, Peter who guarded the gate, had a story of his own. It was just so difficult to think that someone who stood by their gate with an empty stare ever thought much about anything, imagined things. She wasn't aware that he had a wife and children; it seemed he was always in the Adivi house anyways, but she supposed it possible. It was hard to consider the inner life of servants, but it was even harder to imagine that of beggars, their lives so ani-malistic, living from one meal to the next, and Anjali felt ashamed to think it but couldn't deny that when she saw a pauper with his begging bowl, she first thought, "My God, how horrible," and it wasn't for that beggar's plight but because of the horror of his appearance, that beastly half-nude person, so unclean, so far from anything cultured that he seemed nearly inhuman. She almost felt angry at them for being so poor. Sometimes, if she saw someone particularly wretched, she felt herself fouled and would feel her day ruined. "How awful I am," she thought. "Where is my compassion?!" That compassion it seemed was so much more easily accessible from inside the gates of her home, when she considered the poor as an idea in her mind, not a real and wretched mass of illness and hunger and filth. Anjali still could not look at the frail old coal thief imprisoned opposite her, that toothless mouth, the tattered sari, her bony hand pushing her cup against the bars of her cell like a begging bowl at the foot of the goddess.

The wrought iron bars of Anjali's jail cell prevented entry and egress of human bodies but not of light, which swept through the dank, hot, little cell and illuminated the faintly blue whitewashed walls. In the display of squares of light that moved across her cell as the sun set, Anjali carved a map of India with a nail on the wall, the paint chips cracking and flecking off, revealing a pale green undercoat.

In jail the only comfort she found was in the solace of her own mind—her memories and her imaginings, the fantasies of places and stories and people. There was no more stirring a description than that of the foliage—Alexandre once told her of leaves like gold, or as red as falling sheets of fire covering the East Anglian countryside. Anjali would look up at the grey ceiling of her cell and would close her eyes and see a dreary, grey English sky, and then look down and imagine at her feet fields of pyrotechnic leaves. Or, lying in her hard bed at night, she would sing softly, remembering that Sarojini, who had seen the lakes of Switzerland and the Tuscan hills, had once told her that there is no more compelling sound than that of the human voice, and when hundreds strong it can be no more ignored than choirs of angels, or an onslaught of arrows.

In Anjali's life, she would walk to Dandi, for a stretch holding the frail arm of Gandhi, and alongside Sarojini, an unarmed army in white. She would walk with her cane and sometimes stop to cry; it was no easy task for her. That day, Anjali's rough cotton sari flapped like a flag in the wind, but not that white flag of surrender; she sought no mercy. Just that bolt of white fabric wrapped around her, she marched along the sea barefaced and so nearly naked, the strong sun like a baptism of light. She felt weightless and after so long, tethered no longer by family or custom. The air smelled of salt; she felt the rolling ocean inside her chest. "This must be what it is to be young," she thought. They would marched alongside villagers and industrialists, at a steady pace to the sea, at long last lifting up salt crystals baked on rocks at the line where the land met the wide Indian sea; Sarojini would cry out "Hail, Pilgrim!"

ANJALI WOULD BE jailed again, for having taken an axe to the Kali Temple in Munshiganj to force open the doors to untouchables. Approaching the temple in the May heat, Anjali felt the weight of her weapon. It was made of steal and wood and she carried it as if it were a natural extension of her body, an elongation of her right arm. She looked up to see a statue of Kali-Devi, the fierce one, for whom Rama had collected 107 blue lotuses, and looked at herself, reflected in the mirror work of the temple, axe in hand, and felt as though her own body were engulfed in flames. Anjali's hands throbbed, reddened in pain; she was sweating all over, exhausted, her face, hands and feet dirty with dust and exertion as she wielded that axe and threw it down against the steel chains and locks on the doors, cutting down the wooden doors with all her might. And as she turned to face the crowd, the doors behind her busting open, her hair loosened by her exertion, she yelled, howled from her heart, tears streaking her cheeks, a violent wildness loosed from within, her whole body twitching with strength and power; she trembled with that freedom found inside, and the women behind her found Anjali a swarthy Madonna, axe in hand, dazzling and brilliant. For a moment, the life had turned on inside of her. A heartquake; a rumbling, shaking, explosion of life.

That particularly soaring feeling when her soul was as free as the day she was born, she felt it fly inside of her like a birthright, like a flag staked on a new land, before all the shackles of duty and tradition were laid on her body like weights.

As the policemen took the axe from her hands, Anjali laughed as if intoxicated and surrendered to them easily, her eyes flooding again with tears as she saw inside the temple a blinding, golden-limbed statue of the goddess, a garland of heads about her neck, in her hands: tridents and swords.

ALL THROUGH HER life, at times of pain, or fear, she would retire in her mind to that perfect moment of floating in Alexandre's arms in the sea as girl, her view from all sides an endless sky of tear-inducing blue.

Everything girlish was gone and what a horror, when it happened that she realized it, that childhood was over. Alone again in her jail cell, Anjali pressed her knees to her chest and wept and tried to once again remember that moment in the sea, but this evening she could no

longer recall how it felt. That such a thing could be lost frightened her
the most: losing something never had.

At night she dreamt she was adrift in the sea, everything around
her blue, palm leaves and vines in her periphery, her eyes full of grey
sky, streaked through with glowing veins of lightening and a pale veiled
moon, fearsome darkness and seabirds encircling her.

Anjali was tired. In jail the difference between sleep and wake-
fulness was not so distinct, and at night she slept poorly and during
the day was often nearly half-asleep. She felt an emptiness inside. The
Naidus had taken her in, but her relationship with them—however
affectionate—was fraught with formality. She missed the intimacy she
had had with her grandmother, that woman she could talk to without
fear of looking weak or arousing pity. Anjali had long had a small and
secret wish, one she felt was too absurd to say: she had long wanted
to be a mother, and she would sometimes feel a flicker in her breast, a
pang that reverberated in a hollow space.

She thought of the woman who had become a surrogate mother
to her: Sarojini, who for all her maternal affection, for all her passionate oratory as the president of the National Congress, was a quiet and
retiring woman at home. She had so many of her own concerns, and
Anjali felt ridiculous burdening so important a woman with her own
trivial feelings. Sarojini felt she had abandoned her poetry for politics,
and at home she would tell Anjali she was afraid of losing her voice.
Sometimes, in the evenings, Anjali would find Sarojini bent over a notebook, tapping a pen against her desk.

One night, Sarojini, again trying to write under the light of a burning kerosene lamp, saw Anjali out of the corner of her eye, that burdened gait en route to the restroom. Sarojini looked up, "When I was

young, I could write an entire poem in a day. When I was thirteen I wrote an epic and a play in one month . . . " She smiled, tired, the flame of the kerosene lamp flickering in her eyes. And like that, Anjali saw the flame reflecting in Sarojini's eyes as if it were coming from deep within the older woman, whose once-Greek profile was softening with age. When she was married she was tiny, looking as a child does, but now she had also a woman's weight and a wizening streak of silver spun throughout her otherwise black hair. "Anjali, I feel as though the muse has left me . . . " Sarojini sighed and put her pen down, extinguishing the lamp. "I'm going to sleep." And Anjali, no less lonely for that conversation, too retired to her small room in the Naidu home and lying down looked up at the ceiling.

She had given in long ago to an orphan's affliction: she searched for her parents everywhere. She saw them in her dreams and in crowded markets: her father's profile in the faces of strangers, her mother hiding just outside her vision, in the shadows.

ONE DAY, DURING a monsoon, as Anjali knelt on her bed under the cell window, the jailor came by. "Adivi, you have mail," he announced, and he dropped a package into her cell through the iron bars. Anjali let her legs fall from the bed, sitting up; grappling for her cane, she placed a half-read copy of *The Brothers Karamazov* on the bed. Prison allowed her to become ever more substantial, literarily speaking; she wanted to read more of the great works of great men, men of letters and poetry, and yet it was through that window, the small glass square, that she would throw her gaze when the stories were not enough. She sought there the city sounds that allowed her at night in jail to sleep. Anjali wiped her hands on her shawl and scrambled to the floor, taking the brown-paper-covered package into her hands. It was heavy for its size, she thought. Sarojini's address was scribbled on the back.

Anjali tore open the paper wrapping and ran her fingertips over the gold-lettered title of the book inside. "*Lautens's Grammar of Telugu*," she whispered to herself. She opened the book and ruffled the gold-edged pages. Inside, it said, "as translated from the original French by Ian Paulson, University of Cambridge, Faculty of Philology." Anjali pressed the book's open pages to her breast; tears rolled down her cheeks. She smiled deeply as she turned the pages, reading sentences in English with the curving Telugu script below, and below that the transliteration in Roman characters. She looked at the table of contents and read the headings: 1) Nouns and the Nominative Case System, 2) Verbs 3) Adjectives and Adverbs. There were seventeen chapters in all. After briefly flipping through the pages, she turned to a page toward the front of the book entitled "Author's Note":

Dear Reader:

I congratulate you on your interest in the exotic languages of the Orient. The following grammar will provide you with enough of a lexicon in Telugu to form a finite number of sentences. My primary reason for writing this book, and for studying Telugu at home and in India for so many years, however, is to share with Western linguists the unique structure of this Dravidian language, thus allowing for further growth in the fields of historical and comparative linguistics.

For those of you with knowledge of the ancient language of Sanskrit, much of Telugu's lexicon will seem familiar; for those of you without much prior knowledge of the linguistic landscape of the subcontinent, the language I present to you will seem quite unlike those of Europe.

It is a beautiful language, called by Da Conti, the Venetian explorer, the "Italian of the East." It is an agglutinating language and as such has a rich system of nominative cases; native speakers and students of German will have some understanding of this type of system. Its verb tenses are many and complicated. It is my goal that by reading this book, you will soon be able to simply translate basic words like tiger (pulli), peacock (keki) or monkey (koti). But with daily readings and dedicated practice, you too should shortly be able to make the first steps at speaking Telugu, or, to put it perhaps more correctly, as the poet Subrahmanya Bharati once said: Let us sing in sweet Telugu.

Let me briefly present you, reader, with some facts on Telugu, about the history of which much is known and much is yet to be discovered. The name Telugu, according to my Indian friends, and the language's own pundits (to use a Sanskrit word), comes from the Telugu word tene, honey. Telugu is therefore, among her speakers and admirers, considered to be "the sweetest language."

Telugu is of the Dravidian family, of which the other well-known members are languages such as Tamil, Kannada and Malayalam. The earliest examples of Telugu come from as far back as four hundred years before Christ. Currently, Telugu is spoken in a large area on the eastern coastline of India; it is spoken in the northern part of the Madras Presidency, in the area between the Krishna and Godavari rivers.

The scholar Al-Biruni (Alberonius) called the beautiful script of Telugu Andhri, many centuries ago.

The Telugu lexicon has borrowed extensively from Sanskrit, and is the most Sanskritized of all Dravidian languages. It exhibits the rare feature of inclusive "we" (manamu) and exclusive "we" (memu). Telugu has a system of seventeen vowels. As mentioned previously, it has a very rich system of agglutination. Special attention must be paid to the nominal case system; some of these cases will be very familiar to European students, like the possessive, and others will be more exotic, such as the sublative (/paina/, "on to the house"); benefactive (/kosam/, "for the benefit of the house"); and termanitive (/varaku/, "as far as the house") cases.

Anjali read the introduction slowly, and with joy. She took in each sentence carefully, as if, between the lines of his academic work, she could glean something of Alexandre, whom she missed. The last paragraph read:

Finally, I would like to thank my editor and colleagues for their support and aid in writing this book. Their input has been invaluable. In preparation for this book, I was able to spend time in India with the kind and generous funding of the Department of Philology at the Sorbonne and the French Government's Department of Colonial Affairs. Whilst in India, I had the good fortune of experiencing the kind hospitality of

the Adivi family of Waltair and Mr. Anthony Davidson of the
British Royal Botanical Survey. To both, my eternal thanks.

Anjali read the paragraph again and then silently reprimanded herself: she was looking for her name.

THE FIRST EGAS Moniz was praised in the Lusiad for defending
Portugal. "The valiant Egas, as a god appears / To proud Castile the
suppliant noble bows / And faithful homage for his prince he vows."
Egas pledged fidelity to King Alfonso, the first king of Portugal, against
the invading Moors in the 1100s.

In 1874, António Caetano de Abreu Freire Egas Moniz was born
in Avanca, Portugal; by the time he accepted the Nobel Prize for
Medicine seventy-five years later, he was known simply as Egas Moniz,
yet another hero for Portugal, as per his godfather's wishes. His uncle,
an abbot, was his first teacher, and in later years he would continue
his schooling at Paris and Bordeaux. By 1911, he was an accomplished
neurologist, the head of medicine at the University of Lisbon.

Running late in the autumn of 1919, Alexandre dashed through
the buildings of the medical college toward his office. He was working
more now, as his academic star continued to rise. Since returning, he
suffered Madeline gladly. He no longer felt content in their home or
marriage but felt unaccountably ill at ease and felt his unhappiness was
penance for some undefined betrayal on his part. His children were no
longer babies and had lives of their own; their happiness was dependent no longer on that of their parents. Something had changed in
Madeline—she was no longer his bride but his wife. The last traces of
girlhood had fallen away from her; she was a real woman now, slightly

thicker, slightly greyer, and more concerned with how the house was kept and if the children were doing well in school and if her dresses were good enough for the spring season than with him. He knew she was proud of him. She talked up his achievements at parties and to her family, but if it weren't for these instances, he would not have known she noticed that he was accomplished, a rising academic star. It was not just her, of course, for he had changed too, and there were days he loved her more and days he loved her less, and those days too when he felt like being cruel.

In the corridor, on a wall, a poster caught his eye: it was a beautiful photo, he thought. Like lightning among cumulous clouds. Below the photo was information for a lecture later that week regarding "cerebral angiography," and only then did Alexandre realize he was looking at a photo of blood in the human brain. He traced his fingertip across the bright lines, which could so easily have been bodies of water across a continent. He attended the lecture and the following week, he sent a letter to Dr. Moniz, who had invented the process of cerebral angiography.

It was because of something he had known all along, anecdotally, that aging made it harder to learn a new language. He, a linguist, who had grown up speaking French, German, Italian and English, had had a hard time with Hindi and Sanskrit. He was in his thirties by the time he began learning Telugu and that had proved endlessly frustrating.

"Dear Dr. Moniz," he began, and Alexandre provided the requisite introduction and then complimented Dr. Moniz on his research. He told Dr. Moniz about his trip to India, about his book.

"We both study the human brain, Dr. Moniz, you from within, and I from without. I am currently looking into the question of second-language acquisition. Why do children learn languages so quickly, while intelligent adults struggle to do so? I have a nascent theory—stupid, perhaps—that language acquisition happens quickly in children not in spite of their cerebral immaturity but because of it. I assume that children—having not yet developed higher reasoning skills—use their reptile brain much more than the average adult. I believe that as higher reasoning facilities develop in the child, and learning is now dominated not by the amygdala but by the neocortex, language learning slows. Language has patterns, but it doesn't necessarily follow reason. A brain primed to seek logical answers to questions may not be the one best suited to learning language, which is so very often illogical. In fact, it may actually slow the ability to learn language, which may explain why children can learn not just first but second, third and fourth languages with such ease, and why for adults (such as myself) this same task is often so laborious and time-consuming. Perhaps, like fear, or love, language is an instinct and not a skill. As the neocortex develops in humans, the rate of language acquisition slows. Is this merely a coincidence? Or is one directly related to the other?"

Years before, when Alexandre had just returned from India, Matthieu would often play with his toys under Alexandre's desk, running wooden train cars over Alexandre's feet, repeating after his father: "*Naa peru Matthieu. Maa Naanna garu peru Alex. Naake chocolatlu ante chaalaa istam.*"

"And what does that mean, my love?" Alexandre would peer down at his son, smiling up at his father, a chubby hand on his knee as he repeated the Telugu phrases Alexandre had taught his children.

"My name is Matthieu . . . "

Matthieu closed his eyes for a moment, thinking.

"Yes . . . ?" Alex prodded.

"My papa's name is Alex."

"And?"

"I love chocolate!" Matthieu giggled, running a tiny red engine car up Alexandre's leg.

He reached down and held Matthieu's face in his hand. Matthieu's face was soft, and his cheeks pink. "My boy," he grinned. He was proud of his children but quietly jealous of how quickly they were picking up a language it had taken him months to grasp the basic structure of.

MONIZ HAD MANY times held the human brain in his hands, and it never failed to seem miraculous to him: some three pounds of nerve cells, blood, fat, axons, fiber, dendrites that together lay claim to the sum of human experience. Even though the samples he'd handled were from cadavers, he felt sometimes like he was holding a soul. Somewhere in that structure were memories of a mother's cooking and the scent of grass, and the ability to make sense of calculus and map the Alps. He replied, flattered that he had been sought out. "Dear Dr. Lautens, I am flattered that you ask for my assistance. I am afraid the science has not yet advanced to the point where we can pinpoint brain activity, so I regret to tell you that I cannot offer you any firm evidence to prove your theory. Angiography, at least at its present state, focuses primarily on the health in the brain of the venous and arterial systems, not on the development of the so-called grey matter itself.

"What is more, I do not yet have any cerebral angiographies of children. In terms of hunches, however, I do believe you are on to something. I will be in touch soon after I've had some further time to consider your hypothesis. I will tell you this now, which I'm sure you already know. At the root of us all is a reptile's brain. Instinctive, reactive, survival based, lacking in altruism—only meant to keep us alive. It reacts to fear and works on impulse. The point where emotional life begins in the mind is the amygdala, next to the hippocampus, nothing more than a little bundle of nerves, small, pink. What a wonder that so much comes from it: love, fear, joy, and if you are right, the matrix too from which our first utterances originate."

Smiling, Alexandre pressed the paper of the letter to his lips. He knew now where his studies would lead him.

ANJALI LOOKED UP at the ceiling of her cell, as the light flickered valiantly before dying and darkness fell over the whole jail. After a moment she heard the snapping, hissing sound of matches being lit as the guards illuminated oil lamps, throwing into the hallway the striped shadows of cell bars.

She had been imprisoned this time for several weeks, picked up in November 1919 for organizing a small local riot. She had some vague sense it was now December but wasn't sure. Down the hall, she could hear the raspy voice of a woman wailing to the guard for water.

The sun had set many hours earlier and she could see black night outside the window, and then she heard the *plink-plink* of raindrops hitting the glass.

Anjali heard the hiss and pop of small fireworks, and then the happy sounds of cheering children and more fireworks exploding.

Anjali got out of bed and pushed the chair in her cell under the window. From the direction of the constabulary, she heard the voices of men singing "Auld Lang Syne." Allahabad, with all its history and all its institutions, lacked the one thing Anjali would have loved to hear the most, the sound that, if it bounced around the walls of her cell, would make her most glad: the sound of the sea. It was everywhere in Waltair, but Allahabad was farther inland. She stood on the chair and stood as tall as she could, trying hard to look outside at the city around her that had come very much to life.

She leaned forward, pressing her small hands to the walls of her cell. She strained her neck upward, exposing her long, brown throat, and opened her mouth for rainwater, squeezing her eyes shut as she began to cry.

❋ 14 ❋

DURING A VERY low tide, horse-drawn carriages on the sometimes island of Neuwerk can reach the little fishing villages on the icy shores of the North Sea. It was in one such village, Cuxhaven, on the river Elbe, that the *Imperator* was built, and in June of 1913 it set sail for the first time to New York across the choppy Atlantic sea. She was the pride of the Hamburg-Amerika fleet, the largest ship afloat, an answer to the less luxurious *Titanic* of the rival White Star company.

When, after the Great War, when she had spent much of the time rusting in the Elbe, the *Imperator* was seized by the Americans and used to bring surviving Yankees back home to industrial coastal cities and university towns and midwestern cornfields. She was afterward given to the Cunard ship company to compensate for the German U-boat-struck *Lusitania*. Arthur Ballin, a Jewish entrepreneur from Hamburg who had built the *Imperator* and who had once been a guest of the kaiser, seeing his life's work destroyed under the pressures of war, overdosed on sleeping pills and died before the war ended. The *Imperator*, out of commission during those war years, was claimed as an Anglo-American war prize and rechristened the *Berengaria*.

Sarojini, no foreigner to travel, enjoyed the trip but spent much of her time on the *Berengaria* inside her quarters, writing speeches and poetry and corresponding with her many friends—poets, like George William Russell and Arthur Symons, her mentor; Nehru; Gandhi and of course her family, whom she always felt suffered the most for her politics.

ANJALI, AFTER MEALS, walked out on to the deck and felt the breeze move through her clothes, the salt air in her silks. There had been a flaw in the building of the ship: in Ballin's desire to outdo the grandeur of the Cunard and White Star lines, the many mirrors and tiles, the marble pillars and oak furniture weighed so much that the bottom of the ship rocked frequently in otherwise modest winds, but Anjali loved the swaying, the wonderful sensation of danger, the way that the English girls on the deck's croquet courts would moan when the waves made the game balls go astray in the course.

Most of the male passengers spent their evenings in the smoking rooms, the ladies in the rooms with plush red European furniture, well-cushioned and surrounded by plants. The first-class cabins and recreational areas dripped of luxury. The swimming pool for the first-class passengers was modeled after an ancient one in Pompeii.

A day's distance from the dock she could see no land at all. The seagulls floated on the airy current above her, diving down now and again to flit over the water. Inside the ship were drawing rooms and a swimming pool—a floating palace: a marvel of marble and Oriental rugs and cherry wood furniture. Anjali gasped when she boarded, astonished that such a thing could be, that she would spend her days here on the great steamship as if by magic skirted on the seas toward another place, America, a place that had long ago rid itself of the British. The Americans had polluted their oceans with tea.

Anjali liked to look at the silver-blue ocean, its mesmerizing waves so powerful, moving in accordance with the moon. Alexandre had once spoken to her about the stars and the heavens and how they governed the motions of the seas and seasons. On the deck she could let her weight fall down into her hips and allow the rocking of the ship to hold her up. But at night, from where she stood on deck the waves were terrifying, concealing depthless depths. She sometimes felt she could fall down below, leaving everything. She could fall down below into those unimagined depths, to the blackest black below, below the underwater volcanoes, the great sea beasts, the beseeching undertows. She could lean into death.

ANJALI FOUND THE autumn in America lovely, the golden foreign foliage sweeping up the avenues of the grand urban landscape of New York City, where Sarojini's American speaking tour would begin. Haridas Muzumdar, a friend of Henry Miller's and a Gandhi enthusiast, would be Sarojini's escort around America. Some years later, Muzumdar, who marched to Dandi and would die in Little Rock, Arkansas, would lay garlands upon the Liberty Bell in Philadelphia to celebrate the Indian National Congress's declaration of independence.

After Sarojini's talk at the Society for Ethical Culture on the Upper West Side of Manhattan, they were to have dinner at Rossoff's restaurant in Times Square, where Anjali marveled at the gigantically tall and grey buildings and the panels of electrical advertisements that decorated them.

They wore saris—Anjali as a matter of course and Sarojini as a matter of principle—and the white ladies in their dresses and hats and the gentlemen in their suits eyed them not unkindly but with great curiosity. Whatever repulsion they may have felt at the sight of their uncommon brown skin was mitigated by the beauty of their silks, which fluttered about in the cool New York autumn from underneath sweaters lent to them by the idealistic and generous women of the society. "I had forgotten how cool these northern climates can be," Sarojini said to Anjali, shivering slightly.

Anjali wanted to see the Statue of Liberty and the Brooklyn Bridge and the Singer Building. Alexandre had once told Anjali that the statue was a woman to whom Bartholdi had given a triumphant, American gesture but whose proud expression was French as per her parentage. Anjali remembered the phrase he used to describe her clothing: "skirts of copper" that blew freely above broken steel shackles. He told her about the politics of the gift, how perhaps it had been from the French as much a snub to Britain as it was a gift to America. But Alexandre, in his particularly grave and low-toned idealism, offered too that perhaps people everywhere feel a sense of joy at seeing the achievement of freedom of people anywhere.

Anjali tried to pay attention as Sarojini reviewed the following day's schedule. But how could anyone be made to survive the street lamps illuminating the golden foliage of a New York evening, she wondered. How to endure the low happy murmur, the clinking of glasses, the peals of laughter from the crowds that spilled out from the nightclubs and dancing halls? The sounding horns of the streetcars, the women in their evening gowns; Hercules, his arm lifted in a declaration of glory, heralding the modern age from the top of Grand Central Terminal. There was that foreign chill in the air, the calamitously violet nightfall, and Anjali braced the iron bars of the horse-drawn carriage that returned her and Sarojini to the hotel. Sarojini, after some minutes, became lost to Anjali in the drowsy reverie of the poet. Tomorrow's schedule was set.

Anjali sucked cold air into her aching lungs, bracing as those deadening waves of despair overcame her like heavy blankets. She tried again to think of tomorrow. Would there be a particularly good cup of coffee? Perhaps one of their hosts would take them to a Broadway show. Or a nice meal at one of the many charming cafés. Maybe every-thing could change. But along the sidewalks, there were men in their wool suits and women wearing gloves, the children skipping along; Anjali looked at them beseechingly, desperately, would just one call her name? She focused on the rolling rumps of the beautiful horses pulling the carriage. She let her mind be comforted by dreams her own death. Anjali bit her lip; a lump of fury formed in her throat as the Americans walked past the carriage on their way to the places they were expected. The Americans, Anjali thought, moved with light step, a sense of gaiety if not immediate upon their faces, always inching upon the visage from the periphery, as if something not just good but indeed very good, were just out of sight. Anjali held the metal bars tighter. She really did want to love them.

EPILOGUE

PARIS, APRIL 1951

THE DREAMT-OF CITY of her imagination radiated through its postwar death mask with the promise of springtime. She had loved this city nearly all her life, though never before had she stepped foot in it, only inhabited its grand avenues and back alleyways in her dreams. And finally she was here. Alexandre's resonant voice narrated and guided her through its museums and shops, its cafés and gardens, through this modern city and its squares and circles.

Age had caught up with her. Age and the polio she had so long tried to live with as if it were only an inconvenience. But now, in the mornings, as she lay in bed, unable to will herself up, to find reason to move, she was most distraught that her body told her this was right; it was right to lie still. Now, when the morning sun poured into her room and she considered her life, the hopelessness she felt ran straight to her stomach and was as true a gut feeling as ever she had had. She tried to think back to the last time she was desperately sad and thought of the time when her grandmother died and remembered that though sad, the grief was a feeling affiliated with life, while the cloud-like melancholy that engulfed her now was more of a deadening weight from under which she was not sure she could emerge. Such a task was living.

But now, oh Paris! The city was floral and luminous, and when the wind picked up and the foreign foliage swirled in orange and red circles at her feet, she had faith enough in this world to leave it without fear.

Her hotel sat upon the Seine, and while sitting waterside with the locals, she sipped coffee sweeter and weaker than that she was used to. There was also a small plate of fruits from which she ate casually as she watched the glamorous and exotic city dwellers carry on in their daily lives. She imagined Alexandre in a crowd of his countrymen, refined in a grey overcoat, avoiding the rain in a hat, one of those finely dressed women on his arm. She could still remember how he felt, his solid, warm body exuding heat and the smell of wood and musk as she clutched him along the coast of Waltair as the fishermen hauled up sacks of fish like silver coins, the early sunlight illuminating his hair. Her birthplace was called Visakhapatnam now that the British had left.

The women of Paris walked past her, like a parade of the lives she had never lived, casually wielding their femininity like a weapon. "How cruelly and ignorantly they handled its unknown strength," Anjali thought.

A STEWARD AT the hotel told her to wait in the lobby with the same French accent she remembered coloring Alexandre's voice when he spoke of Paris to her in English in her garden in Waltair.

She caught her breath at seeing him—still so youthful, somehow, still so lissome in carriage and graceful in his stride; she was too taken to wonder how it could be, after so much time. Because he entered as if from a girl's dream, tall and handsome and strong, his pale hands exactly as she remembered, the translucent skin and the blue veins, clutching a small box, that same long-strided walk, and only as he neared did she realize upon closer inspection that it wasn't Alexandre at all. The light moved across his face, his beautiful face, made an angel of him and redoubled Anjali's sorrow.

To her old eyes, and in her heart, which had grown weary with sorrow after so much time, the man carried with him more hope than she could muster into words.

"Miss Adivi?" he asked. And then she felt her heart fall; though the voice too possessed beauty, it was not the one she had loved listening to for so many cool nights in the blue, Indian moonlight. He sat as tears blurred her vision and she could no longer find words.

"Miss Adivi," he repeated, a gentle smile spreading across his face. He set down upon the table a small wooden box. "I am Matthieu Lautens . . . " he waited for her with an infinite patience. "I am Alexandre Lautens's son." He placed his hand upon Anjali's. "Dear Miss Adivi, how long I have waited to meet you. How very long." He took a look about the lobby. She thought how strange she must have looked in it, how insignificant her life. She straightened her sari over her shoulder, refolding the pleats under her hand, trying to gather her courage. He answered before she could ask. "My father died last year, Miss Adivi." Matthieu reached into his pocket and retrieved a kerchief, which he handed to Anjali. He held her withered brown hand as tears filled her old eyes. She had of course known all along, but still the finality of this knowledge stabbed at her stomach and heart with a sharp, forceful violence.

"My father had kept something in the family account in Switzerland for safekeeping during the war. We retrieved it from the bank before he died. He had wanted to give it to you himself. He always wanted to go back to India. He used to tell me he'd left something there. But when he was dying, I promised him I would do it." Matthieu smiled sadly and sighed, "He had waited all these years to give it to you."

She could see now that Matthieu was a young man, handsome like his father, but his face yielded a sense of joy that Alexandre's never had. Matthieu's face was bright and young. He lifted the small box and handed it to her. Inside was a note, written in Telugu:

Dearest Anjali, February 1914, Paris
If I have come to you, and we are in India, you must show me the new country. This new place, your India.

> *Or perhaps you are here, in Paris? You are near the Louvre. I'll take you to go there, to see a David painting, of Brutus waiting for the bodies of his sons. It inflamed past generations, during the revolution. Brutus was a supporter of the Roman republic . . . to ensure its stability, he ordered his own sons to death.*

> *Here, in France, not so very long ago, the prince died alone, orphaned and weak, in a stone tower. He was a child. His sister could only hear his cries for their mother, whose severed head had long before been lifted before cheering crowds. The boy did not know she was dead. Must children always be sacrificed during revolution? What is necessary is often ugly.*
Yours,
Alexandre

ANJALI RAN HER fingertips along the smooth edges of the tissue paper inside and lifted up the scent of sandalwood into the air; Matthieu propped his elbows on his knees, his eyebrows high on his forehead like a youngster in anticipation. She thought for a moment of all the boxes that in her young mind she had hoped for from Dr. Lautens after he left India: boxes of the chocolates he had described, postcards, handmade French lace, love letters. She lifted up, out of familiar fuchsia crepe paper, her grandmother's pearl necklace with the ruby pendant, the earrings with the ruby flower and the pearl flourish. And now she felt the full sorrow of missing on earth those whom she loved most in this world.

IN PARIS, IT was cool now; the low light of spring filled the evening with a warm, pink glow. She could see its beauty now—a promise of the modern city, and like Waltair, a specter of the ancient. She closed her eyes and saw in her mind's eye for a moment Dr. Lautens's boots kicking up dust as he alighted the horse-drawn coach, descending for the first time upon her natal home.

Anjali was alone again after Matthieu left her. She strolled the streets and bought boxes of chocolate and stopped into the Guerlain shop on the rue de Passy to buy a bottle of *Après l'Ondée*, and then walked in cool darkness back to her hotel. There, she looked out through the window of her hotel room. She rubbed the perfume into her neck and wrists and melted chocolate after chocolate in her mouth. She inhaled the smell of ozone and flowers. It came upon her that all these limits and the artifice of modern morality and the supremacy of safety were curtailing her living. She felt inside of her an angry beast.

It began to dawn on her that greatness was not an amplification of goodness, that they could be opposites. That it would be hard to be great without taking risks, that all those around her, who purported to be good, that their lives didn't stand up to scrutiny. That goodness and greatness were sometimes composed of opposing qualities. That the imposition of reasonableness and social mores stifled her hunger for life. That her leg prevented her perhaps from marriage and thus perhaps even from having children but that those demands were somewhat artificial ones and that in some small way she was given the gift of being freed of the burden of her biology, because she lived in a grey area, neither man nor woman, not fully human yet in that human realm. She remembered Sarojini once reading Apollinaire to her; Sarojini laughed, "He says the Marquis de Sade is 'The freest spirit that ever existed.'" Sarojini had smiled and repeated the words, "the freest spirit," dreamily. Anjali thought that sentiment so beautiful; she wanted to have a fuller soul to keep herself company. Duty imposed on her a smallness she wanted to shake off. Smallness wasn't her destiny. She realized with shame that when she was infected with polio the world had jailed her into a eunuch's existence, and she had bowed her head and submissively entered the cell. That she had worked for those who never felt any responsibility toward her.

She turned out the lights and lay down on the bed in her hotel room. Several months before, she had had a moment when bravery and terror hit her in equal parts and she had made a single slash at her wrist before losing her nerve, and now she ran her fingertip along that pale scar. Sleep had longtime been her dearest companion. She wished to sleep deep and long, and wake up—in spring, in India. In her mind she heard the bells of anklets chiming as she and Mohini walked through marigold fields as girls. She had long wanted to see those golden flowers again, to smell the roses and the jasmine on her father's estate. She longed to hold her grandmother's hands to her face. She wanted to go home. For a moment she fancied walking from Paris to Visakhapatnam by night, to pay obeisance to nothing so artificial as country borders or other imaginary and invented things. "And then I would walk to the mountains and die in the snow of the Himalayas," she thought.

IN 1800, THE nawab of Oudh sent his engineers to Lucknow to design for his British court representative the Tower Residency edifice. The representative was a man with two masters, the nawab and the queen. Fifty-seven years later, when the brown-skinned sepoys mutinied, the white residents of Oudh rushed to the stone Tower Residency there in Lucknow.

The sepoys mutinied because they were forced to give up their India Pattern Brown Besses, the same guns used to free the American states from the British. In 1856, they were issued Pattern 1853 Enfields, whose cartridges were greased with beef and pork fat. For the Hindu and Muslim soldiers, this was akin to giving up their gods. It was the final insult, and word began to spread among villages and towns that the company's end was near: *Sub lal hogea hai*, everything has become red. For eighty-seven days, Oudh's British residents withstood cannons. The city around them was on fire, but the lonely Union Jack at the residency flew as artillery shells chipped away at the building's red stone.

All around India, all other British flags were lowered, burned and trampled under horses' hooves. Officer William Hodson, with his fifty horsemen, rode out to Humayun's tomb and captured Bahadur Shah Zafar, and later his three sons. At the Kabuli Darwaza gate, Hodson shot Zafar's sons. His men stripped their bloodied bodies and hacked off their heads. Hodson collected the heads and handed them to Bahadur Shah, the last Mughal emperor, whose empire had once held most of India in its embrace.

On the fourteenth of August in 1947, minutes before midnight and ninety years after the sepoys mutinied, the British at long last lowered the Union Jack on the Tower Residency. The British officers swung axes at the flagpole and destroyed the cement foundation in which it had been planted so no other standard would ever be strung up there. In Manhattan, Ivan Kerno, the acting secretary-general of the UN, supervised the lowering of the Imperial Indian Blue Ensign and raised in its place a khadi Tirangā. Sarojini was sworn in as the governor of the United Provinces.

Four million people would move as the country divided; two great migrations. Hindus to Delhi, and Muslims to Lahore. And in two weeks, the train cars between the cities would begin to arrive full of corpses, the floors slippery with blood, in their bodies the shards of the axes used to hack the bones and flesh; their murderers believing them to be the children of a lesser god. Everywhere death, everywhere guts and limbs and hair. Wheeled luggage carts were piled high with limp brown and red bodies; blood was mopped off the platforms.

Anjali watched now as the French tricolor whipped in the wind, and it reminded her of her own *Tirangā* and she felt, after so much, through good and ill fortune alike, a sense of pride. She had helped to deliver her country from the tyranny of colony. And sad too, because a country wasn't something that could really be captured or held in the hand; it was an idea and not a heart.

For years now, she had had only one thought, again and again: she dreamt of a strong and merciful rope around her neck and dreamt not of returning, not of a heaven full of choirs of angels and treasures of gold, but of sweet, silent death, of melting into that earth that had bore long silent witness to her pain for so many long years, and dreamt, open eyed and awake, again and again for the comfort of a quiet demise.

DAVID PAINTED BRUTUS in the shadows. Amid the weeping of his wife and mother and daughters, Brutus sits, his arm weakly lifted, as if to acknowledge the victory of the republic. Despite this glory, Brutus's face is a mask of quiet sorrow. Anjali had gone at last to the Louvre; Alexandre, as a ghost of her own conjuring, accompanying her. She walked along the Champs-Élysées and alongside the arterial river of the great city. She saw the river and the crowds and saw that through all these things—the world wars, the revolts, the struggled-for tricolors of France and India and Ireland—the Seine flowed with slowness. The movements of the people outside for a moment seemed to lose continuity. They moved in finite gestures like rapidly taken photographs, each articulation distinct from the one before it and that one after, each movement only a suggestion of what was to come and not a promise, and then, after such a time of tirelessly fast spinning, the world for a moment seemed still.

ACKNOWLEDGMENTS

I AM INDEBTED TO the The Edward and Sally Van Lier Fund, the Asian American Writers Workshop and Quang Bao; their early support of this book gave me the gift of time. I would like to thank Erin Lem and Claire Dippel at Janklow & Nesbit, for their committed championing of this book and without whom I would not have met my wonderful agent, Alexandra Machinist, who took this book on only as a labor of love.

I would like to thank my family, especially my Mom and Dad.

I have the good fortune to have the most wonderful friends in the world, all of whom have been a fountain of support, and I would like to thank all of them, especially Antara Kanth, Michael Smith, Grace Lu, Katie Pulick, Sabrina Esbitt, Wendy Kuo, Laura Beck, Joy Meads, Kristyn Caminos, Daniel WK Lee and Grace Kim.

Finally, my deepest thanks to Liz Parker, Kelly Winton and Julia Kent at Counterpoint, who have been wonderful to work with and have provided constant comfort to a very jittery first time author.

Printed in the United States
by Baker & Taylor Publisher Services